Twenty-Four Hours A Day

Also by Faith Baldwin
in Thorndike Large Print

Enchanted Oasis
Beauty
Make-Believe
No Private Heaven
"Something Special"
Give Love the Air
He Married A Doctor
The Heart Has Wings
The Lonely Man
And New Stars Burn
For Richer, For Poorer

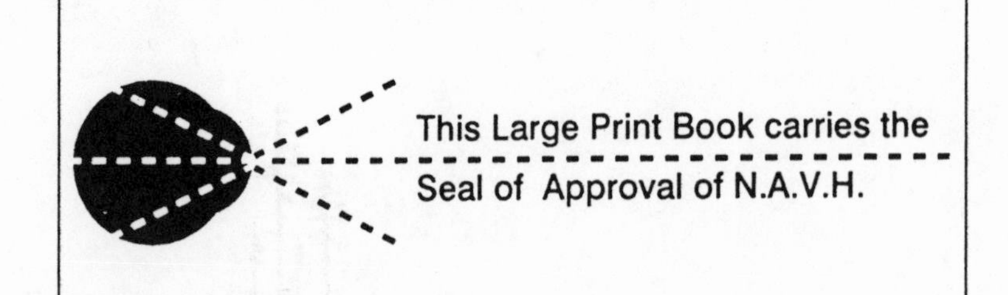

Faith Baldwin

TWENTY-FOUR HOURS A DAY

Thorndike Press • Thorndike, Maine

Library of Congress Cataloging in Publication Data:

Baldwin, Faith, 1893-
Twenty-four hours a day / Faith Baldwin.
p. cm.
ISBN 1-56054-273-X (alk. paper : lg. print)
1. Large type books. I. Title.
[PS3505.U97T94 1992] 91-34433
813'.52—dc20 CIP

Thorndike Press Large Print edition published in 1992
by arrangement with Henry Holt and Company.

Large Print edition available in the British Commonwealth
by arrangement with Harold Ober Associates.

Cover design by James B. Murray.

The tree indicium is a trademark of Thorndike Press.

This book is printed on acid-free, high opacity paper.

To Janet Kinley and John Robert Gregg

(who always return books —)

with affection

1

One memorable night in spring Christine Carstairs stood in a crowded theater lobby, between the first and second acts of the most sensational theatrical production of the season and, declining her host's offer of a cigarette, looked at the people milling past. Her younger sister, Janis, was exclaiming excitedly over the various celebrities whom she was audibly recognizing. Janis was smoking, and, vaguely, Christine wished that she would not. There was no harm in it, of course, but rushing out in the entr'acte to flip the flame of a lighter to a cigarette seemed to her so terribly impatient.

She turned her mind from Janis, so patently enjoying herself on this unexpected party, reflecting that, after all, a youngster down from college on vacation has a right to be impatient and avid for good times, and looked more closely at the women, not of her party, who were near by. Her host, Nelson Yorke, was speaking to her.

"But you smoked after dinner," he was

commenting in mild astonishment.

"Yes — I often do after a meal. But not much. I don't care for it really," she told him, smiling. "I think it's because of the smell of stale smoke in one's hair and frocks, which I dislike so much."

She spoke abstractedly, noting the details of the women's gowns there in the lobby. She was trained to notice such details, as she had been employed for some time in the exceedingly successful establishment of Hilda Staneways who, as rumor and Staneways herself had it, dressed "everyone who was anyone" in New York, Chicago, Hollywood and the more affluent suburbs.

There was Mrs. Evanston in Staneways' "Secret Laughter." A very silly name, thought Christine, and a very pretty frock. Mrs. Evanston was a shade too dumpy for it, but it had done wonders for her just the same.

The very good-looking man beside her, whom she had met for the first time that evening, and whose guest she was, spoke. She started a little, realizing that he had been talking for some time.

"I don't believe you've heard a word I've said," he accused her with faint astonishment.

"I'm so sorry," apologized Christine. "I was looking at the clothes."

"So you won't leave your career behind you

in the shop," he said, "or can't you — which is it?"

"Can't, I suppose," Christine answered frankly. "It's rather idiotic of me."

"Are you so terribly ambitious?"

"Yes," she admitted. She leaned against the railing and surveyed the house, "I'm afraid I am."

"What do you want to do?" he asked her.

"Design the best clothes in New York," she told him calmly. "No, why limit it? The best anywhere!"

"For Staneways?" he inquired, smiling. He knew something about Staneways; he knew something about almost everything. It wasn't likely, he thought, that this attractive young creature — how young? — twenty-six, twenty-seven? — would be permitted to realize her goal within the four decorative Staneways walls. Hilda Staneways kept a tight rein on her assistant designers.

"No," Christine told him, "for myself. In a place of my own."

Her sister Janis came up to them then, followed by Francis Austin, whose father was the Carstairs' lawyer, and who had arranged, at Yorke's urging, this particular party which included dinner at Yorke's celebrated apartment and the theater and afterwards a night club.

Janis was chattering, at top speed, and Yorke looked from one to the other of the sisters, smiling. They presented a very interesting contrast, he thought, liking contrasts. Christine was small and slender, with dark gold hair, and long brown eyes faintly tip-tilted in her oval face. He liked especially the dark eyebrows, which had never been submitted to plucking but were heavy, beautifully groomed and definitely crooked. He liked her vital hair, which had retained the springing natural wave of childhood, and the fact that it was not very short, but caught into a little knot at the nape of her pretty neck. Lipstick, drawn across the firm molded lines of her controlled but exciting mouth was, he felt, a mere gesture, a modern signature, delightful with her clear creamy skin, faintly flushed at the high cheekbones.

Janis was taller, very lithe, unconscious seemingly of the grace of her long body. She had a short, curly chestnut mop, and wide blue eyes and a good skin. She hadn't Christine's purity of coloring, but she was quite charming and she could have posed for the Typical American Girl at Twenty, thought Yorke, dismissing her from his mind, although his smile, practiced and caressing, appeared at the moment uniquely dedicated to herself.

Janis smiled in return and said, in her quick, high-pitched voice:

"Look — who's that going down the aisle . . . if he isn't the *best*-looking specimen!"

Christine thought uncomfortably, and there's another thing . . . Talking about people . . . or about herself — about anyone — at the top of her lungs. In public places. I hate it, it's such bad taste. But if I say anything she'll say I'm a prig and too old-fashioned to live . . . and that everyone does it. I suppose everyone does. It's the reason, possibly, for gossip columns.

Yorke's regard followed that of Janis. He turned back to Christine and said lightly, "But *you* must know who it is, Miss Carstairs. . . ."

"I haven't the faintest idea," said Christine indifferently.

There were two men in the party in question: one elderly, with a short, white, carefully trimmed beard, and a breadth of shoulder and a height which marked him in any crowd; the other was perhaps thirty-two or so, as tall, as broad and very dark. He was, as Janis had remarked, very good-looking; and he was also the son of the older man if the great resemblance was to be taken at its literal, face value.

"Yet that," explained Nelson Yorke, smiling, "is Clarkson, Inc. That is to say, Howard Clarkson, lately retired from the presidency but still on the board of directors, and his son Lawrence, the new president."

The warning buzzer sounded and Yorke's party made its way to their seats, not unremarked, a fact which filled Janis with enormous pleasure.

When the second, and last, act was over Christine found herself looking for Lawrence Clarkson. But he was nowhere to be seen. On the way to the supper club, a little later, she confided to her host:

"I was so interested in seeing Lawrence Clarkson . . . I had no idea he was as young . . . I have just finished designing a line for the Clarksons . . . under the Staneways label, of course."

"Tell me about it," urged Yorke, with flattering promptitude.

Christine told him while Francis and Janis talked of the play. The rest of the party had gone on in the Austin car. Yorke listened, watching intently the play of light and shadow on Christine's mobile face.

"It will be an innovation for Clarkson's," he commented after a time. "I don't know much about shops, of course, and less about women's clothes" . . . he was, she thought in a flash of intuition, lying so far as the second statement was concerned; he knew a good deal about women's clothes, from the angle of one who has paid for them liberally and who has his own well-defined tastes . . . "but a moderately priced line for Clarkson's seems rather out of the picture."

"I know. But it appears that they had to — in order to compete with the other shops. I understand that the senior Clarkson was against the idea but that his son . . . and the buyer, Miss Allen, whose idea it was, won him over. You see, she persuaded them that with a line especially designed and bearing the Staneways name the curse of the inexpensive label would be taken away. It's a line for youth, of course . . . after all, debutantes nowadays haven't the money to spend which they once had. The Clarkson tradition has always been ready-made clothes at custom-made prices."

"I've met both Clarksons," said Yorke. "And I ran into Miss Allen in Paris once . . . a very attractive woman, knows her business. . . ."

Francis interrupted with a casual remark, and the conversation became general.

Their entrance into the supper club created a little stir of interest and comment. Nelson Yorke was very well known, and Christine, watching his smiling progress to their ringside table, was amused by the differences between him and her old friend Francis Austin. Francis was attractive and pleasant and utterly undistinguished. He had been for some years comfortably established in his father's office and for many years before that Christine's devoted and admiring shadow.

Francis and his father had proved themselves towers of strength when, some years previously, the not inconsiderable Carstairs fortune had crashed and with it the mental and physical life of Christine and Janis's father; and with it also all Christine's glowing postcollege ambitions.

These, which were centered about art school, portraiture and ultimate fame, had vanished. In their stead Christine had accepted the training at Cooper Union, the apprenticeship in a Paris cutting room instead of a Paris studio, and eventually the position at Staneways', which enabled her to carry much of the burden of her household and to educate her sister. Mr. Austin had helped. It was he who had financed her Paris venture and who had advised her at every turn of the strange, new road.

That her mother and Mr. Austin would certainly have welcomed an alliance between the daughter of one and the son of the other, Christine knew. To Mrs. Carstairs, perpetually bewildered by the tragic change in their fortunes, advantageous marriages for her girls appeared the only possible solution of their troubles. But Christine had not concurred. She was fond of Francis, she liked him very much indeed. But she was not in love with him. And latterly she had begun to suspect that he was turning from her to Janis.

She had experienced a certain hurt pride, wounded vanity in this realization, being human. But Janis, at twenty, casual, lighthearted, irresponsible, was certainly worth loving. And she was so pretty and so vital! Christine, saving every possible cent against the proverbial inclement weather, against the dear dream of, someday, a shop of her own, was aware of Janis's constant and careless inroads upon those savings, her affectionate demands upon her sister's generosity. It would solve a great deal if Janis were to forget her procession of enthusiasms, her bright parade of flirtations, and turn, seriously, to Francis Austin. But Christine would not have her coerced. She had a rooted conviction that the only possible excuse for surrendering yourself and your privacy was because you were so terribly in love that you couldn't help it. And it was curious that on the evening she met Nelson Yorke she admitted something of this to him, when during the leisurely dinner in his delightful apartment, chaperoned by the elder Austin and a desiccated cousin of Yorke's, the conversation had turned, under his guidance, to marriage.

Yorke, forty-odd, a bachelor by choice and through the medium of the divorce courts, probably appeared at least a hundred to Janis. Yet in some ways, reflected Christine, he looked younger than Francis. His eyes perhaps, they were uncommonly youthful. He was a stocky man, who carried himself so well that he appeared to possess more height than his actual inches measured. He had thick, unruly gray hair, and his close-shaven skin was tanned and smooth, his jaw dogged, jutting, and his mouth fine, if rather indulged.

They danced together, and he danced well. Christine, moving with effortless ease in the circle of his arms, wondered about him. She knew little. He was reputedly very rich and amused himself, according to rumor, in backing horses, theatrical ventures, lost causes and scientific research. Beyond that she knew nothing of him save that he had seen her at Twenty-one with Francis Austin and called Francis the next day to demand her name, quite coolly, and to announce that he wished to meet her. This, thought Christine, when Francis laughingly told her about it, was decidedly highhanded, almost arrogant, but, of course, flattering. Francis had been immeasurably entertained, which was a certain sign, Christine thought, a little ruefully, that she no longer commanded his heart. "Not a bad man to know," he had suggested, his nice gray eyes amused, and she had agreed with him, if without much enthusiasm. "It's a pity," she added, "that he hasn't a wife to dress. But by all means trot him out, Francis. And be sure you include Janis — she's coming home next week — she'll be thrilled to death."

So Francis had made his plans, only to discover the party taken gently but firmly into other hands than his. He was therefore a little amazed to find himself calling for Christine and Janis and escorting them to Yorke's astonishing penthouse overlooking Fifth Avenue. And he laughed outright when he saw the corsage orchids and gardenias they displayed.

"I must say," Christine told him, "your friend is lavish, if superbly unmindful of the conventions."

"I suppose you know they call him Duke?" asked Francis absently. He shrugged his shoulders, in defeat. "It was to have been my party," he explained, "but he wouldn't have it. He says he's tired of speakeasy atmosphere and until a return of the era which provides rank on rank of wine glasses and a delicate, rather than a desperate and deliberate, drunkenness, he prefers to entertain his friends in his own home. I quote him verbatim. I hope you don't mind awfully, Christine?"

She had not minded. She had enjoyed dinner, preceded by the fine old sherry which Janis had eyed with the distrust of her generation. She had liked the beautifully proportioned drawing room in which she had encountered her host for the first time. She had been entertained by the elderly cousin, Mrs. Henderson, a mid-Victorian objet d'art, complete from pompadour and fringe to bugles and a black velvet ribbon threaded with seed pearls about her neck. And she was enjoying this dance.

Supper was exactly right, enough to eat, not too much, and the champagne was iced laughter. Janis was little-girl-greedy, almost dipping her nose in the bubbles. Christine, afflicted with hidden merriment, saw Francis motion the waiter away when he came prepared to fill the younger girl's glass for the third time. And Janis, pouting, shrugged and rose to dance.

Mrs. Henderson, astonishingly, still managed a mean fox trot although not given to anything more spectacular. She danced with Yorke and with the Austins, father and son.

During one interval Yorke and Christine were alone at the table.

"You have," he remarked, "a very pretty little sister. I take it that you believe this to be a responsibility."

"Heavens!" cried Christine in concern. "Do I betray it to that extent?" Her long, tip-tilted eyes, narrow rather than round, looking as the texture of velvet feels, regarded him in consternation. "Well, yes, I admit it. There are seven years between us. She's in college, as you know. She'll be going back next week. . . . You're giving her a pretty grand wind-up to her vacation, Mr. Yorke."

He said lightly, "My friends call me Duke."

"It suits you," she agreed, as lightly, "not that I've ever met a duke, and no doubt he'd be disillusioning if I did . . . but . . . not having met one, I repeat, it suits you."

She did not, he noted, accept the invitation, challenge, call it what you will. He rather liked her for it. He was a little tired of the incessant, *Duke, darling*. . . .

He said, "I must tell you again that it was good of you to come. You know that night I saw you dining with Francis wasn't the first time I'd seen you."

"No?" she asked indifferently, aware that he was probably stating a fact. She was seen in the best places and by the best people, she reflected a little dourly, but with some entertainment. Staneways' assistants always were. It was a condition of their employment.

He said, "I hope you'll let me see you — often . . ."

"I'd like to," she told him instantly, "but I haven't a great deal of time."

"Aren't you permitted to lunch, at Staneways'?"

"We're compelled to lunch," she said gaily, "and at what are known as the right places. To see and to be seen. It's all part of the game."

"Then," suggested Yorke smoothly, as the others returned, "how about — let me see — Tuesday? At one?" He named the place on Park Avenue and Christine said, "I'd like to very much."

The Austins took the two girls home. Janis said, lying back in the car, "I had the most marvelous evening. Wouldn't it be sweet if every evening were like that? . . . Every evening is, I suppose, for some people."

"They get fed up," Francis reminded her. "You'd be like the little girl who wished that every day would be Christmas and got her wish."

"What happened to her?" asked Christine, laughing.

"Just what you'd expect. She stood it all right for the first four or five days but in a couple of weeks she was so tired of toys and so ill from plum pudding and turkey and mince pie and candy that she begged and begged to take back her wish."

"She was a sissy," said Janis definitely.

They laughed, and Francis asked curiously, "What did you two think of Yorke?"

Janis spoke first, yawning. "I think he's perfectly divine . . . of course," she added calmly, "if it weren't for his money and his way with waiters and all that he'd just be an attractive middle-aged man!"

Mr. Austin sighed and Francis shook his head. "Honestly, Janis, there are times when I'd like to turn you over my knee. Middle-aged! Well, I suppose," he added, astonished, "that he is. . . . He must be forty-five and that's middle-aged in your language."

"It is in any language," said his father; "yet to my disadvantage point of going-on-sixty, he seems almost a callow youth to me."

Janis put her hand through his arm.

"I didn't hurt your feelings, did I?" she asked him anxiously, with her disarming smile, "because . . . well, I love you to pieces, and as far as I'm concerned you're younger than any of us."

"The amende honorable," he commented,

and patted her hand.

"We haven't heard from you," Francis reminded Christine.

"I don't know," she replied slowly. "I like him. He's interesting, and, as Janis says, attractive. But . . . he frightens me a little."

"Now, why?" asked Francis, while the others laughed.

"He's so awfully sure of himself," she answered. "There's something inexorable, the steam-roller quality, about men with quantities of money who have always been able to buy everything and are so sure of themselves."

Janis laughed again.

"You must be scared to death of him," she said. "I heard you make a date with him for Tuesday, when I came back to the table."

There were times when it would be a relief to slap Janis, much as one loved her.

2

Christine fell silent, forgetting Janis and Nelson Yorke, her thoughts turning on the glimpse she had had of Lawrence Clarkson and his father. They had looked, she thought, a very likable pair. It was curious that she had met neither of them. But Staneways had arranged the designing of the ready-to-wear line and had attended all the conferences. It had merely evolved upon Christine to submit sketches and suggest materials, and the glory, if there was any, had gone, she assumed, to Staneways herself. Not that it mattered. She looked from the car windows at the lights. She would never tire of Manhattan, stimulating and unforgettable.

Janis was talking about Nelson Yorke again. She dug an elbow into Christine's resentful ribs. "Don't you wish we were rich?" she sighed, and Francis frowned, slightly, while his father laughed tolerantly.

No one answered, but then Janis hadn't expected a reply. She was off on another tack, while Christine thought, Janis puts a great deal of emphasis on money. She was not off the gold standard no matter what the new administration had decreed. Christine had noticed this with increasing frequency of late. Francis, she told herself, sensing his close attention to her sister, had enough for any reasonable girl in material things, and more than enough in his nice dependable self.

"How did Duke Yorke make his money?" Janis was demanding. "I hear he has one of the biggest yachts afloat." She broke off to sing a snatch of "Every nice girl loves a sailor — " and concluded, in a pleased tone of voice, "Perhaps he's a bootlegger. I don't mean the kind that comes sneaking around with suitcases, but the head of a ring or something."

Francis and Mr. Austin laughed, but Christine said sharply, "Janis, don't be childish."

"Why is it childish?" demanded Janis indignantly. "I think it would be keen! Bootleggers are all the rage nowadays. I know a girl who spent a week-end with one — oh, there were other people along," she added hastily, as Christine exclaimed in horror, "but anyway she said he was the life of the party, aside from the refreshment he provided. Quite the little gentleman. He had an armored car and a bodyguard."

"You've been seeing too many movies,"

murmured Francis, and leaned from the small seat to touch Janis's hand, conscious of his heightened pulse as her fingers encountered his own in a fleet pressure, "and moreover the bootleggers' day is almost at sunset — we'll hope. For your disappointed information I might add that Yorke's money was made quite soberly, from your point of view, in mines and shipping and railroads, by his father and his grandfather before him. I admit he does some curious things with it, but that's up to him, after all."

"How dull," murmured Janis sorrowfully. "Here we are at our own modest flat!"

Later, getting ready for bed, patiently waiting until Janis, taking her own good time, saw fit to surrender the occupancy of the bathroom, Christine dutifully narrated the evening's events to her mother. Mrs. Carstairs, plump, pretty, faded, curled up on the edge of Christine's bed and listened, with pyrotechnic comments. Christine, looking at her in the mirror, laughed suddenly.

"What on earth?" asked Mrs. Carstairs indulgently.

"Nothing. . . . Just — such a transparent little face! I can just see you thinking . . . 'Yorke? Wouldn't he be entirely suitable for Christine? Of course, it's a pity he's so much older and has been divorced, but even so — ' "

"Nonsense," denied her mother, sharply, flushing, "I had no such idea — Christine . . . how can you . . . ? Being in business has hardened you," she decided sorrowfully.

"It should," agreed Christine cheerfully. "I wish it would harden me more." And her mother sighed, remembering a younger Christine barely out of college who, when the subject of Francis Austin was broached to her ever so delicately, had cried, with violence, "Never! I'll get a job!"

Well, she had the job, and they were the better off for it financially, but Mrs. Carstairs was not resigned. Of course, Christine's work was, well, ladylike. She shuddered when she thought of Janis with her nebulous ambitions to become a model, take a screen test, go on the stage. Here, at least, Christine seconded her mother's disapproval. But Mrs. Carstairs felt that she could not cope with the present generation. If only the girls' father had lived. She thought of him, as always, with shock and despair and a sort of curious, futile anger . . . not at him, really, but at the nature of his passing . . . he, who had so loathed the sensational.

Janis whirled out of the bathroom, darted on to kiss her mother good night, to announce that she had put her gardenias and Christine's orchids in the ice box. "We can't starve," she added, "we can eat 'em if funds get low. Chris, Duke Yorke fell for you like a ton of bricks. I never saw anything like it. Personally, while affronted that he passed over my immature charms, I think you're on the right track. Stick to him and you'll wear penthouses."

Christine laughed, and her mother smiled, a very little, while ejaculating in her vague fashion, "Surely that's in very bad taste, Janis!"

"Oh," cried Janis, "you antediluvian darling. I take it you are not amused. If I were Chris I'd know how to play my cards!" She yawned, displaying sound teeth in a healthy setting. "Good night, lambs. Chris, you never answered me — aren't you seeing Duke Tuesday?"

"You didn't ask me, you stated it," said Christine calmly. "And he's Mr. Yorke to you, darling. Yes, I'm seeing him."

"It won't be the last time," prophesied her sister gaily; "sweet dreams of strawberry leaves," she added wickedly.

"What did she mean?" asked their mother, bewildered, when Janis had left the room. "Strawberry leaves?" Her nose wrinkled in distaste. "Surely not something — Freudian?" she inquired darkly, lowering her voice.

"Mother," said Christine, "you are priceless." Later, lying in bed, she remembered this and laughed aloud, and then almost instantly slept, to dream of neither Nelson Yorke nor the symbolic strawberry leaves but, oddly enough, of Lawrence Clarkson.

Janis was right, for during the next few weeks Christine continued to see Nelson Yorke with increasing frequency. She lunched with him; she dined with him, either alone at a restaurant, or, with other people, at his home. The columnists made the usual comments . . . "Is it possible that Duke Yorke has decided to take a Duchess?" they inquired simply; or "Christine Carstairs, the socialite lovely who helps design those too, too charming folderols at the celebrated Staneways, is being seen with Duke Yorke who has backed more successful plays and more successful horses than you can shake a stick at — if you're sufficiently interested to shake a stick. . . . "

Janis, back at college, wrote that she was "thrilled." Obviously she read the papers. Francis Austin was perturbed and said so frankly. "I didn't mean to let you in for all this," he told Christine remorsefully. But she laughed at him. "Nonsense! Staneways is delighted. It's very good publicity." Mrs. Carstairs was, sincerely, shocked. She belonged to another era.

Nelson Yorke's own reactions were rather mixed. Not that he minded being pilloried in the gossip columns. He was accustomed to the stocks, he would have noticed being left out of them. No, he minded for Christine, which was odd. He remembered, with regret and a sense of stirring up old ashes, his sensational affair with Sara Thorpe. His name and hers had been coupled with an almost cloying frequency in the public press. He hadn't minded that nor had Sara. She had laughed about it. She had said, "I'll be forced to make an honest man of you yet, Duke," and then without warning, had burst into tears. Now he tried to forget that he had remembered Sara. He hadn't seen her in a long time and, while he assured himself that he had nothing to reproach himself for, the swift memory of her small accusing face, wiped blank, as writing on a slate is erased, of all her careful sophistication and revised into sheer grief, disturbed him . . . even now.

Sara had loved him, he knew it, reminding himself of it without vanity. Christine Carstairs, he was equally certain, did not. But if she came to loving him . . . ? He was, he admitted to himself, very much attracted by her. He had been ever since the first time he had seen her. He had been wondering ever since the night at the theater whether she was involved emotionally with Francis Austin — who was, of course, a good enough chap, if a little on the dull side. He thought it quite unlikely that Austin should not be involved with her. However, on the evening of the party Francis had been just as attentive to the pretty rattle-brained sister — although how a man in his senses could prefer her of the two —

Before the dinner party Yorke had made certain careful inquiries. On the night he met Christine Carstairs he knew as much about her as people did who had known her for years. The fact that she was working heightened his interest. He did not like idle women. At the same time the nature of her employment pleased him. A lovely woman whose gift for making other women lovely appealed to him. It argued a sense of beauty, an exactitude of eye, a feeling for nuances. It argued the artist, without, he hoped, the quality which for lack of a better term we call temperament. Writers, singers, actresses, he found too egotistical and uneven in disposition and businesswomen too self-confident.

Nelson Yorke was extremely fastidious when it came to women. This sprang not so much from an integral trait as from an experience suffered in his youth. He had married, directly after completing his university education, a beautiful girl of excellent family and background, who had proved to be extraordinarily coarse-grained and insensitive, possessive. The fact that she had been generous, earthy and authentically in love with him hadn't balanced the scales in her favor. Eventually despairing of holding him she had become a little too generous, and he was free to divorce her. Instead, he had permitted her to divorce him, made an ample settlement on her and assured himself that he would not marry again. If he had not married Evelyn he might have gone on for the rest of his days believing her as fine as her profile, as delicate as her ankles.

Later he grew to recognize, without despising them, the earthy and generous qualities of other women; and to enjoy these so long as he did not have to live with them day in and day out. He had had some amusing and satisfactory friendships, and more than friendships, with women whose tastes ran, while not at all counter to his own as a free man, counter to the tastes he required of a woman he would marry. So long as none demanded marriage and possession, he was tolerant and indulgent of them.

But his association with Christine Carstairs was beginning to disturb him. If he fell seriously in love with her? . . . Nonsense, he had no intention of committing suicide! He told himself, she is charming, she pleases me, she likes me — rather — and I enjoy being with her. . . . And told himself further, but without much conviction, that if ever he discerned the first symptom in Christine of a possessive interest in himself, he would, as he had done in other cases, take immediate refuge in flight. Cut and run, was the way he phrased it.

Spring was lovely that year and during the early part of May Christine motored more than once on Sundays to Westchester or the Island with Nelson Yorke. He had a powerful foreign car which he drove at a terrific rate of speed. She asked him one day, her teeth chattering with terror, "Do you always drive like this?" She had to shout, and he shouted back, "Of course . . . why not? Not afraid, are you?" When he saw that she was, he slowed down. He said remorsefully, "I'm sorry. . . ."

"Are you never arrested?" she demanded, straightening her little hat and composing her heartbeats.

"Oh, now and then. Not if I see the motorcycle first," he told her cheerfully. "Do you like planes?"

"Not very much," she answered candidly. "I haven't had much experience. I did fly to Washington once. Janis was visiting there, and was taken ill. It was a dreadful trip, wondering what was waiting for me . . . at the end of it." She shuddered in retrospect.

"Oh, Washington." He dismissed the country's capital as if it were a mere drop in the aerial bucket. "I meant a real flight. There's nothing like it."

"I suppose," she ventured, "you have a very fast plane." She said it demurely; it was a commonplace remark but her long eyes twinkled and Nelson laughed with her.

"It's very fast," he admitted. "I've two, by the way. I flew with the Lafayette Escadrille, you know — "

"I hadn't known."

"This talk about war and its horror," he said, after a minute " — is all very well. But — will you understand me when I tell you that when the war ended I felt as if I had lost my best friend?"

She said, after a minute:

"Other people felt that way — with plenty of reason."

He shrugged. "Now you're reproaching me. Brutal, hard-boiled, selfish male animal, you're thinking. Aren't you? Be honest!"

"Not — exactly."

"Near enough. . . . Look here, life's cheap, doesn't mean a thing, any one of us can be replaced, instantly. There are too many of us in the world. Dying doesn't matter. Perhaps it's struggle and a long sleeping and six feet of earth and no more. Perhaps it's the gateway to adventure. I don't know; no one does really. We've no proof."

She said, "If you'd ever cared for anyone, and that person died, you might feel differently."

"I did," he said at once. "I cared very much for someone. . . ."

Christine resigned herself to hear the story of some woman he'd loved, his legendary wife, perhaps. But he said, quietly:

"A youngster — my cousin. I was devoted to him . . . he had all the qualities. I can't tell you how fine he was. I killed him."

"You *what?*"

"Oh, not literally," he said, "but — There was a little excitement in, say, Mexico — a matter of guns. It was all very long ago. It amused me to take a hand in it, financially. Robert was a great deal younger than I, he had no people, I'd more or less adopted him. He was crazy for excitement. I understood that. I let him do the hero act . . . that of go-between. Well, they shot him. There was nothing I or money or the government could do . . . I pulled every wire . . . I haven't forgotten."

After a long time she said, "I'm sorry," and

he turned on her almost belligerently.

"Well, perhaps he wasn't, who knows? Perhaps that's the way to go out, with nothing exhausted, with no memory of boredom, with the sun in your eyes and the wild music of the rifles. . . ."

At luncheon he said, over a table on the porch of an almost deserted roadhouse:

"I don't suppose you understand the way I tick, at all. You haven't had much to do with gamblers, have you?"

"No," she admitted, "I haven't." She raised her eyes to his and looked at him for a long moment. "I was just thinking, perhaps if you hadn't come back from the war — "

"Well!" he said, on a long, astonished breath.

Christine flushed slightly. "I mean . . . so many boys died, of wounds, of disease, who had had nothing from life . . . none of their potentialities realized. But you, you'd had everything . . . most of life thereafter would just be a repetition to you. Can't you see that?"

He said, smiling, "I don't know whether to love you for that or dislike you very much. I think you've found out how I tick, after all. Boredom. I'm afraid of it; it's all I'm afraid of. That's why I gamble. I gamble on a horse, a show or a woman. I put money into scientific research work because God knows that's a gamble. I lend it to friends; that's another. I stake it on the fall of dice, the turn of a card, on a polo pony, a hockey player, a prize fighter. Generally, I win. It isn't the winning. It's the moment of suspense . . . the moment before one knows — *Do I win or lose?* . . . I am thinking," he went on with a change of expression, "of staking it on you."

"On me?" said Christine, amazed.

"Yes. You told me what you wanted, the night we met. A place of your own, a chance to make good. Very well, it's yours, without the asking. I'll set you up in your own shop. Carstairs Inc. We'll find the best location for you, we'll turn it over to the decorators — under your guidance. You'll hire the best people in New York, you can go to Paris and find some miraculous female to make your hats . . . Staneways boasts of hers, so I've heard. There must be better. We'll put on shows that will knock Staneways' eye out, and I'll see that in the background you have the best publicity man money can buy. There'll be ample advertising appropriation . . . well, don't look so dazed."

"But I am dazed," she told him truthfully, her heart pounding.

"How about it? I'll launch you, I'll make good any deficit you may encounter for, say, three years. When you begin to show a profit you can cut me in, as silent partner. Or, you can repay me over a term of years. We'll make it all very legal once the terms have been agreed upon. We'll have lawyers and contracts and all the rest."

She said indignantly, "If I couldn't show a profit in three years I might as well not attempt it at all!"

"Then you will?" he said, delighted. "Good, I thought so. That's the proper spirit. I like spirit," he added, "as you may have noticed."

"Not so fast," said Christine. She pushed her plate aside and regarded him. "I haven't said yes."

"You haven't said no," he reminded her.

She said slowly:

"You tempt me very much. Everything I've dreamed of . . . within my grasp. But how can I take it?"

"Go on and say it," he said. "Ask me, 'What will people say?' Ask me, 'Are there any strings to it?' What do you care what people say? I haven't given a damn since I was old enough to listen. You must learn not to. If you're clear with yourself, that's all that matters. So far as that goes, if you'd rather we covered the trail, we'll do it differently. I'll arrange for you to borrow at my bank . . . I'll put up the collateral. It will amount to the same thing except when people ask you who is backing you, you can reply with your absurd honesty, 'I borrowed from a bank.' And as for the strings . . . there aren't any. I may pull wires but I am not interested in strings."

She said:

"You must think me very ungrateful, Mr. Yorke."

"I told you before that my friends call me Duke."

Christine ignored that and went on. "But," she said steadily, "the trouble is, I can't decide. Not right away. It would take long and very careful thought. It means so much. I—I'm not as good a gambler as you are," she admitted smiling.

He said genially:

"Take your time. Think it over. But don't take too long. The autumn is the time to launch a venture of this sort and we'll have our work cut out for us, you know."

Yes, she thought, looking down at her coffee cup, they would. But with unlimited means at one's disposal, obstacles would vanish, difficulties would be overridden, the time element would be of less importance.

She said, after a moment:

"You're extremely kind. I appreciate it more than I can say. You've opened a doorway for me, given me a glimpse of something very close to Paradise. It frightens me a little. One of those too-good-to-be-true moments."

"All right. That's all I wanted to know. Think about it. Let me know what you've decided. Now we'll talk about something else."

It was clever of him, when all she wished to discuss was this astonishing proposal. But he did not mention it again until they were starting home. In the car he said, briefly, "While you're thinking about this I'd like you to know that I believe in you. I think you have something. I am not offering to permit you to prove it for the sake of your very attractive eyes. I'd like you to know that."

"Thank you," she said, smiling.

"Naturally," he said lightly, "if you were not so easy on the sight I might not have made the offer. Wait, that's not strictly true. I once financed a woman in the cosmetic business. You'd know it if I named it. It has since repaid me liberally. The poor creature was thirty-five and painfully unattractive. She was interested in beauty because she herself had none and had spent what little money she could lay her hands on to acquire it. Later, of course, she made the round of plastic surgeons with very little, if any, result. But she had two formulas for creams and a lot of ideas. So I backed her. We found a very pretty girl, a relative, and brought her down from her upstate village — she became our front. But the presiding genius, the owner of the business, was and is a very ugly woman, with ill-assorted features, whom no one ever sees. So perhaps, after all, I might have made you the offer no matter what your appearance. But, since you look as you do, I'll never know!"

He was amusingly honest, she thought, and then wondered briefly if the honesty was an act.

They passed a high brick wall with a door set in it. The door was open and Christine looked past a lodge to a long tree-bordered road, carefully landscaped grounds and a big brick house, not beautiful but substantial, almost noble in its solidity and dignity. She said, "I wonder whose place that is?"

"It's the Clarkson place," replied Nelson; "they use it summers. I understand that when the son marries the old man will retire and live here permanently. It was built a good many years ago, and will stand a good many years hence. It has a four-square look I've always admired. One expects to see a captain's walk. The original Clarkson was a clipper ship's captain who on retiring from the China trade set himself up in a little shop downtown —

Division Street, I think — and laid the foundations of the mercantile fortune for his successors."

He left Christine at her apartment house before dark, held her hand no longer than was necessary, and said without warning:

"I'm going to Hot Springs tomorrow. I'll be gone a week or two weeks. I don't know. When I return I'll get in touch with you. Perhaps you'll have made up your mind by then."

"Good-bye," she said, "and thank you . . . words are awfully inadequate . . . I'm not much good at them. I'm better with a pair of scissors."

"So is the least attractive of the Fates," he told her. "I think her name was Atropos. Good-bye, and good luck."

She did not go inside immediately. She watched him cross to the curb and drive off. The car was a symbol of speed, of power, as was the man himself. She still felt dazed when she went upstairs to discard her wraps and answer her mother's patiently probing questioning.

3

On the following day she forgot her wakeful night of indecision and doubt when on entering Staneways she was met by the information that Lawrence Clarkson wished to see her. Madame Staneways had made the appointment for her, for eleven o'clock and was not now present to offer any explanation.

Christine, curious and astonished, kept the appointment. Curiosity was uppermost and a feeling of breathless excitement, when, entering the pleasant, private office Clarkson rose from his desk to greet her.

Christine, taking stock of him during his first greetings, his pleasantly complimentary references to the line she had designed for Clarkson's, under the Staneways label, was aware that Janis had been right. Lawrence Clarkson was excessively good-looking, in a way that depended upon a combination of irregularities . . . good teeth, widely spaced eyes, a fine forehead, an almost brutally determined jaw and mouth. His smile was disarming and his hands, she noticed immediately, were beautifully shaped.

Presently he was not talking generalities. He was asking her to become a member of the Clarkson staff, as one of several designers for a new custom department which he contemplated. He went on rapidly to sketch his plans, admitting that he had met with opposition from his father, "Clarkson's has always stood for exclusive design and quality in the ready-to-wear field," but he added with some satisfaction that his father had been won over. "He realizes that our competitors have established custom departments and I have convinced him that the American designer has long since come into her own. . . . Would you consider such a position, Miss Carstairs?"

He added, suddenly, that he had not realized she was so young. He might have said, "or so pretty," as he was thinking just that. At the moment she was prettier than ever, flushed, a little confused, saying slowly that she was greatly honored but that she must have time to think it over, and adding frankly . . . "You see, recently I have considered a place of my own."

"That's a gamble these days," he told her swiftly. "Not that I have any doubt of your ability . . . but your work here would *be* your own, Miss Carstairs. You would receive full credit. And you'd have a big organization back of you. I am in a position to offer you eight thousand a year, and commission on any sales that you make personally." He rose, tall, broad-shouldered, and smiled down at her. "And now, will you let me take you around? And then perhaps you will think things over and give me your decision in, say, a week?"

He took her through the shop, presented her to Miss Allen, their buyer who had been instrumental in persuading Clarkson's to order the Staneways-designed line. Miss Allen was smart, veneered, a dark, good-looking woman in her late thirties. Lawrence, smiling, told Christine that she was "one of the family" as indeed she was, having come into Clarkson's as stock girl at seventeen and having risen to her present position through hard work, dogged battle and the influence of the senior Clarkson who had taken an interest in her and her abilities. Long after Christine and Lawrence had gone Miss Allen sat in her office and considered her future. As buyer, department head, floor manager, she reigned supreme, under Lawrence. She had sided with his father against the innovation of a new department, she had debated it bitterly with Lawrence. But, if his mind was made up and the thing went through, she knew that she must withdraw all her opposition outwardly and co-operate with him up to a certain point.

There might be, she reflected, ways and means beyond that point . . . but open hostility toward him, toward this girl he had brought in, was not politic.

On returning to Staneways, Christine had an interview with her employer, who was one of the cleverest businesswomen in New York. She left her office little wiser. Staneways had encouraged her to accept the position, pointing out that Christine had gone as far in her establishment as she could . . . and that, if she considered going out for herself, she would meet with many obstacles . . . "unless of course you have proper backing," she added with a rising inflection. Christine did not answer, but sat there, her eyes on the floor, thinking. And Staneways remembered the clipping she had seen, the gossip columns linking Christine's name to that of Nelson Yorke. She held her own counsel. Back at Clarkson's, Rita Allen was remembering too, and when Lawrence mentioned to her before luncheon that Miss Carstairs was considering a venture of her own, she deduced carelessly, "Nelson Yorke, of course . . . they've been together a good deal," and no more. But Lawrence frowned slightly. He knew Yorke and his reputation. And his temper was not improved when, lunching with his father, as was their custom, in their penthouse over the store, the older man grunted disapprovingly over Lawrence's report that Miss Carstairs wanted time to make up her mind.

"She must be out of it," he said. And added, "What's she like?"

"Very charming," replied Lawrence inadequately.

"I see," said his father, his bright blue eyes a trifle malicious.

"You don't see at all," contradicted Lawrence irritably. "I never saw her before in my life until today —"

During the week which followed Christine weighed both offers in her mind, as carefully as possible. She knew it was of no use to consult with her mother or Janis. Instead, she went to Mr. Austin and over luncheon at his club explained her problem to him. Mr. Austin considered her gravely and after a time rendered his decision.

"I am greatly flattered, Christine, but I wonder if you want advice or if you want to be told that what you intend doing is the right course. I don't know what you intend, you have given me no hint. From a purely business standpoint, I advise you to take the Clarkson offer. The other is too great a risk in this day of uncertainty . . . despite the fact that Yorke is financially reliable. With things as they are, it might be years before you would be free and clear. I don't suppose you have seen the President's message to Congress, regarding the National Industrial Recovery Act? You youngsters don't read presidential messages, I take it. There is little doubt that Congress will pass the bill. Under whatever provisions the various codes dictate, a new business would have to make unexpected adjustments. Clarkson's is established. And, from a purely personal standpoint, I'd rather see you there than under obligation to Yorke."

Thus, Mr. Austin. Christine went into conference with herself once more and made up her mind. She told herself firmly, The fact that I find Lawrence Clarkson very attractive has nothing to do with it! If he were a hundred years old, bowlegged, bald-headed and toothless, it would still be the sensible thing to do!

She had heard nothing from Yorke. She wrote a note to Clarkson formally accepting his offer and asking for an appointment. This was made, by telephone, and when she left him it was to give Staneways her resignation and her two weeks' notice, which Staneways, congratulating her, waived.

By the time Yorke returned from Hot Springs and heard her decision, Christine was deep in organization. Clarkson permitted her to select and engage her own special staff of fitters and seamstresses. The other designers — three of whom had been engaged, two women, and the man who would design the classic tailor-mades — would have the same privilege. Christine hunted up a fitter who had left Staneways rather recently for personal reasons, and one of her seamstresses came also from Staneways. She was dissatisfied, was leaving anyway, and Christine felt no particular compunction in taking her. The others she found easily; there were plenty of competent girls out of work. And now it was nearly the end of May and that meant that she would have to work for all she was worth to get her designs and finished models for the formal autumn opening.

While the showroom, model rooms, the fitting rooms and the upstairs workroom were being made ready, space assigned and altered, Christine had a temporary workroom of her own, with good light, in which at a long table she made her sketches and worked with remnants of material on a miniature figure, draping, cutting, pinning. The other designers worked there also, and at first there was a spirit of helpfulness and eagerness and a pleasant association, everyone anxious to do his or her part to get things under way. To this room the fabric salesman came and the material samples were exhibited and discussed and the first inevitable little bickerings began, as there were few really good unusual materials which were not wanted by more than one designer. Nor was all the material purchased for Clarkson's custom department; Rita and her designers had the privilege of selecting materials for their departments as well, under arrangement with their manufacturers.

Summer went, much too quickly. Christine rented a small house on the Island during July and August for her mother and sister. Janis went on a round of visits and Mrs. Carstairs was plaintive. She didn't like being left alone with a maid, miles from nowhere, although, she added, the neighbors are quite kind.

Christine went down for week-ends, driven down by Francis Austin, and occasionally by Yorke. Yorke had been extraordinarily pleasant about the whole affair. When, on his return, he had telephoned her and she had told him of her decision and the Clarkson offer, he merely said, "Well, that's that. Have dinner with me just the same. I won't try to persuade you."

He had tried, of course, laughing at his own persistence, but had finally given way. "All right, anything you say goes," he told her, "but remember, the offer still stands . . . any time you care to reconsider it."

He was a lifesaver during the hot summer

weeks. He did not remain in the city but he kept his apartment open and entertained there when he came to town from a yachting trip or a stay at some resort. He also took Christine out, to roof gardens, to summer theatricals in Connecticut barns, to lunch in the coolest places in town, to dinner. He was a very amusing companion.

Francis, in town most of the summer although courts had closed, took her out too, and told her seriously that he did not like the idea of her being cooped up alone in the apartment. But he was more concerned about Janis, who had acquired several new cardiac complications since spring. She was, he thought, too young, too pretty and too unthinking to be gadding about as she was, house parties, clubs, beach parties. So Christine should do something about it.

"What?" Christine demanded. She pushed back the damp hair from her forehead and regarded him, as they motored down to the cottage one hot August Friday evening.

Well, he didn't know. Couldn't she talk to Janis?

Christine said that she could, but to what purpose? Janis wasn't doing anything she shouldn't. She was simply having a good time, which was what Christine wanted her to have . . . the gay, normal time a girl of her age should have, without undue responsibility. She wasn't, to Christine's knowledge, floating unchaperoned around the countryside.

"I can't understand you," complained Francis, "you used to be so concerned over Jan. This new job of yours — I believe you sleep and eat it."

"Especially the pins," she admitted. "I dream they're sticking me, and that I'm one vast pincushion. And I have a recurrent nightmare about an enormous pair of shears which comes at me slowly, moving under its own power, its pointed sharpness headed straight for my throat!"

What he couldn't understand, she thought wearily, was that she was working this hard in order that Janis should have a good time, the sort of good time she herself had had during her vacations from college and which had ceased so abruptly and, she thought, prematurely.

She saw a good deal of Lawrence Clarkson. The department was organized under his immediate supervision, and every alteration which took place in the building came under his jurisdiction as well. They had come to be on friendly terms, which, she assured herself more than once, meant little, the Clarkson policy being what it was. She had met Howard Clarkson shortly after her new status had been established. He had been pleasant enough, she found herself liking him, his miraculous grooming, the carefully trimmed beard, his bright blue eyes. But it was perfectly plain that she was there on sufferance and that he washed his hands of the whole business.

Rita Allen was friendly also. She helped Christine more than once, saved her from several errors, pointed out various pitfalls, guided the personnel manager in his employment of the new models. Later, she explained that when Christine had been there longer she would doubtless be able to influence Mr. Harding and make her own selection. In the meantime, Miss Allen recommended several girls whom she herself had used during seasonal rushes. She would need extra help herself, for the fall showings, but meantime she wanted to help the new department, these girls knew the shop, the type of customer, and the work.

Howard Clarkson was not in town during the heat. This left Lawrence free at the luncheon hour and a custom arose of lunching weekly in the apartment with Christine, and the other new designers, Ellen O'Day, Mimi Forsythe, Janet Gaines and Harold Norton. More often than not Rita was included. During luncheon, problems were discussed, plans made, policies formulated. The weekly departmental meetings had the same purpose, but Lawrence decided that the very informality of the luncheon meetings made for a better feeling and understanding. How it came about that, during August he and Christine lunched alone, he never quite knew, nor did she. But he walked into her now adequate workroom one day and asked her, "How about lunch?" and there it was. The other meetings had by force of habit come to take place on Thursdays. This was a Wednesday.

They went out to a place on Park Avenue, under a green canvas which gave the illusion of coolness, and bordering on a court with a fountain. Christine was talking of work, of the short time left before the opening. The girls were working hard under the handicap of the heat, she said, her mind in the big workroom with the purr of machines, the heat of the ironer, the clatter and confusion.

Two of the girls had fainted during the recent hot spell and Christine marveled that more did not, sitting there, making their tiny innumerable stitches, in fine perishable material.

She herself loved fabrics; the color and texture and feel of them; sliding her sharp scissors into the shining or dull folds of sheer color was always a delight . . . exciting . . . an adventure . . . like setting brush to palette, she told him, smiling.

Rita Allen came out into the court with a young blond man in tow. She saw them almost instantly and hostility went through her in a great sickening surge. She waved her hand and smiled but shook her head as Larry, rising, beckoned. No, her bright glance said, no, thanks, I've my own luncheon date, surely you can see that.

She went to a table as far away as possible. Laughing with, and at, her blond young man, ordering the cocktail she shouldn't drink because of her figure and her skin and the season; and she was thinking, I knew it . . . I knew it. She hated Christine for her youth, her effortless grace and the way she wore the little black linen suit of her own design, with the turquoise linen blouse, cool as the sea, and the floppy rough straw hat. She hated her because of her long eyes, turned back to Lawrence's now, and her charm and her growing popularity in the shop. The workroom girls, from apprentices to the forewoman, adored her, they'd probably do better work for her than anyone else. Sooner or later Rita could murmur that information into willing ears. Not yet. The department would open with a bang and Rita would help, she would cooperate if it killed her. The new venture would do business, and when vigilance relaxed slightly and Carstairs began to feel secure and walked with less caution, Rita would step in.

Rita had told Lawrence that she liked Christine Carstairs. This was not true. She had not liked her. She was honest enough to admit to herself that she might have, in other circumstances. But as things now stood she disliked and feared her. It was not alone that she felt her own supremacy in the store, her importance, threatened, but she felt that her influence, as a woman, might also be. It had been no source of happiness to her to realize that she was in love with Lawrence Clarkson. She detested women of her age who went around falling in love with younger men. They were fools. She was a fool. But she couldn't argue herself out of love with him. She had at first entertained no special hope of marrying him and in their situation anything else was out of the question. Rita Allen hadn't reached the age of thirty-seven to fall in love for the first time. There had been other men. There had been offers of marriage; and other offers. She had refused them all. If two or three times in her life there had been emotional episodes which had nothing to do with such offers, and which she had been able to take in her stride, as a free woman, self-supporting, and clever enough to be cautious, no one in the store knew anything about them, although gossip might have been faintly stirred at one time or another. Rita kept herself and her own counsel and no one had any proof of indiscretion.

Latterly she had begun to hope that because of their daily contact and their reliance upon each other, Lawrence might come to feel that his life would be incomplete without her, in business or out. She did not believe that Howard Clarkson would make any great objection. Howard was, always had been, her friend. She owed him everything, but even that obligation could not deter her from falling in love with his son. Over this neither she nor Howard had any control. Once, when Lawrence had first come into the store, he had shown a more than passing interest in one of the girls in Rita's department. Rita was assistant buyer at the time, and it was she who handled the situation for Howard Clarkson. He had not discussed it with her but he was aware of what she was doing, and had approved.

The girl had been pretty, and meretricious. She was not ambitious, the work with her was a means to an end. The end, of course, was Lawrence, once she set eyes on him. Rita had been clever. She had persuaded her superior, and the girl herself, that Miss Petersen had a flair for design. Miss Petersen had been taken off the selling force and put to work with the designers who adapted the Paris importations, and created their own ideas for their manufacturers to follow. Miss Petersen hadn't done at all well in the venture. Skillfully she had been removed, and as there was no sales position open for her on the floor, she was set to modeling. She had the figure for it. The Clarkson models were not so famous then as they were to become a little later, but they were a carefully selected group. And Rita, continuing her interest in Miss Petersen, fed her vanity with excellent fuel. She saw that Miss Petersen heard about commercial photographers and did some posing for them during her seasonal layoffs. She saw that she was featured in the fashion shows, with the not very astonishing result that presently Miss Petersen began to think that, after all, she might be wasted on a mere store owner's son, who worked so hard that he had little time left to take her out to the right places. There was something to be said for the idle rich. And having met one or two of the species, Miss Petersen ceased to model at Clarkson's and drifted from the Clarkson orbit.

Howard congratulated Rita. It was the first time Miss Petersen had been mentioned directly between them. He said, "You're a clever girl, Rita," and she said, smiling, "I knew that if you gave her enough rope — gilded rope — " The subject was dropped for an instant. There was a companionable silence, and then Howard spoke heavily. "I wouldn't like Lawrence to become involved, seriously, so soon. He's young, he has a long way to go and his job's cut out for him. I want him to marry, of course, at the proper time. And I don't want him to marry in the store. This may sound brutal to you, but I needn't defend myself. You know what I think of the majority of our people. There are a half-dozen girls here this minute I'd be pleased to welcome into the family — except for the fact that they are already part of my business family. An alliance of that nature would create quite a situation. I imagine you see that."

She saw it; she still saw it. Yet she fancied that now, with Lawrence a mature man, and given Howard's reliance on herself, that old objection of his might be overridden.

Rita felt that she had earned her place in the Clarkson sun and her rest. But with new blood in the store, new methods, new rights, threatening her own, she would have to be prepared to do battle again. She did not want to. She was thirty-seven and she was tired. She merited peace. She had fought her way up from unpleasant beginnings. She never spoke of that. She had not been born to ease and security, safe in a background that counted for something. She knew — when she forgot to forget — far too much about squalor and misery; she knew too much about heat in summer and cold in winter and the hollow pinch of hunger. She had heard things, in the night, women who screamed in childbirth and men who stumbled on echoing stairs. The cards were stacked against small, skinny, undernourished girls, only one in a thousand escaped. She had escaped. She had secured almost all she desired, because she had so hungered for it. She had learned how to dress, and how to walk, and how to modulate her voice and control her accent. She had studied, nights, and Howard Clarkson had helped her to attain the poise and the ease and the patina. He was the only person now living who knew from what she had come, and even he had probably forgotten it by now. She thought she had, yet why was she so hotly hostile toward the gently bred girls who drifted into Clarkson's now and then and asked, with disarming candor, for jobs? And why was she so inimical toward Christine Carstairs aside from the natural enmity of a department head who feels her supremacy imperiled?

She looked over at Christine and Lawrence. They were patently absorbed in each other. Clever! she thought, and knew how stupid she was. Must it be cleverness on Christine's part . . . wasn't Lawrence sufficiently attractive? Seeing him with the younger woman was like seeing him divorced from the store. She'd never viewed him apart from Clarkson's, even since she had loved him. He was Clarkson's, had been since his boyhood when he had clerked, vacations, when he had bitterly railed against college, because it kept him from actual work. He had railed against her too when she sided with his father. She remembered the time when during summer vacation in his junior year he had gone abroad to make an intensive study of foreign merchandising methods and to meet the exporters with whom Clarkson's dealt. She and his father had seen him off and he'd put his arm around her and kissed her under Howard's tolerant eyes. "Good old Rita," he'd said.

Well, in those days she had thought of him as a boy. She no longer thought of him as a boy. But . . . had his pigeonholing of her place in his life ever changed?

What were they saying, those two?

Lawrence was demanding, his eyes on Christine's:

"Tell me about yourself. Oh, I know the business background and all that. Let's not talk about work, now. I know what you're doing. It's fine. But of yourself I know so little, actually."

"There's not much to tell," she began obediently, yet somehow she was telling him a good deal, even about her early ambitions, when to be a good painter was the sum and substance of her ambition, when art had been spelled with a capital A. "But I would have been second rate," she ended ruefully, "and I can't stand anything second rate; better a first-class designer than a mediocre portrait painter. . . . I've come to that conclusion."

"You couldn't be second-rate anything," he said abruptly, and looking up she was aware of his intent and kindled regard.

She looked away, confused, but not aware of the depth or significance of her confusion until that night, shortly before the opening when, with her mother at home and Janis back at college, she dined with Yorke. She was worn out with all the excitement, expectancy and irritation attendant on the coming event . . . and when driving home, Yorke kissed her for the first time, she found herself submitting. She was keyed nervously to the highest pitch, and under Yorke's expert caress the tension broke, she was marvelously relaxed.

After a moment she pulled herself away.

"I shouldn't have let that happen," she said remorsefully.

"Could you have prevented it?"

"Oh yes. And I know your friends call you Duke. So do I now. But it ends there."

"Perhaps," he said coolly, "but you weren't exactly unresponsive."

"No," she said frankly, "I wasn't. Put it down to fatigue, excitement, a cocktail too many. After the opening next week perhaps I'll be myself again. However, tonight's tonight, and it's over. Will you remember that?"

"I'll remember," he promised, "tonight."

She would too. In her room at home she viewed herself in the mirror, pale with excitement, her eyes glowing, her lids drooping, her red mouth soft . . . too soft. . . .

"You look as if you'd been kissed," she informed herself.

When the lights were out she tried to think of the play they had seen. She could recall little of it. She couldn't think of anything except that Nelson Yorke had kissed her and she had let him, and had even returned his kiss, because with her eyes closed, and her heart pounding, she had imagined him Lawrence Clarkson.

4

She thought it would be better if she did not see Duke Yorke again, yet she knew that it would be best if she did not see Lawrence Clarkson. Idiotic, humiliating, terrifying, to be forced to admit to yourself that you were headlong in love with a man who never gave you a second thought, except in a business way. But she knew that if she were told, Very well, you need not see him again, she would die of the agony. So, seeing him, every day, she controlled her voice and her hands and her eyes, and told herself, You can't throw away a job you've just begun because your absurd emotions have run away with you!

She did not re-encounter Yorke until the opening, for which Clarkson's sent out their announcements, pointing with pride to their new custom clothes department and the brilliant young American designers who would labor to dress the Clarkson clientele as no clientele had been dressed before. And the invitations to the opening went out, and the publicity and advertising department knit their eyebrows over lists and combed the blue books and social register and saw to it that everyone who was anyone was invited, as well as the charge customers.

Mulberry and green, Christine's suggested color scheme, the custom salon burst upon the especially invited gaze, on an autumn evening. Crystal chandeliers, and pier glasses. Champagne cocktails, Russian cigarettes, and thick ivory-tinted programs with little gilt pencils. The loveliest models, tall girls, slim as every woman's dream, with little or nothing under the frocks they paraded . . . a runway, lights, and an orchestra playing, and Christine elected to do the announcing, in a Carstairs gown, the soft green she loved, perfect with her dark gold hair and with unexpected details of sable brown, the color of her eyes.

The frocks had silly, entrancing names: "The Third Kiss" was a dance frock, pure, clear scarlet; "Do Not Forget" was a dressmaker suit, the color of burgundy, with a high collar and vest of mink. There were dozens of others, day wear, afternoon wear, dressmaker suits and an evening suit, one of the first, in velvet, a Carstairs . . . they were called "Hearts Are Trumps" and "October Fields" and Heaven knows what else. And there were dinner gowns and formal attire and the beautiful tailored things in fine Scotch tweeds which Harold Norton did so superbly.

The stage came, and society, and the people who frequented cocktail bars and literary parties, and the women who wrote for the shopping columns, the weekly magazines and the newspapers. It was an enormous success, that opening.

There were men there, some reluctant and some rebellious and some frankly interested, not in the women who had brought them, but in the girls who came down the runway and turned, and moved their hips a little and walked with their sleek artificial glide back and forth . . . redheads and brunettes and blondes. . . .

Among the men, Duke Yorke. He knew, it seemed, half the people crowding the salon on their little gilt chairs and on the divans against the wall, drinking their champagne cocktails and smoking their cigarettes. He talked to many of them, and, when it was over, drew Christine aside, no apparent remembrance of their last meeting in his cool eyes.

"You've done it. I'm proud of you."

"But I haven't done it all," she assured him, laughing, "you forget there are other designers."

"Naturally I forget them," he said, and Lawrence Clarkson, coming up with his father, overheard.

Nelson Yorke greeted the two men imperturbably, congratulating them, smiling; and stood aside with Howard while Lawrence took Christine's hand and said something to her, low. Yorke said easily, "A very clever young woman, Miss Carstairs, you're fortunate to have secured her," but the elder Clarkson grunted.

"Maybe you're right," he said, "but you can't tell from this. It doesn't mean a thing. In six months, in a year . . . well, I'll answer you then because then I'll know."

Rita came up, radiant in a shade of dull red which greatly became her and put her arm through Christine's, detaching her. "It has been marvelous," she said, "but *too* marvelous. Now if my own little show will go as well . . . You do look tired, Christine," she added gently.

First names, intimacy. That was better than formality, than putting your opponent on her guard. Disarm her, attach her to yourself . . . more rope.

"I am, a little," admitted Christine, "it's been pretty exciting."

But she could not go home yet. The Clarksons were giving a little party for the new department and store executives upstairs in the penthouse after the guests had left. It was a gay party complete with orchestra, with

Howard at his genial paternal best with his employees. That was the Clarkson way. Christine wondered whether in practice it worked out so well as the strictly impersonal attitude. Already she sensed jealousies, undercurrents, grievances which were personal among the Clarkson hirelings. Yet that there was affection and to spare she did not doubt.

But certainly Howard took a high hand with his hired help. If he was lavish with wedding presents, tolerant of honeymoons and of time off for babies, if he adored giving advice, there were times when he meddled. He had to approve of the marriage, the selected two weeks' vacation, the baby! It was a trifle heavy-handed, Christine thought. She thought, too, that while the majority of the subordinate employees basked in benevolence . . . vacations with pay, indulgences, doctors and nurses and hospitals when they were ill, they were, on the whole, not particularly well paid. She knew something about this now from the salaries permitted her seamstresses, the daily wage of the models, the pay checks of clerks. Perhaps, she thought, watching those higher up drink Howard's good champagne, perhaps it would be better in the long run to withdraw benevolence and the paternal guidance and permit these people to stand on their own feet . . . on higher wages. Let them pay their own doctors, and fight their own battles and finance their own honeymoons.

But this was treason.

"Of what are you thinking?" Lawrence asked her when, later, they were dancing.

"Of the shop," she replied truthfully. And she was thinking of it, as a whole, the stepped-back structure, proud and pure of line, the hushed departments, the entire lack of display, the thick-piled carpets, the hurrying clerks . . . hurrying under the kind, the heavy, the watchful shadow of Howard Clarkson. It didn't matter that he was no longer "active" in the business. Lawrence was his representative. And the concern was a family affair. Howard held the majority of the stock and after him came Lawrence. What little was left had been judiciously distributed among friends and relatives.

Lawrence's eyes kindled. "It is — pretty fine. And you put on a grand show tonight, Christine."

He had never called her by her given name before. Her heart stirred treacherously and she smiled at him. "It wasn't altogether my show," she said.

"So far as I am concerned it was," he told her warmly, and they were silent a moment regarding each other. Then Lawrence remembered. Nelson Yorke had said something very like that to Christine earlier in the evening. His ardor, awakened by success, by Christine's nearness, by his father's champagne, was suddenly chilled. He remembered Rita and her stupid gossip.

He spoke of something else and Christine sensed the sudden change in him; her own mood altered and was as flat as the pale amber liquid standing in a forgotten glass.

After the opening Christine found herself almost incredibly busy. Once the department was under way, it appeared to be every man for himself. Naturally the temptation to urge the purchase of one's own design upon a prospective customer was strong, but it had to be withstood. You couldn't lose a sale for the department as a whole simply because a pet client was lukewarm about your "Tomorrow Night" but might be enthusiastic about Ellen O'Day's "Surrender."

There was friction about fitters. Ada Regan proved herself the most valuable member of the fitters' staff and, although she was assigned to Christine, the others borrowed her with increasing frequency, if she was not occupied and their own fitter was busy. This was to be understood, but occasionally when a client of Christine's demanded Ada and she was not immediately forthcoming, there was trouble. However, Christine managed to be friendly with the people in her department and, to do them justice, they were likable enough. The one person she did not like was Nancy Redding, Rita Allen's niece, placed in the department through Rita's influence. She was about twenty, rather plain, and, Christine thought, far too casual for her job. She had an air of conferring a favor on a customer by waiting on her. But when during the winter Christine spoke to the personnel manager about it he merely shrugged and said, "Well, what can I do? — she came in through Miss Allen."

"Couldn't she be moved to another department?"

"Not without a panic," admitted the personnel manager, sighing.

Rita, Christine was learning, was the power behind the throne. She was not merely in Lawrence's confidence, she had Howard's ear as well. Howard, returning from Long Island, had established himself upstairs in the penthouse and commanded his son's dutiful appearance at luncheon. So the lunches with Lawrence ceased, but Christine saw him every day, as he had taken over the floor management of the department, and she saw him at the weekly meetings, and outside the shop as well. This began early in the season with his suggestion that she attend Mavis Downing's first night with him. Mavis was a customer and Christine had sold her several of the loveliest models in her own fall collection. So Lawrence, strolling through the salon, had asked, "Like to go to the Downing first night?" and she had answered, "I'd love to."

They'd had fun, first at dinner, then at the play and later at a supper club. If, as Lawrence suggested, Christine's interest was more in what women were wearing than in anything that took place on the stage or around them, he didn't seem to mind. That formulated a silly beaver sort of game in which they strove to recognize Christine's handiwork as it strolled past on the back of one woman or another. They laughed a lot, and decided that it was foolish to continue addressing each other formally. They were good friends, were they not? And working partners.

"Do you realize, Christine," said Lawrence, driving her home, "that my father is really coming around? He's beginning to think that after all I'm not going to run the business into the ground. It's hard for him to be apologetic, but I see the symptoms."

"He does spend a good deal of time on the floor," said Christine.

"How's Nancy Redding doing?" he asked idly.

"Oh, very well," Christine answered, and

hated herself for hypocrisy. From her standpoint Nancy wasn't doing well at all, she spent far too much time gossiping in the model rooms and her general attitude was one of easy insolence. Yet you couldn't go out to dinner with the boss and complain about a member of your department, especially one who was related to someone far closer to the boss than you were.

Almost before she knew it, she was busy with the spring collection and sometimes she went home at night so tired she thought she would drop, and would fall into bed and ask her mother to send in a tray with a salad and a cup of soup, and tell anyone who called that she couldn't come to the phone. She had never been so tired at Staneways, not that she hadn't worked hard there. But in this job she had more responsibility as well as more work.

The spring opening came and went. One night, shortly thereafter, Christine, her tray sent away and her muscles crying out for rest, was interrupted by a knock at the door. Her mother came in. "It's Mr. Clarkson," she said, with some disapproval. "He's downstairs. . . ."

"For heaven's sake!" Christine swung herself out of bed, groped for her slippers and looked at the clock. Nine. "What on earth does he want?"

"I'm sure I don't know," said her mother primly.

"Tell him to come up. . . . I'll be there in a second. Keep him busy. Talk to him, anything, till I get there."

Mrs. Carstairs departed, sniffing audibly. She had a poor opinion of young men who worked in shops, whether they owned them or not. She had a poor opinion of trade in general. She was fond of saying, "None of our family has ever been in trade," although just what she considered Wall Street is another matter. She excused Christine's entry into the world of barter by saying, "After all, Christine is an *artist*. . . ."

Christine was not feeling like an artist. She was feeling like a schoolgirl on her first heavy date. She was splashing her face with cold water, dropping powder puffs, losing lipsticks, discarding a pair of stockings that had a run. But in an incredibly short time she was out in the living room, her dark gold hair burnished, and her new sheer wool very becoming to her slender figure.

Lawrence rose as she entered. He and her mother appeared to have reached the best of terms. He laid aside the photograph he was holding and said, "I've been admiring your little sister."

"She is rather nice," admitted Christine,

and gave him a firm, cool hand. But she didn't feel firm or cool.

Her mother lingered a moment, remarked about the weather, "so unseasonable," said plaintively that she couldn't understand the NRA and left. And then Lawrence looked at Christine and laughed.

"I suppose you wonder why I'm here."

"I do, rather," she told him, "but I'm glad."

"Are you? So am I. Well, I'll confess. I was bored. My father is entertaining. He likes a game of poker now and then. It was all very stag, heavy dinner, too much to drink and eat and smoke. And presently I escaped. I took the car with no special idea of where I was going and drove myself through the Park. I let down the windows, let in the air and blew some of the smoke out of my brain. And presently I said to myself, 'I'm not far from Christine's . . . suppose I drop in and see if she's home.' I didn't think you would be, but I took my chances."

It was a pleasant evening. They sat and talked, about everything and nothing. They went out and drove awhile and then went to a neighborhood movie theater and saw a midnight show, a picture they'd both missed. And Christine said, sighing, "I wish I were a Hollywood designer," and Lawrence cried in alarm, "Don't you dare . . . wishes are dangerous . . . they might come true, and we don't want to lose you." And after the show was over they went to an all-night place which served remarkable sandwiches and good beer, and then he drove her home again.

He held her hand a little longer than was necessary and said, smiling, "I've had a very swell time. Let's do it again. Your mother thinks you're the eighth wonder. We're perfectly agreed on that."

She said quickly, "I hope she didn't bore you. You know that mothers are prejudiced."

"No," said Lawrence, "she didn't bore me. May I come again?"

She found herself asking, "What about dinner, some night?"

"I'd like to, very much," he told her.

Christine went back into the apartment and found her mother, a figure of horror, in flannel robe, hair in curlers, waiting for her.

"Do you know what time it is?"

"I do."

"And do you realize that — "

"I realize everything," said Christine and hugged her. "I'm not a bit tired, really. Good night, angel. I've had an elegant evening."

"Well," said her mother, "I can't understand you. You came home so dead you could hardly drag one foot behind you. And when I asked you to go to the concert with me, you almost burst into tears. You said you wouldn't go across the street to see the Supreme Court dancing the rumba to a Salvation Army band. Those were your very words."

"That was then," said Christine. "I changed my mind. And I didn't go across the street to see the Supreme Court dancing the rumba to a Salvation Army band. I went to the movies and I had a club sandwich and a glass of beer and I feel like a million dollars and seven per cent interest."

She was so happy that she was lightheaded. He *did* like her. It wasn't just shop and business association, and cordial relations between employer and employee, it wasn't just the Clarkson policy. It was herself, Christine.

During that springtime she was incredibly happy. She was seeing Lawrence with increasing frequency, quietly, at her own home or dining with him at little out-of-the-way places. Now and then he said something which made her heart turn over. . . . "How I've managed to get along as long without you, Christine!" Sometimes she sensed a rebellion in him, as if such things were said against his will. Early in the summer when the subject of vacations came up, when Nelson Yorke had asked her and her mother and Janis to take a short yachting trip with him, and she spoke of it idly to Lawrence, he astonished her by the violence of his disapproval.

"You can't do that!"

He was at her apartment. Her mother had gone out, after dinner, and Janis was not yet home. The lamplit room was intimate, the windows open to street sounds and a faint city breeze.

"Why not?"

"Because I won't let you!"

She trembled perceptibly, trying to answer lightly, but he went on savagely, though she scarcely heard him. "That man . . . his reputation . . . he's in love with you, Christine!"

She managed to ask faintly, "What of it?" but her hands were ice cold and her heart shook her.

"What of it!" he repeated, outraged. "But . . . *I* love you . . . you belong to me. You love me, don't you . . . and you'll marry me, darling, right away?"

It was a characteristic proposal. But even while she smiled, her eyes were suffused and she said, finding herself in that miraculous, strange, yet it seemed, familiar embrace:

"You know I do, Lawrence, so much, and of course I'll marry you. As soon as you wish."

5

They were married within a month. Looking back on it, Christine believed that four weeks to have been the most incredible in her life, in anyone's life. She went on working, fully conscious of the tempest breaking above her head and serene in her happiness. She expected her mother's tears, Janis's wild wires of congratulation, Nelson Yorke's shrugged shoulders and too casual felicitations; and she anticipated the flurry which would be aroused in the shop, and, sadly, a little resentfully, Howard Clarkson's opposition. . . . She had warned Lawrence.

"Your father won't like this."

"Why not?"

"I'm sure I don't know," she answered frankly enough, "I'm human enough to believe myself fairly eligible . . . but — you haven't known me very long, Larry, and perhaps your father has other plans for you."

Lawrence was furious. A grown man does not enjoy being told that his father has plans for him, especially if he more or less suspects that such may be the case. Lawrence and his father had not discussed a possible Clarkson daughter-in-law. Now and then his father remarked, "When you're married, I'll turn over the penthouse to you and retire to the farm." Yet Lawrence tacitly understood that when he did marry he would be expected to marry well. Which, he considered, he was doing.

What Christine could not anticipate was that Lawrence would assume complete command from the moment of their engagement. She had expected to have some hand in formulating their future. No matter how much in love a woman may be, how ecstatic, how romantically swept off her feet, she remains practical. It is she who plans the wedding, thinks of trousseau, of homemaking, of honeymoon. But to Christine's amazement she found everything arranged for her, with the utmost speed. Later she had time to examine this and even to resent it, but at the time Lawrence's highhandedness was merely a part of his enchantment for her.

Therefore, during the few weeks before her marriage she found herself as docile as a child — and with as little influence. They would be married quietly, in her apartment, decreed Lawrence, no fuss and feathers, with just his father, her mother and Janis present. They would spend their honeymoon in his hunting and fishing lodge on Peconic Bay, two whole weeks together, and then they would return to work and take up their residence in the penthouse. A marvelous solution, he thought; he didn't want the girl he married to be all worn out with wrestling with domestic difficulties, househunting, furniture buying, servant problems.

He fully expected that she would want to return to work. When his father asked, "Do you expect Christine to carry on in the shop?" he answered, amazed, "Of course I do . . . why not?" And when her mother fluttered and wept and said, tearfully, "But *surely* you won't permit Christine to go on working?" he laughed and patted her shoulder. "Permit her! I wouldn't dream of anything else. I'm too loyal to Clarkson's to deprive it of one of its greatest assets!"

He did not inquire whether Christine, herself, wanted to go on with her job. He simply assumed that she would . . . and Christine herself assumed it too. Certainly, had he suggested that she stop, fold her hands, become the perfect housewife and forget she'd ever held a pair of shears, she would have protested volubly. But even then it did strike her, penetrating vaguely through her dreams, her bewildering rapture, that Lawrence took it all pretty much for granted. But then hadn't he said, "Partnership's the most important thing in marriage — I couldn't love a woman, Christine, unless I considered her as much a part of my business as I did of my private life. We'll have the most amazing times together. We won't be like other people. . . . I'm sorry for the married men who come home to women who are utterly ignorant of their problems and of the daily routine of the time spent away from them. Such marriages aren't complete. Can't be, possibly. Ours will be!"

Of course, he was right. She found herself parroting his views to those of her relatives and friends who questioned the wisdom of this arrangement. The elder Austin was especially gloomy, she thought.

"Not that I don't approve of married women holding down jobs," he said, "theoretically. But sometimes in practice . . . One must make so many adjustments in marriage, my dear; and when it's marriage and business . . . I'm afraid you've got your job cut out for you."

"But it is my job," she told him, radiant, "and I'll love it. I've been so happy working with Larry."

"Because you were in love with him all along?" he asked shrewdly.

"No," she replied after a minute, flushing. "Well, perhaps a little . . . but not altogether. You see, I like my work, and to work with someone who understands, who co-operates . . . it's been wonderful. It will be more so . . . a mutual goal, something shared, comprehended by both of us . . . a vital partnership."

"Well," said Austin, "I wish you luck." He smiled at her. "I wish it could have been Francis, but as it isn't . . . all happiness to you, Christine."

Her mother was lachrymose but overjoyed. When Christine and Lawrence had announced their engagement to her she felt like a woman whose dearest ambition has been, halfway, realized. For there was still Janis. But meantime Christine was marrying sensibly and well. Mrs. Carstairs wasn't sure whether she was marrying suitably or not, as she still retained her notions about "trade." Still, Lawrence Clarkson was a personable and attractive young man, with an assured income and, it appeared, a position in society, trade or no trade. But something of her satisfaction was reft from her when she learned that Mrs. Clarkson would continue, as Miss Carstairs, to function in the shop. She fought against it, feebly. It was all too modern. It was absurd. It wasn't fitting. "And," she whispered, a little embarrassed at her own "modern" lack of delicacy, "what about children?"

Christine laughed at her and kissed her.

"Lots of time," she said cheerfully, "for all that."

"You're twenty-eight!" her mother reminded her. "When I was your age — "

"Yes, I know, darling. But twenty-eight's still fairly youthful according to new standards. And thirty! And thirty-five! And suppose we do have children, sometime," she added calmly, "what of it? There are people much better fitted to bring them up than I am. I don't know the least thing about them. And after sufficient time out I can go back to the job — our job."

Her mother sniffled, groped for a handkerchief and replied that she had always thought a married woman's home, husband and babies constituted her job.

"They'd still have time over, nowadays," said Christine. "Here's my handkerchief, you goose. And remember what happens to idle hands."

Christine was never given an exact report of what took place when Lawrence told his father of their engagement. She still believed the older man was hostile to her although Lawrence assured her that he was not. "He was delighted," said Lawrence untruthfully, "and you and your mother are to dine with him tomorrow night. You don't mind, do you, darling? He's old-fashioned . . . a little. . . . "

What really had happened was in the nature of a scene. "Absurd!" snorted Howard. "Poppycock! You're out of your head! Oh, a thoroughly nice girl, I admit, clever and very good-looking . . . but —"

"I'm in love with her," said Lawrence, and set his jaw. "I'm sorry, father, if you don't approve, but we're going to be married, and as soon as possible."

"I hope," said his father, "you'll have the decency to expect her to stop working."

"On the contrary," answered Lawrence quietly, "I expect her to keep on working." He grinned at his belligerent parent suddenly. "In fact I'm really marrying her for dear old Clarkson's, just to keep her in the business. She's our ace designer."

"I'll fire her," threatened his father violently and then looked ashamed as Lawrence chuckled.

"Oh no, you won't," he said gaily; "you forget you've retired."

Howard muttered something about control of stock and the board of directors and then reluctantly grinned back. Lawrence had plenty of stock of his own. The Adams family had quite a bit and Lawrence's mother, who had died during his first year at college, was an Adams.

"You'll wish I had, someday," prophesied

Howard grimly, and added unexpectedly, "I knew her father. He wasn't a bad sort. Good blood and all that. But he hadn't any guts. Couldn't stand the gaff. Lord, if I'd killed myself every time things went wrong I'd have to have had as many lives as a cat!"

This was not strictly true, and Lawrence knew it. There had been many times in the history of Clarkson's before Howard's time and since when there had been wars and rumors of wars, panic, depressions, a slowly falling market. But the backlog of their personal fortune was sound enough. No Clarkson had starved. They'd retrenched, put the money back into the business and waited; they had been clever and patient and cautious, and presently the money came back to them.

At the end of the long evening Howard had capitulated. He had to. Lawrence was all he had in the world and he suffered for his son a sort of idolatry which frightened him and which he concealed as best he could beneath a gruff casualness of manner, belligerence and violent disagreements. But if Lawrence was happy, nothing else mattered. If Christine didn't make him happy, he, Howard, would take steps. What steps he couldn't tell, as yet.

"All right, all right," he said testily, "marry her and between the two of you run the business. You're a grown man. I needn't warn you that the situation will have its difficulties. You'll find out soon enough. I suppose I must call on her mother?"

"It would be nice," said Lawrence, smiling, "but I doubt if she expects it. It isn't done nowadays."

"Don't tell me what isn't done nowadays," grunted his father. "I suppose we should be grateful that you haven't eloped. Tell you what. Have 'em here to dinner, tomorrow night. I — do you think she'd like your mother's pearls for a wedding present, Larry? . . . And would you want the square diamond? It will have to be reset, and maybe your girl has other ideas about engagement rings, but somehow I've always thought your wife would wear it."

So she did wear it a little later, in its new setting, and came to dine with Howard and Lawrence, and Howard and her mother got along famously, much better than anyone would have expected. Howard understood women like Mrs. Carstairs, small, rather helpless, petulant women who hadn't forgotten that they had once been great beauties; he understood business-women too, harder, cleverer, more on the defensive; and in his understanding, you married the former type and employed the latter.

Mrs. Carstairs was impressed by the penthouse, by the pine-paneled walls of the dining room, from which the Clarkson ancestors looked down, the clipper ship captain in seagoing uniform, painted against a background of uneasy seas, t'gallant and r'yals, and the succeeding clan with muttonchop whiskers, in frock coats . . . together with their wives, an austere if not uniformly handsome collection. The room spelled solidity to her, tradition and background, against which the incredibly elderly butler fitted perfectly.

Speaking of butlers, Lawrence had disposed of the housekeeping with the greatest of ease. Christine would have a housekeeper to run the place for her. There would be competent servants whom the housekeeper would engage. Christine need not lift a finger. Pomfret, the butler, would go with his father, as would the cook, who knew his father's diet to perfection, and by the time they returned from their honeymoon everything would be in order. His father would be established on the Island, and engaged in his hobby of raising Llewellin setters. He raised them successfully and never sold them, giving the puppies to those of his friends of whom he was especially fond. With Howard would go his more personal belongings, but the actual furnishing of the penthouse would remain as it was — "You like it, don't you, darling?"

She did like it, very much. The place was beautifully done. It was massive, masculine, substantial, comfortable. It did not occur to her, then, that she might have had a very happy time setting the mark of her personality on it, even if the result were perhaps less successful. She thought vaguely, Of course, there will be little changes . . . they will come with time.

So it was settled. The store buzzed with talk, with excitement. Rita Allen learned of the engagement at first hand. Lawrence told her, "Wish us luck, Rita," he asked, smiling at her.

She took it standing. She wished him luck, heard the news that Christine would remain in the shop with no more than a barely perceptible lift of her eyebrows and altogether acquitted herself marvelously. She was much more outspoken to the other designers when, after the news had been made public, they spoke to her about it. . . .

"I hear she's staying on?"

"Yes, of course. Mr. Clarkson feels she can't be spared," said Rita evenly, with a definite sting in her voice, "and of course," she added, "she has done very well indeed. One can't help feeling, however, that in a sense it's a pity . . . there are so many who need the work," she added.

Which was what a good many felt in the store. Rita had merely given the signal that it was quite all right to put it into words, provided one was careful who overheard.

Christine knew nothing of this. Neither did she notice the slightly altered attitude toward her, the fact that people no longer gossiped so freely in her hearing. The great Clarkson diamond blazed on her finger and soon, very soon, she and Larry would be going away together, alone.

Janis came down for the wedding, excited, as pleased as if she herself had made the match. Howard took an instant fancy to her, he liked her looks and her youth and her affection for her sister. He did not like Christine. He told himself over and over that he had no reason to dislike her, she was pretty, well-bred, brilliant, an asset not alone to his business but to his personal life. He would not probe deeply enough to find the root of his hostility established in the fertile soil of jealousy. Yet he would not have been jealous of another type of woman, of a girl like Janis, for instance, a little scatterbrained, brimming with vitality, thoughtlessness, youth. Perhaps it was because Christine herself was so poised and so assured that he feared her and her influence over his son; perhaps it was merely because he had not selected her for Lawrence.

But he was charming to her; he never did things by halves. He put the pearls around her neck, after the simple ceremony, and kissed her. He regarded her with the impartial eye of justice and admitted to himself that he had never seen a prettier bride save, of course, his own. She wore the loveliest afternoon frock of her own spring collection, and a big wide flattering hat under which her dark golden hair waved, drawn back from forehead and cheeks to show the pure outline of her oval face. Her dark, tiptilted eyes were luminous and the color came and went over her cheekbones. Her mouth was curved into the loveliest smile — and Howard thought, She *is* in love with him.

He hadn't believed it — quite. He'd told himself, She set her cap for him from the first, and why not? Yet in a way he had to believe it, for wasn't his son worth loving, for himself? Now he was sure of it. The girl did love him. Well, that was all that was necessary and his hostility toward Christine decreased although he liked her no better.

After the wedding a few close friends of each family came in: the Austins, a distant relative or two on the Clarkson and Adams sides, and Rita Allen. Christine herself had included Rita. She remembered Lawrence's saying, "Rita's one of the family." Rita, longing to refuse, had told herself, I'll go if it kills me; and so had gone. She made herself especially agreeable to Janis, with unforeseen results because among other things she told Janis that she would be perfect as a model. . . . "I wish I could persuade you," she said, smiling, "but of course your sister would have first claim."

"Chris? She'd just as soon kill me," said Janis, laughing. "I've had a yen to model for some time but she wouldn't hear of it."

"Oh," said Rita thoughtfully, and tucked that bit of information away for future examination and possible use. What she meant to do with it she didn't know, but any weapon seemed fair in this particular war; and Janis thought, When I graduate . . . I can't sit around and fold my hands . . . I'll have to do something, and what's the use of having a sister married to one of the best shops in town if she can't find me something to do?

Rita went home early from the reception, with a severe and authentic sick headache. She went back to her small, pleasant apartment, with such a good address and done in the best possible taste, shattered an expensive piece of pottery and tried not to cry . . . at thirty-seven tears are difficult and quite devastating. But when the pottery smashed against the eggshell-tinted walls she felt a lessening of tension, a certain relief. Well, it had happened, there was nothing she could do about it. Or was there? She would have to go on working day in and day out with Lawrence Clarkson and Lawrence Clarkson's wife. She had been clever enough to cultivate Christine and her friendship. She felt that Christine considered her a friend. And things had run smoothly for Christine. But if they didn't run as smoothly . . . Rita believed that she knew Lawrence better than Christine did, better than his father, better even than himself. Part of his admiration for Christine, something aside from emotion but very important, to a man of his type, was his pride in her, in her success, in her business acumen. If Mrs. Clarkson were to prove less clever than Miss Carstairs?

Mrs. Clarkson wasn't thinking of Rita. She wasn't thinking of anyone. She and Lawrence motored down to the lodge on Peconic Bay and were for two weeks completely and superbly happy. The lodge was simple, comfortable, and large enough to afford some privacy. An adequate couple, the caretaker and his wife, looked out for them. It was early summer, or late spring, depending on whether you regard seasons by calendar or weather. The air was warm and golden, and the bay was blue as heaven in the depths and clear green in the shallows. Perhaps it rained a day or so, perhaps one day was cloudy and windy and a little chilly. But they didn't know it. They sat in front of a log fire and were supremely content, or they put on rough outdoor things and went walking in the wet woods and smelled the good smell of drenched earth and of growing things, drawing vitality from the rain and reaching up toward the sun which would shine again very soon. And one night there was a thunderstorm, and Christine was afraid and Lawrence was amused and tenderly pleased. He rather liked thunderstorms himself.

They talked of the shop and of their work, and of people and of the world and conditions; they talked of themselves and of what they were going to do with their united lives; and they were silent.

Their emotional weather was completely fair, or, if stormy, exciting, thrillingly so. The only chill wind which blew was when Nelson Yorke was mentioned.

Nelson had been the cause of one slight difference of opinion during their brief engagement. Christine had said, "I wonder if I should invite him?" and knew that she should not. Oh, Yorke had never asked her to marry him, he didn't figure at all as the rejected suitor — she'd always thought it bad taste to flaunt rejected suitors at one's wedding — but then he had definitely displayed an interest in her and so perhaps she'd better not ask him. On the other hand, he had been kind and generous, a good friend. She could afford to forget the episode of one emotional moment in his car.

"I don't want him," said Lawrence. "I don't like him, and what's more important, I don't like your liking him."

This was pretty arbitrary and naturally she soon found herself advancing all sorts of arguments as to why Nelson Yorke should be invited. And so they almost quarreled; and then when Lawrence surrendered, too much in love, too newly in love to refuse her anything, saying, "Well, why not, if he hadn't asked you on that idiotic yacht of his I might not have got up my nerve to tell you that if you were vacationing with anyone it had to be with me!" she was sorry he had capitulated. Yet she asked Yorke to the small reception, "just a few friends, informally, to wish us well," and he had gratified, and affronted, and flattered her by refusing.

"I do wish you well," he had written, "but I won't come to the reception. I have a rooted objection to kissing the bride."

He had sent a gift, or rather gifts. He had sent an exquisite bowl of handmade silver, a museum piece, and he had sent an amazing Chinese robe, heavenly blue, with strange symbols, marvelously embroidered, and with jade buttons, a robe which had once belonged to the Old Buddha, the Dowager Empress. It was from this robe, exclaiming over it, its richness, its incredible workmanship, that Christine derived the idea of the Chinese influence in the autumn line she designed, on which she went to work almost as soon as she returned to the shop. The lines, the severity, the beauty, appealed to her enormously and she yearned, as soon as she set eyes on it, to translate those lines into modern apparel for the modern American woman. She spoke of this to Lawrence on their honeymoon, and he agreed with her, watching her draw the rough preliminary sketches to illustrate. "See, the fastening here, Larry. It's beautiful . . . not every woman could wear it . . . but those who can — they'll be out of their minds about it. Simplicity, perfection of line, luxury of material, formalized design."

Lawrence could see that. He had a flair for design himself, a real comprehension. But he could have wished that the idea had come to her through some other medium. Later he did not like to see her wear the robe, and after a time she no longer did.

Then, the two weeks were over and Mr. and Mrs. Lawrence Clarkson returned to the city to take up their respective jobs in, and their residence over, Clarkson's.

6

Lawrence's secretary, Miss Hanson, a marvel of middle-aged efficiency, had found Christine the impeccable housekeeper, Mrs. Finley, who greeted them at the penthouse and offered for their inspection a spotless kitchen presided over by a small, dry, Finnish cook, whose husband, Oleson, butlered to perfection. It seemed to Christine that she had stepped into a well-oiled and smoothly running machine. She felt more like a visitor than the mistress of this unique establishment. But Lawrence was delighted. He approved of the Olesons and of Mrs. Finley, and he said, with an arm about his wife, "You won't have a thing on your mind. . . . You can leave here in the morning and not give the house another thought."

He had announced that they would automatically lunch together in the apartment; would entertain business connections there. All Christine would be called upon to do would be to tell Mrs. Finley how many and at what time and the rest would be up to that incredibly silent and obviously competent individual herself. "For," Lawrence reminded her, "you can't do two jobs. I've seen too many girls dashing off to work in the morning and coming home to supervise their housekeeping, too tired to do it properly and far too tired to give the proper attention to their liege lords. We can't let that happen!"

No, she assumed, they couldn't. But as the pattern of the first few weeks fell into place she found that she was not losing the sense of being an honored guest in her own home, or perhaps a resident of a hotel. She resented this and yet took herself to task for the resentment. Mrs. Finley was a far better housekeeper than Mrs. Clarkson; and she admitted to herself that perhaps she wasn't overly domestic, she might not have made much of a success of supervision and the innumerable little details which make up the running of a household. Mrs. Finley kept the Olesons busy and as happy as was compatible with their slightly gloomy natures and she had found the Perfect Parlormaid, who doubled in brass as occasional seamstress and personal maid for Christine. A more beautifully run establishment could not be found in Greater New York.

It was obvious that Lawrence was proud of it. He intimated to Christine that when the summer was past and people began to return to town, they would do a good deal of entertaining. It amused Lawrence to play host. And a great many of the most important Clarkson customers had enjoyed being Clarkson guests.

They went away week-ends: to see Howard, to stop off and see Janis and Mrs. Carstairs, or to some country place on the Island or in Westchester. Lawrence insisted upon these jaunts . . . a day or so away gave one a new perspective, stimulated spirits fagged from heat and fatigue. Christine, coming upstairs on Friday afternoons, during the period when the shop was closed on Saturdays, and viewing the packed bags and sensing the car panting at the door below, was filled with a sense of haste and hurry which appalled her. She often thought that there would be nothing she'd like better than to go to bed in a high cool bedroom with the Venetian blinds drawn, flitting green light on the polished floor, and a tray containing iced tea and a salad for dinner. Then, too, the small, perfectly appointed terrace was pleasant on summer evenings, and she and Lawrence could be serenely happy alone there, with the dusk filling the city, the clamor softened and stars shining. But Lawrence was tremendously vital, completely absorbed in whatever pleased him at the moment

— a tearing drive out of town, a swim, a sun bath, a game of polo, a tennis match. He couldn't understand why she wanted to stay home occasionally. He was so proud of her and of his newly acquired status. He wanted to show her off. He liked being away from the shop and coming back to it, fresh, tanned, permeated with health and vigor.

As for the store, the seasonal slump had set in but Christine was fully occupied. She spent time on the floor, of course, but she was more often in the workroom or the designers' office. She was present at the fittings of all her own frocks and she adapted a good many originals to her customers' individualities . . . a neckline was too trying for this one . . . this figure needed a more graceful draping and the other less sensational sleeves.

In between she was up to her pretty eyes in the designing of the autumn line, with the Chinese influence.

Her personal happiness was deep and satisfying and a little frightening. But sometimes she wished she had more time to examine it closely, to gloat over it perhaps, to worship at its shrine. But that would take solitude and of solitude she had little. Sometimes up in the workroom, or bending over her drawing board, or draping lovely material on one of the models in the big model room, she would stop for a split instant whatever she was doing and think, amazed, her heart pounding, But *I'm Larry's wife*.

Before autumn came she realized that other people were fully if less emotionally cognizant of the fact. She was still scrupulously called Miss Carstairs by her associates. But now and then as she approached a group chatter died, and once when she found one of the models in tears and asked the reason, instantly sympathetic, the girl, who had always confided in her more or less, shook her head and was stubbornly silent. It took Christine a little time to realize that as the wife of the president her position had changed greatly. And there was another side to the picture . . . associates who had hitherto paid little attention to her were now most careful to accord her a good deal; and more than one asked, if not outright, then at least not subtly, her influence with the president on one matter or another.

More often than not the matters for which her patronage was solicited were of small moment. Before her marriage to Lawrence she would have thought nothing of ranging herself on the suppliant's side, if that side seemed the right one to her, and asking his advice or co-operation. But now she found herself hesitating, unwilling to take advantage of her influence as Lawrence's wife.

Lawrence was constantly about the shop. He did not believe in hiding behind a flat-topped desk, a barrage of typewriters and a guard of secretaries. The Clarkson policy laid down by that clipper ship captain who had known a great deal about silks, and who had employed the best dressmakers of his day to make them up, was one of working partnership between employers and employees. The original Clarkson had not felt that an executive should sit in an office, look over daily and weekly reports and study his balance sheet every six months and preside like a remote god at departmental meetings. He believed that the executive should be on the floors as much as possible. He believed that he should know how to sell and how to buy and that he should know so much that, when he advised his subordinates or gave them an order, he would be backed by a superior knowledge of the problem rather than mere authority.

The Clarksons who followed him had adhered to this. Lawrence's father spent more time with customers and salespeople than he had spent in his office. Lawrence had no intention of changing this. He had been brought up in the business and he loved it. It had color and excitement and adventure — there was color in figures, not merely the color of black or of red, but the color of life itself.

Not long after their return from their honeymoon the young Clarksons had a purely business encounter. It was in the custom salon, and Christine was busy with a customer when Lawrence strolled in through the department, regarding it with the eye of affection, for was it not his creation? He liked the uncommercial air, which distinguished all the Clarkson floors, the thick-piled carpet, the Chinese screens, the divans and smoking stands and the absence of exhibited goods. It was a slack afternoon and there were not many people about. He saw his wife before she saw him and observed her with pleasure as nearly impersonal as it was possible for the man who loved her to achieve. She looked cool and smart in her linen frock, miraculously cut, and her astonishing hair was beautifully waved back from her forehead, as he liked to see it. She had unutterable distinction, he thought coolly, and then his coolness vanished; he was thinking, It isn't long till closing time . . . when we'll go upstairs together, be alone, by ourselves, when I can tell her how much I love her. . . . At this minute he perceived that the customer was making herself unpleasant.

"It's absurd," she was saying. "I won't stand for it. . . . I'll tell my friends."

Lawrence knew a good many of his customers, both socially and by sight, but he had never seen this large, florid woman. Christine said something low, placating, and then turned a little, and saw him. He was delighted to observe that she flushed.

He came up without haste, and asked, smiling, "Is there anything I can do, Miss Carstairs?"

This was one of their private jokes. Not all the customers knew Lawrence or his relation to Christine.

This one did not. "Well, young man — whoever you are, I don't know whether you can do anything or not, but I have been very much upset — and this young woman here is not in the least helpful."

"I'm sorry," said Lawrence smoothly, as Christine, scarlet now to the roots of her hair, but not with astonished pleasure at the sight of him, said hurriedly:

"This is Mr. Clarkson."

The large lady was placated. She turned a wintry smile on Lawrence and pronounced her name. He had never heard it before, but he judged quite correctly that she was an out-of-town customer. She continued to talk, in full spate and from her conversational torrent the facts emerged.

She was Mrs. G. S. Elbron of Detroit. She had bought her clothes at Clarkson's for some time, twice a year. She was in town for a few weeks before sailing for an extended visit to Europe. She had allowed herself to be persuaded into a custom-made frock. It was absurdly high in price but she had been promised that it would "do things" for her. Well, it hadn't. The frock which she had been practically blackmailed into ordering made her look a fright. She wouldn't wear it. She would throw it back on their hands. And so far as the account went, they could sue her for it.

Lawrence said, quietly:

"We will take back the frock, Mrs. Elbron. Of course, it is not our policy, with custom-made garments. But," he smiled at her, "while I cannot imagine the accuracy of your statement that you look a 'fright' in anything, a dissatisfied customer is not the best advertisement of Clarkson's."

Mollified by her victory the lady empurpled and murmured something about "that's more like it — " with a vicious glance at Christine. And when a moment later she complained bitterly that she had so little time, that she must supplement her wardrobe before sailing, Lawrence blandly suggested the ready-to-wear department and himself escorted her downstairs, said a word or two privately in Rita's responsive ear, and left the redoubtable

Mrs. Elbron surrounded by models and completely pacified.

He went back to Christine, grinning slightly. Christine greeted him with a still heightened color.

"I did it very well," he informed her; "no, don't bother to congratulate me."

"But," she said, "two hundred and sixty dollars back on our hands . . . like that!"

"What frock was it?"

" 'Morning at the Lido.' It was entirely unsuitable. I didn't sell it to her. I was called in for the fittings. I tried to dissuade her, and she wouldn't listen to me. Oh, why," wailed Christine, "will women who are fifty if a day and who weigh one hundred and eighty, if a pound, persuade themselves that they will look just like Gwen Davis, modeling a frock, size fourteen, aged twenty-one and one hundred and six on the hoof!"

"Lord knows!" said Lawrence. "Don't be downcast, darling, your 'Morning at the Lido' will go on sale here at the end of the season with the other originals. Or you can ship it down to Rita if you like. You'll soon learn to judge people. That dreadful woman might lose us a good deal of out-of-town business. With someone else we might take a different attitude. You may remember Mrs. Turner, last winter? One of the O'Day line came back from her, and there was an ungodly row. We took the frock back, remember? And later it was reported to us that she was seen somewhere in its replica. She'd had it copied by some clever little dressmaker. Well, we could afford to lose Mrs. Turner's trade . . . it hadn't amounted to much, and she is, let us say, on the fringe. So we began bothering her for a long overdue account. But this is different."

He touched Christine's shoulder, as casually as he could, said, "I'll be seeing you," and walked away. She looked after him with something very like anger. He had handled it all so smoothly and easily. She couldn't have done it. She hadn't the authority. In the last analysis he would have had to handle it. It gave him just the fillip of superiority over her which, being a woman, she adored and resented in the same breath.

Autumn came and with it an increase in business, such an increase that Christine often felt rushed off her feet. And she was having trouble with Nancy Redding. Rita's niece was paying less and less attention to business and becoming more and more a liability to the department. She would have to do something about it soon, she thought in exasperation, Rita or no Rita.

She and Lawrence went to Mavis Downing's opening, the first really important theatrical opening of the season. Miss Downing played, as usual, a sort of perpetual rose in bloom, a type which still had its followers. In the lobby between acts Rita came up to them, looking especially handsome, and commented on the play. It was too bad that dear Mavis still thought of herself as sweet sixteen. One could bear it on the stage, but not off . . . the stage still possessed some illusion. But away from the footlights Mavis gave the lamentable impression of a baby parade, and, added Rita, "she's forty at least, and looks it."

That, thought Christine, who was making Miss Downing's offstage frocks, is a direct dirty crack.

Rita was saying, on a sudden breath, "Oh, I'm sorry. I forgot she was a customer." She laughed and shrugged. "And of course she isn't the sort of person you can guide in her choice. She still has a picture of herself as an ingénue with daffodil curls."

She departed, leaving the distinct impression that any fault with Miss Downing's appearance lay with the dressmaker who should have been able to persuade her to be at least approximately her age.

When Rita had gone, Christine said hotly, "I did try to persuade her . . . but, after all, she's a good customer and the clothes do become her, even if they are a little youthful."

"You don't have to defend yourself to me," said Lawrence instantly. "There's the curtain."

However, the episode did not cause Christine to feel very tenderly toward Rita and on the next day she and Nancy Redding had words. As usual, Nancy was spending most of her time in the model room smoking and talking, and was requested to assume the perpendicular and come out on the floor. Christine was extremely busy. She had salesmen to interview, reports to get up, a new, difficult client who was good for thousands a year if properly handled, and Nancy was not in evidence to do the things she had been hired to do — greet customers, summon whomever they wished to see, run errands to the workroom, telephone. . . .

Bidden, she came into Christine's office. No one else was there, and she stood sullenly by the desk. Christine said:

"I'm sorry to have to send for you to find fault, Miss Redding, but you are taking no interest in your work. You were informed of your duties when you came. They are not onerous. Nor am I the only person on the floor who has been hampered by your negligence. I am perfectly aware of your relationship to Miss Allen. But your aunt is a businesswoman and the welfare of the store is her deepest concern. I am sure if I explained to her that you might be happier elsewhere — "

"Oh," said Nancy, "so that's it! Want to get me out of here. I got that crack about coming in through my aunt. Well, everyone knows through whom you came in. And you got what you wanted, didn't you? But that doesn't give you any right to ride me. You've ridden me ever since I came into Clarkson's and I know why, if you don't."

"I'm afraid," said Christine evenly, "I do know why. But what reason can you offer?"

"Don't play dumb," advised Nancy. "You ride me because my aunt got me the job. You were jealous of her . . . everyone knew that if it hadn't been for you she and Mr. Clarkson — "

She stopped, flushing, and flung herself out of the room, aware that her temper had betrayed her into saying too much. Carstairs, having married Lawrence Clarkson, could get her fired. Or could she? Nancy went directly to Rita's office, and closed its door behind her.

When Nancy had gone Christine sat looking after her and adjusting herself painfully to the situation. She had heard gossip . . . she couldn't be in the store and not hear it, but she had always dismissed it. Rita Allen was *years* older than Lawrence!

Later she went downstairs to see Rita. She was some minutes too late. Rita listened to what Christine had to say. She did not mention the personalities, merely remarked that she felt Nancy would be more suited and more suitable elsewhere.

"Why, of course," said Rita smiling, "if you feel that way about it, Christine. I think I can talk to Nancy, however, and you'll find that things will be smoother. She's young and a little spoiled. I had wanted her in your department for various reasons. I believed she would work in nicely, and hoped she would show an interest in design, and I have no place for her with me. But if you really feel that she won't get along . . . " She stopped a moment and then added, "I'm glad you came to me. After I talked with Nancy — oh yes, she's been down here — I was afraid you might think it best to go — elsewhere."

She's warning me, thought Christine, not to go over her head.

For the first time she sensed Rita's definite hostility toward her. It made her a little sick. It simply could not be on emotional grounds, she tried to persuade herself. It must be that she resented the department. Then why pick on her, why not be as hostile toward the other designers?

She said, rising, "Thanks, Rita. I do feel that the work doesn't interest Nancy but if you can assure me that she'll make an effort — "

It was a direct challenge. Rita recognized it as such. She said sweetly, "I do assure you, Christine," but when the door had closed and she was alone her expression altered. Nancy would be spoken to, and sharply. She must watch her step. She could be very useful in Christine's department — to Rita.

At luncheon Lawrence ragged her because she seemed abstracted. "Up too late last night? Not that you need a beauty sleep — "

"I had plenty," she told him, smiling.

"Anything wrong?" he persisted, looking at her closely.

She couldn't tell tales. Especially in her position. But this was business, he was intimately concerned, being married hadn't anything to do with it.

"A little friction in the department," she admitted after a moment, "nothing much."

"Nancy Redding," he stated calmly.

"How on earth did you know!" asked Christine, wide-eyed.

"Rita told me, just before I came upstairs. Don't take it seriously. Rita will set the kid straight. She practically brought her up, and has done everything for her. She's the child of a much older sister, now dead, whose husband deserted her and Nancy."

"But she's entirely useless," argued Christine, "she's forever in the model room gossiping. It isn't good for discipline. And I think she carries tales from one department to another."

"You're exaggerating. In ordinary circumstances we'd give her a trial elsewhere, and if she didn't make good, fire her. But this case is different. Forget it, will you? Let's not ruin our luncheon which, by the way, is very good. And you haven't told me that you love me, since breakfast."

She didn't tell him now. She said slowly, "Larry, don't dismiss this from your mind. It isn't just a case of youth and inexperience. Nancy Redding dislikes me. She was impertinent. She intimated that I had come into Clarkson's through you simply because of your personal interest in me — "

"Well," he said, laughing, "that's true, isn't it?"

She stared at him, and a little color left her cheeks. "No," she said, "it isn't. I came because you liked my work, wanted it."

"Of course," said Lawrence instantly, "that was why I sent for you in the first place. But after sending for you I'd seen you — close . . . not at a distance . . . and wild horses couldn't have kept you out of Clarkson's, darling."

"You can't persuade me to that," she said stubbornly. "I won't be persuaded."

"Why not, when it was love at first sight?" he asked, laughing; then, with a change of mood, "What difference does it make? Rita's part of this shop. She helped to build it up. She's even a small stockholder. Now and then we have to overlook things — play ball. If, as you say, the Redding girl isn't any good, she'll soon fire herself. I didn't think you were so petty, Christine."

"Petty! I!"

"I mean, that you'd make an issue of this just because the girl offended you, personally. Of course being a woman I suppose it's only natural. . . ."

She looked at him in horror, rose and precipitately fled. When he followed it was to find her face down on the bed, crying bitterly.

"Christine, for heaven's sake!"

He took her in his arms, kissed her wet cheeks, her eyelids. He said distractedly, "Look here, we weren't quarreling, were we? Over Nancy Redding! I'll fire her tomorrow . . . I'll talk to Rita. . . ."

"No," said Christine, muffled. "No, I'll work it out myself . . . it will be all right. I'm sorry, Larry."

She knew the instant his arms went around

her how powerful were her weapons. Now, in this first year of their marriage she could persuade him, she could convince him — of almost anything if she used tears and embraces to fan the living flame between them. But she wouldn't, she told herself desperately, she wouldn't stoop so low . . . using their love for her own trivial ends. She'd fight it out with the insignificant Nancy and with Rita herself. She thought, I'll have to walk carefully, I'll lean over backwards, I won't employ our relationship for — for business purposes. She saw it as a sort of prostitution and it sickened her. Yet she knew that it would tempt her, often, to the easier way.

So they kissed and pledged themselves anew, and Christine went off to wash her eyes and to finish her luncheon, with laughter and no further mention of Nancy. Awareness was coming to her slowly. Nancy didn't matter, she was just a symbol. Yet it would be a long time before she would forget what Nancy had said of Lawrence and Rita. Looking back, she was forced to doubt all Rita's friendliness and sincerity. She doubted, by the same token, her own ability. Had not Lawrence told her that from the first moment his interest in her had been personal?

The honeymoon was over.

7

With the autumn and early winter season in full swing, Clarkson's was plunged into tremendous activity, humming beneath the surface like a great machine. The customer hurrying, or strolling, through the shop, realized this subconsciously, sensing the acceleration, the tempo of trade. There is a pulse, a beat, a rhythm to a big shop that is properly conducted and enjoying success of which the shopper is made aware although he or she puts no name to it. Outwardly Clarkson's ran smoothly, the departments were spacious, precluding overcrowding, the clerks trained to an ultimate of perfection . . . pretty girls, attractive older women, courteous men. Mrs. Jones from Jersey or Mrs. Vanorman of Manhattan purchasing stockings side by side could not be aware that the girl who sold them was aquiver with excitement because her best friend, the blonde who ran the third lift on the right-hand side as you entered, had been noticed by a great motion-picture director, en route to the custom fur department to order a coat for his current wife, with the result that Maisie would soon be submitting to the routine tests, with the glittering hope that it would be just a matter of time before, via the Twentieth Century and the Chief, she would "arrive" in Hollywood.

Mrs. Jones went on to the shoe department, that large room with chairs which were miracles of comfort and not a shoe in sight, but Mrs. Vanorman went up to the custom salon for her fitting.

Nancy Redding came forward to meet her, a Nancy rather more subdued than usual, yet alert, following a session behind the closed door of Rita Allen's office.

Mrs. Vanorman smiled upon her. It was a brisk day and the market had exhibited some signs of life. Mr. Vanorman was amiable and Miss Vanorman had met an eligible young man in her first season. All was well on the Vanorman horizon and as the outstanding Clarkson bills, long overdue, had been paid, Mrs. Vanorman felt that she could, with impunity, run up a few more. So here she was, for a fitting.

Nancy took her to a large, well-ventilated room with perfect lighting and long glacial mirrors, chairs, ash trays and a chaise longue upon which a lady might recover herself after an ardous ordeal. Presently Ada Regan came in, deft and quiet, the Vanorman model over her arm. Ada knew that sticking pins in a person worth some six to eight thousand a year to Clarkson's, overdue or not, just wasn't done.

"Is Miss Carstairs coming?" inquired Mrs. Vanorman, craning her neck to regard a slashed waistline.

"She's next door with a client," replied Ada, "she'll be along in a few minutes, Mrs. Vanorman. . . . Do you like the draping?"

"Very much," replied Mrs. Vanorman, "but I am a little disturbed about this line." She indicated the deep underarm décolletage, very trying for a woman of her age. She had preserved the good lines of her body with the help of expert massage, but right there — under the arms . . .

She had first seen the dress on Hulda Gustavson . . . Hulda was tall and slender and divinely fair. Hulda was twenty.

Mrs. Vanorman was on the whole satisfied with her lace gown, the color of blue ice. She was satisfied with Ada and with Miss Carstairs and with the fitting room and with all she had seen during her morning shopping. There was a good deal she did not see, at Clarkson's. She did not see the girls in the workroom upstairs, nor did she sense the unrest and hurry, the dreadful feeling that one must always be two jumps ahead of rival designers, competitive shops. She heard no gossip and knew of no enmities and she was quite unaware that her attitude toward Christine Carstairs had altered slightly since last week's fitting.

Christine knocked on the door and came in. She wore a brilliantly cut woolen skirt and a handmade pullover and she looked young and pretty and a little tired. She and Lawrence had been out for dinner and contract the night before and had come home after two. It had been a large, very gay party. And this morning she had shown models to a Hollywood star, en route to Europe and undecided between American goods and French. She had sat for two hours with the important young woman, who leaned back against the mulberry velvet of the divan and smoked impassively, watching the models slither out from behind the Chinese screens. She had procured an order for three frocks, two of which were her own, and of course it had been a rush order, only one fitting. Then she had supervised a final fitting in the next-door room, and here was Mrs. Vanorman, expecting service and plenty of it, and she'd get it too.

"Like it?" asked Christine, smiling.

"Of course . . . but . . . here —" Mrs. Vanorman frowned and indicated anxiously — "surely, that's a bad line?"

She didn't say, a bad line *for me*. She said,

"a bad line." All the difference in the world.

Christine spoke to Ada, moved forward, made an adjustment, and nodded. She said, "You're perfectly right, Mrs. Vanorman. We'll appliqué a little piece of lace in here, at each side. I think that will take care of it."

Presently Mrs. Vanorman was assisted out of the frock. Ada and Christine watched and helped, with a veiled anxiety. Women wouldn't wipe off their lipstick before a fitting, and many of them refused the paper underarm shields offered as a protection. And if delicate costly fabrics were stained . . . that, declared the average customer, was Clarkson's hard luck and not her own.

The frock was removed without mishap. Mrs. Vanorman, in her superb corsets and slip, surveyed herself in the mirror with some satisfaction and remarked, not too peevishly, that she should know better than to try on clothes directly after a finger wave. She put on her street frock and ran a comb through her white hair. Christine asked, after a consultation with Ada:

"You'll come Tuesday for a final fitting?"

"Oh, but I can't! I have a board meeting Tuesday and a bridge and then a cocktail party. No, it's out of the question, Miss Carstairs."

"But you want the frock for Friday?"

"I must have it Friday," declared Mrs. Vanorman firmly; "it's the Bursted dinner for Lord and Lady Manley. . . . "

Christine and Lawrence were going to that dinner, worse luck, thought Christine, feeling that if the season kept on as it had begun she would be in a sanitarium by spring . . . after the spring showing.

She said, "Then it will have to be Wednesday . . . at the very latest. . . . "

Mrs. Vanorman shrugged.

"Wednesday then . . . at twelve-thirty . . . that's the only time I have open."

Christine nodded and spoke to Ada and made a notation in a little book. This meant that her own luncheon hour must be postponed. Larry, who allowed nothing to interfere with the regularity of his noon meal, would eat alone. She watched Mrs. Vanorman putting on her hat and replied to her comments on the weather and thought, I'll have a sandwich and a glass of milk sent up to the office. . . .

In a way it would be pleasant, to be able to relax behind closed doors and look at a magazine and eat a sandwich. Lawrence expected her to be sparkling and unfatigued at luncheon, and there were times when this required an almost superhuman effort, when, after a difficult morning with customers or salesmen or fighting the other designers for the fabrics which, it seemed, all of them wanted, she had no energy left to expend over a luncheon table. At such times the paneled walls seemed to close in on her and the formality of the table itself to oppress her, and she could have dispensed happily with the solemn presence of the Clarkson ancestors.

Marriage, she reflected while Mrs. Vanorman chatted on, would be perfectly idyllic if one could see one's husband only at one's unfatigued best.

"By the way," said Mrs. Vanorman, "if I may venture to be personal, I didn't know about your marriage to Lawrence Clarkson until a day or so ago . . . I don't know why it escaped my notice, after all, I do read the papers . . . I hope you'll be very happy."

"We are," said Christine, smiling, "thank you so much."

"I've known your husband for a number of years," Mrs. Vanorman went on. "I daresay it isn't telling tales to confide in you that I once thought that he and Marguerite — that's my older daughter, now Mrs. Hawthorne . . . she married a very charming Englishman last spring . . . yes, there was a time when . . ." She patted Christine on the shoulder and said, "I hope you'll dine with us some evening. I'll call you up."

Christine left the fitting room with her and walked through the department, uncommercial to the point of emptiness. No display racks and no obsequious salespeople, a model or two walking about, several women talking and smoking on one of the couches, a perfume bottle of beautiful Lalique, on a little pedestal, a sable and lamé evening wrap flung over a petit point chair.

She scarcely touched her luncheon. Lawrence made an excellent meal and then, as it lacked ten minutes of the hour he permitted himself, took her by the arm and led her into the living room. Coffee was brought to them there, and he passed her his cigarette case. Christine shook her head.

"It gets in my hair . . . I hate to smell of stale smoke, on the floor," she said.

"You're off your feed," he remarked, "tired?"

"No . . . sleepy . . . " she yawned slightly, "last night was a little overwhelming."

Lawrence laughed.

"I feel," he announced, "like a million dollars. Look, you let me do all the talking at lunch. Anything happen this morning?"

"Not very much. I persuaded Dolly Painter into ordering three frocks . . . if she doesn't cancel. She informed me that she used to patronize Staneways . . . as if I didn't remember her there — and that she would of course buy her off-screen things in Paris if it weren't for the duty. Then I had a couple of fittings. One was Mrs. Alastair Vanorman . . . she's asked us to dinner . . . sometime . . . indefinite. . . ."

She glanced at him, smiling, her brown eyes very bright.

Lawrence said leaning forward to an ash tray:

"Nice people. I went to college with the son."

"And where with the daughter — may I inquire?"

"There are two daughters."

"I mean Marguerite."

"Oh, here and there." He laughed and ruffled her hair with his big hand. "I see that the customer has been talking. Remember, the customer is always right. Marguerite Vanorman's a very attractive girl." He put his arm around Christine and drew her close, a little roughly. "Jealous?"

"Of your dark past? Not very. Only," she sighed, leaning her bright head against him, "I do wish we needn't know our clients socially. It puts me at a disadvantage somehow. We go out to dinner and I look at our hostess, handsome is as handsome does, in a Clarkson custom-made, and I think of the horror of her fittings and the heartaches and the difficulties and I see her, quite undressed, and I lose my appetite!"

"Christine!"

"Well, I do. And then again, I sit opposite a woman at dinner and she's perfectly charming to me but she hasn't paid her bill for four months and I know it and she knows it . . . and . . . well, there you are."

"You'll learn to forget business after closing," he said.

"Will I? I wonder. By the way, you'd better plan to lunch at the club Wednesday, or something."

"Why?" He frowned at her. "Wednesday? Father is coming to town — for a couple of weeks . . . He'll stay at the St. Regis . . . I planned he'd lunch with us — "

"Your ex-girl friend's mother, Mrs. Vanorman, has a fitting at twelve-thirty. I'll be with her at least an hour," said Christine.

"I see. Well, we'll plan dinner then," said Lawrence.

"Can't. We're going to the Norths' for dinner that night."

Lawrence looked at his watch. "Must go. You too." He rose, pulled her to her feet, kissed her, said, "Comb your hair, or else — " and went whistling down the hall.

Christine briefly invaded their bedroom

and a little later went down in the private elevator with her husband. On her floor, they parted. She was smiling, she felt rested for just the few minutes sitting relaxed in the curve of his arm. But she was met with news of a minor disaster. One of the models hadn't shown up all day. She had phoned she'd be in after luncheon, but she wasn't in yet.

Christine went to the model room. Big, bare, the dressing tables running around two sides of the room, slippers hooked on shelves beneath, mirrors glaring with lights, cigarette stubs in pin dishes, and lipstick on tissues and on towels. On the third side of the room were racks of originals, on the fourth a couch . . . there were straight chairs, one window, and a door leading to a stockroom.

The girls sat around in various stages of undress. The mirrors were decorated with clippings from newspapers, cards, cartoons. The chatter was shrill and lively. Christine looked around. Her appearance created no excitement, one or two of the girls spoke to her, others smiled, and still others paid no attention whatever.

"Helga, where's Gwen?"

Helga shrugged her slim, creamy shoulders.

"I dunno, Miss Carstairs . . . she phoned in she wasn't feeling so hot — "

Christine frowned. She needed Gwen. She had draped and pinned a new frock on the cardboard figure she used, now it was in the second stage and she had planned to use Gwen for further draping and pinning. Besides, she had a mother and daughter coming in later to select trousseau models and Gwen was about the girl's height, weight and coloring.

Well, she'd use Helga. She left the model room conscious that the chatter grew louder and more carefree as she departed. She thought, As if I'd let Janis . . . !

Janis was still set on being a model. "Look at their opportunities . . . commercial photography, and then a step to stage or Hollywood." No, thought Christine, shaking her head, I won't let her.

It was a lazy life, in a sense. Oh, tiring, bodily fatiguing but — lazy. They thought of nothing but figure, skin, a new hair-do, and their dates. They were paid by the day, they skipped their lunch hour to pose for the photographers or the illustrators; as a class they were without further ambition. Some of them reached Broadway or the screen, some became interested in designing, in buying or selling. But these were in the minority. Knowing Janis as she did, Christine knew that Janis would not be one of these.

It was such a *physical* sort of existence, she thought, making her way back to the floor. Lawrence didn't agree with her. He thought that Janis had the right idea. If she wanted to model, why did Christine stand in her way?

Janis and Mrs. Carstairs dined with them that evening and Janis began her old arguments. She couldn't see why Christine was so opposed to her modeling . . . and she was sure Larry couldn't either.

"You'd never last," said Christine, across the table, "it's hard . . . changing fifty, a hundred times a day, standing on your feet, in spike heels, learning to walk, to parade yourself up and down. You'd be fed up the first day."

"I would not," contradicted Janis indignantly, "and think of the chances I'd have."

"There aren't many . . . " began Christine.

"Oh, don't be like that," cried Janis. She began to enumerate the girls who had gone from dress modeling to stage and screen.

"I know," said Christine wearily, "but they constitute a very small percentage."

"Ellen O'Day was a model!" said Janis triumphantly.

Christine nodded. "She was, for a short time. She was earning money to take her art courses, it was a means to an end. She happened to have the figure, that's all. You haven't any interest in or talent for designing. If you had you wouldn't have to model as a start."

Janis's blue eyes sparkled. "You sound just like Francis." She looked over at Lawrence. "Can't you persuade her?"

"I've tried," he assured her, while Mrs. Carstairs said, mildly:

"Really, I think Christine is right. It isn't the proper thing for you, Janis. It isn't at all suitable."

Later, when the Clarkson car had taken the Carstairs home, Lawrence demanded, wrenching at his collar:

"What was that crack your mother made? and why?"

"Crack?" repeated Christine vaguely. She was ready to drop. She sat down in a low chair, took off her slippers and held one slender foot in her hands.

"About modeling not being suitable for Janis."

"I didn't think it was a crack, and it isn't suitable," said Christine unthinkingly. "I don't want her in the shop — or any shop."

The collar was flung on the dresser. Lawrence, fumbling with studs, his hair disheveled, asked hotly:

"And what's wrong with the shop?"

"Oh, Larry!" She sat back, sighing, and regarded him. "Why must you be so sensitive?"

"Sensitive!"

It was, she realized, quite the wrong word. He said savagely, before she could speak:

"I fail to see why your sister should be above this shop — or any other. I'm not above it, nor are you. It gives us our living, and a pretty good one. It stands for something. Work, success, tradition. . . ."

She exclaimed softly, "For heaven's sake, Larry, I'm not an emptyheaded little snob. Of course it does. But Janis isn't adapted, temperamentally, to the job she thinks she wants. She shouldn't have it. It would be very bad for her."

"She wouldn't be the first college girl," he reminded her, "to model in Clarkson's."

"Larry, I know that. Oh, why won't you understand?" She thought of cigarette butts, with the red stains on them, and the telephone numbers scrawled on the white paint of the dressing tables . . . she thought of a number of things. She thought, Larry isn't a snob, yet he's acting like one . . . terribly on the defensive. . . .

She said wearily, "Don't let's quarrel, Larry."

"I'm not quarreling," he said coolly,

"you're making all the gestures. Personally I'd rather Janis wasn't employed by Clarkson's. Family jobs rarely work out —"

He didn't think that about Rita Allen and Nancy, she thought. But he was continuing. "It isn't any of my business what you do with your money, Christine, if you want to spend it on Janis . . . if you want to keep her indefinitely until she makes up her mind to marry Austin, that's all right with me. I merely thought you'd rather have her working, making herself useful, and where you could keep an eye on her. But it's up to you. Only I wish you'd stop bickering with her about it. It doesn't enliven a meal, so far as I'm concerned."

No, he didn't dictate how she spent her money. Clarkson's paid her and she spent it on her mother, on Janis, on her own small investments, whether a few shares of stock or a modern painting. Larry took care of their joint living expenses and deposited, over her protests, a monthly sum in a special account, for her. He was more than generous. She looked at him and laughed aloud.

"What's that for?"

"Nothing. You look like a small boy in a temper. What on earth is the matter with that stud?" She rose and went over to him, in her stockinged feet, stood on tiptoe and kissed him. Her deft fingers touched the stud briefly.

"There!"

"Oh," said Larry, and kissed her, "what would I do without you?"

8

On Wednesday Mrs. Vanorman came for her fitting. She was late, of course. The number of women who kept their appointments exactly could be counted on one hand, Christine reflected. Larry planned to go to the club with his father, and Howard would lunch with them both at home tomorrow.

At one-forty-five Christine went into her office and closed the door. The impulse for sandwich and milk had left her. She would ask someone to go out to lunch with her . . . but almost everyone had gone, or was coming back again. Rita? No, Rita would have gone out long ago. She opened the door and looked out. . . . Nancy Redding was slithering by in her infuriating manner. Christine smiled at her, determined to preserve the peace. "I suppose Miss Allen has gone to lunch?" she inquired.

Nancy responded with her veiled insolence: "She went upstairs with Mr. Clarkson some time ago."

"Oh, I see. Thanks. I thought perhaps

she'd be free," murmured Christine.

She went back to her mirror and reddened her lips furiously and tilted her little hat over one eye. Larry hadn't said a word about Rita joining him and his father. Christine shrugged. Silly to be angry. It was probably a spur-of-the-moment business . . . he'd seen her around, remembered that his father was coming — Howard was very fond of Rita — and had asked her to join them at lunch. He simply hadn't bothered to tell her, Christine. Logically, why should he? All he had to do was telephone upstairs and inform the house-keeper that there would be three for lunch, after all. It wouldn't occur to him that that was Christine's province. Well, perhaps it wasn't . . . perhaps she belonged to the floor, in the workroom and fitting rooms, and not upstairs, in the butler's pantry.

Rita and Howard would have an elegant time talking shop!

She went out, conscious of the pre-Christmas crowds on the Avenue, the crisp clear air, the golden sun which had been obscured for a day or so and was now shining bravely. The street teemed with shoppers, gay red packages under their arms. She'd have to take a little time off and do some shopping herself, she reflected, drawing the sables Larry had given her a few weeks before more closely about her. She wondered what on earth she could give him. He had — everything. She stopped to look in a window and a man said, "Fancy meeting you here — it's a small world, as I always tell the missis."

It was Nelson Yorke, smiling down at her, looking very fit. She was inordinately glad to see him. He represented something far removed from Clarkson's and fitting rooms and hurry and organization politics.

"You're looking pretty grand," he commented, "what are you doing abroad at this hour?"

"Going to lunch. I was held up, in the store."

"How about coming with me?"

"You've probably had your lunch."

"No, I was on my way to the Plaza. That can wait. Let's go somewhere. I was walking for my manly figure. But we'll taxi."

He stepped to the curb, raised his stick and hailed a cruising cab. Christine said, hesitantly:

"I can't take much time, Duke."

"Nonsense. You're allowed an hour." He grinned at her cheerfully.

"But what about your date?"

"Merely a man, on business. His business. I'll see him later. I'll phone from our destination."

"Which is . . . ?"

"More fun not to know," said Yorke.

He gave the driver an address and they drove to a small French place on the West Side. Good food, no music, subdued lights, and excellent liquor . . . "one of the few places not ruined by repeal," explained Yorke lightly.

He telephoned the Plaza and had his man paged. Christine, waiting for him outside the booth, was convulsed with laughter. She could not hear what he was saying but his face expressed contrition, sorrow, regret, humility, in altering degrees, and he made sweeping gestures. When he came out she said severely:

"I hope your friend was properly impressed. Too bad that television is around the corner. He would have been overcome. You looked as if you were reciting 'The Wreck of the Hesperus.' "

"He'll buy his own lunch and meet me at the office at four," said Yorke serenely. "After all, he has something to sell, he can afford to be co-operative. He has an invention he wants me to see."

They went into the dining room and Nelson ordered a superlative meal. While they were eating he told her the various amusing things that had happened to him since they last encountered each other "a hundred and fifty years ago, by the clock . . . now tell me about yourself."

"There isn't much. I'm awfully busy."

"Good. Everything running smoothly?"

"Well — does anything really run smoothly?" she countered. "But it's all right."

"Happy?"

"Yes, very," she answered simply, and looking at her, he believed her. He said, after a minute:

"I suppose personalities are out of order. But your marriage gave me something of a jolt."

"That," said Christine placidly, "is your imagination," but her heart quickened a little, pleasurably. The woman hasn't been born who wouldn't react to the implication.

"No, I think not," he told her gravely. "It's a little late to tell you now and I am speaking out of turn, I'm aware of that, but until I met you the thought of marrying again never entered my head."

She tried to laugh. "Duke, don't be silly. It never entered your head after you met me, either."

"I'll admit that too," he agreed, "that is, not until you married Clarkson."

"That," said Christine, "is idiotic. If it's true, it's just because I was out of your reach.

Not very flattering. I mean . . . as if you had looked over an interesting piece of, say, pottery, for your collection and decided you didn't want to pay the price for it. Then someone else came along and took it — and now you're sorry!"

"I don't think it was quite like that," he told her. "However, have it your own way. I know what I know."

"You sound like Public Enemy Number One," she told him, "mysterious and a little menacing. No, Duke, I'm afraid that if I hadn't married Lawrence thoughts of domesticity wouldn't have occurred to you. But as I did . . . and the acquisition has become impossible — "

"Let us, rather, say improbable," he interrupted, "I like it better."

Christine stared a moment, and then laughed. She said, her slender hand poised over her coffee cup, "I didn't dare tell the waiter two lumps. He would have set me down as very bourgeois."

"You changed the subject sweetly," he told her, smiling, "but it isn't changed for me — yet. While there's life there's hope . . . even when there's wife."

"That's a very bad joke," she told him, "and in very poor taste." She looked over at him and her whole small face sparkled. "My poor

Duke, you're just providing yourself with a sentimental alibi. Next time you meet a woman who has an urge for the hearthstone and you feel yourself slipping, you have but to tell her, sadly, 'Alas, I love one woman only and she is wed to another!' "

They both laughed. Nelson Yorke said, after a moment:

"Perhaps you're right, but I think you're wrong. We'll see."

It was close on three when they returned to the shop. Christine's conscience was clear enough. She had one appointment only, for three-thirty. Nelson got out of the taxi and helped her to the street and paid the driver. He would walk, he said, to his office. As they stood there, the cab just pulling away, Lawrence and Howard Clarkson emerged, not from the private side door but from the main store entrance.

Christine saw them first and waved to them. She said, as they came up, "Hello, you two." She gave Howard her hands, smiling. "How are you?" she asked. "No, don't tell me, you look marvelous. I was kept very late by an appointment, and ran into Mr. Yorke on the Avenue. He gave me such a good lunch."

She was conscious of explaining too much under Howard's keen blue eyes. She felt guilty, which was absurd, as she was innocent. The three men exchanged greetings, and preholiday wishes. Presently they separated, Howard and Lawrence to walk away in the opposite direction from Yorke, and Christine to enter the store.

When she went upstairs after closing, conscious that she must hurry if she wanted a rest and a long, relaxing tub before dressing for their dinner engagement, Lawrence was not there. He came in, some time later, and she turned from her dressing table.

"You're late," she accused him, "you'll have to hurry."

"I know," he told her amiably. "I walked over with Father to the hotel and then came back and got balled up in a lot of work. I left before closing, had to see a man outside. I'll step on it."

It wasn't until they were in the car driving to the Norths' that he spoke of Yorke.

"Funny, your running into him like that, wasn't it?" he asked casually.

"Yes," she said, unthinking and then, on a swift indrawn breath:

"Larry! You don't think — you're not trying to say that I *didn't* run into him!"

"Of course not," he said slowly, "but . . . it did look a little odd. You made such careful arrangements . . . several days ago . . . you wouldn't be home for lunch today, Mrs. Vanorman would keep you late . . . and . . ."

She said stiffly, "Very well; if you don't believe me, there's nothing more to say."

Her lips shook, in the darkness of the car, and she clasped one hand tightly over the other.

Larry said, "I do believe you, darling. It just — looked odd. I found myself explaining to Father —"

She turned on him, in anger.

"And why should you?" she demanded, and now her voice shook too. "There wasn't anything to explain. I was kept late, as I knew I would be. At a quarter to two I thought I'd go out rather than send for something. There wasn't anyone around . . . I asked where Rita was, thought she'd go along, if she, too, happened to be late. But I was informed that she was lunching with you and your father. So I went out alone and ran into Nelson Yorke outside the shop. He offered to take me to lunch, and I saw no logical reason why he shouldn't. After all, you changed your plans, it's your privilege — and mine too."

"There's no reason to go off the handle," said Larry, tinder to her spark. "I had every intention of lunching at the club, but Father came along early, we went down to talk to

Rita . . . and decided . . . Oh, hell, what's the use?"

"Exactly," murmured Christine.

They were silent a minute. Then Lawrence said, stubbornly:

"I've no particular objection to your lunching with other men; no, that's not true. I don't like it, especially. But it wouldn't bother me, at all — "

"How modern of you," said Christine.

"You needn't be sarcastic," he told her. "It's just — Yorke. I don't like him, and never will; and he — he's in love with you, Christine!"

Her anger vanished miraculously. She laughed and put her hand over his.

"Darling! So I may have lunch with men who aren't in love with me?"

"If there are any," he told her.

"That's the nicest thing you ever said to me. But there's only one. You. At least — so I've been led to believe," she ended inquiringly.

He put his arm around her, held her.

"Look here, we both have tempers. Mistake to lose 'em at the same time, don't you think?"

"I do, indeed."

"And no more Yorke?"

"No more Yorke," she agreed. "But you're

mistaken, Larry. He isn't in love with me, really. He likes me, he's always liked me. And I was never in love with him, not for a minute, not even before I met you. There, does that satisfy you?"

"I suppose it will have to."

"No — for heaven's sake. All my make-up ruined! And here we are at the Norths' . . . where we'll have to be stately all evening. Larry, will you please behave yourself?"

But hours later, with the Norths' Old Guard dinner party safely behind her, when, after Larry slept, she lay awake, pleasantly drowsy, listening to a wicked little wind howl around the terrace, she thought, Why didn't we talk it all out? Duke and this business of Rita's going up to lunch and of Larry's discussing me with his father? I can just hear them! Why didn't we? But we didn't. We were too busy kissing and making up. And I was pleased as a pussycat because he was jealous. That seemed to be the thing which was most important. But it wasn't. It wasn't important at all!

She hadn't even asked him if he and Rita and Howard had discussed anything of interest to her. She did so the following morning at breakfast but he shook his head, grunted vaguely and went on reading his paper. It was Howard, coming briskly to luncheon that noon, who spoke of it.

"Satisfied with your department, Christine?"

"Very . . . have you seen the reports?"

"They look all right. Novelty. First year isn't what counts. Wait and see," Howard warned her. "Women rush to anything new. Takes years to build up a regular clientele. They'll rush away just as fast, you know. Or don't you?"

"Yes," said Christine, fighting her annoyance, "I know, all right."

"Rita," said the elder man complacently, "plugs right along. I'm afraid you haven't quite sold her yet, Christine. She still insists it's a duplication. She's right. Her department has aways stood for the unusual and exclusive in the ready-to-wear line. Few of each line offered . . . no one else carries them . . . the alterations are clever, and each number when it leaves the shop is as if made for the customer who bought it. You won't see its exact counterpart."

This was pure Rita! Christine had heard it all before. She said, smiling determinedly:

"Well, we'll show you. Has Larry talked to you about the enlargement of the beauty salon?"

"Yes, and I don't approve," said the old man. "No sense to it. Big enough as it is.

Didn't want it in the beginning, put it in as a concession to a lot of cackling females . . . must say it's done well enough. Personally I thought we'd do better with it if we let the Stairs-Maine people run it, but Larry didn't agree with me."

The Stairs-Maine Company was a big concern which operated beauty salons in a number of specialty and department stores. But Lawrence had held out against it. Clarkson-operated or not at all, he had said.

Christine said, pacifically:

"I still think the alterations will pay. It doesn't take care of enough customers now. Women who plan a morning's shopping here don't want to go elsewhere for their titivation. We are trying, through advertising, to sell them the idea that they will look better in the new Clarkson hat or frock if they have a different hair-do created for them in the salon first, or a facial, with proper make-up. Likewise, if they are tired after shopping, an hour's facial or scalp treatment will rest them."

"Well, maybe," said Howard grudgingly, "but it's a lot of money — in these times."

"We charge a lot," said Christine coolly. "Most of the women who come here expect to pay. They wouldn't be interested in a two-dollar facial or a five-dollar permanent no matter how good. The woman who insists on the original French model in hats wants original model facials to go with it. Granted that our copies are as good, sometimes better, and a lot less expensive, and granted that for half the price of a Clarkson facial she'll get more than her money's worth. Her mind just doesn't work that way, Mr. Clarkson."

She couldn't call him "father." She'd tried, but she couldn't.

"Well, time will tell," was all he would say, and turning to Larry, spoke of something else.

There wasn't much use. Any suggestion from her would antagonize him. He was charming to her — except on matters of store policy. He treated her with the utmost courtesy. But, she thought, he didn't like her. And she was sorry. She liked him. She couldn't help it, for in many ways Larry was so like his father. She wished she might win him over . . . she had tried.

She spoke of it to Larry later.

"I wish your father liked me."

"He does, darling. What an idea!"

"Not very much. I wish he were really fond of me," she said wistfully. "He's such a dear, really. But you disappointed him by marrying me, Larry, and he just won't see any good in me or in the marriage. He's trying, because he's a grand old sport."

Lawrence said uneasily, "I think you're mistaken. Perhaps he isn't overexpansive. And he takes a long time to make up his mind, that's all. And you — you *do* hold him off, Christine. Look at the way Janis treats him, as if he were a combination of Santa Claus and Casanova! She makes a terrific fuss over him and he loves it. Those two get along like a house afire whenever they are together."

"Yes, but Janis isn't married to his son. And . . . I'm not demonstrative, Larry. Oh, don't look at me like that," she added, flushing. "I mean, with anyone but you. I suppose I'm shy, really. Go on and laugh and see if I care! But I am. And if I tried to make a fuss over him as you put it, I'd always be thinking that perhaps he'd think there was a motive in it — "

"Wouldn't there be?"

"Yes, of course. You confuse me, Larry, I wish you'd stop. But a perfectly sincere motive. But he might question the sincerity. I do understand his feeling. You're all he had, he'd resent any woman coming between you and especially one he hadn't selected for you."

"Selected for me! I should hope not!"

On Friday night they went to the dinner for Lord and Lady Manley and Christine had the pleasure of regarding Mrs. Vanorman in her perfect frock — the appliqué had been a great success — and of meeting the nobility. She was unprepared for Lady Manley's whoop of amazement when, turning from her host to her other dinner partner, she discovered Lawrence Clarkson. "How very quaint!" said Lady Manley, viewing Lawrence with astonishment. Later it transpired that Lady Manley had encountered Lawrence in Clarkson's that very morning. She had had a slight altercation with a shoe salesman, and Lawrence had come up providentially and settled it. And here they were side by side at one of the season's important dinners. Very quaint, indeed.

Lawrence didn't seem to mind. He got along marvelously with Lady Manley who was, primarily, a good egg. She wore her teeth on the outside, her voice was slightly sawmill in quality and she was so painfully British that it was no surprise to Christine to learn that she had been born in Iowa some fifty-six years ago. No, Lawrence didn't mind at all that Lady Manley found it quaint to sit next to Trade at dinner. Christine minded. She minded a lot. Customers, she told herself savagely, should be seen and even heard . . . but not socially.

There was something wrong with the shrimps that night. Larry was susceptible to shellfish at times, especially those shellfish which had been too long removed from their native habitat. Shortly after reaching home the shrimps went to work on him, with devastating effect. He was a very sick young man. At first he was afraid he would die and then he was afraid he wouldn't. No, he didn't want the doctor. Would Christine please go away and let him suffer?

She was up with him most of the night, consulting Mrs. Finley about remedies, heating water for hot-water bags, sending the gaunt housekeeper back to bed. Mrs. Finley was very helpful. Her husband, she said, used to have the colic. A mustard plaster for the stomach did the trick.

Larry didn't like the things they gave him to drink, and he was sure one hot-water bottle leaked and the electric pad got too warm and altogether he was in a bad way. They burned him, he howled, with the mustard plaster. "Go away," said he, "and let me die. No, I won't have the doctor."

It was the shrimps, all right, but it wasn't ptomaine. The next morning he felt like a new person and ate the largest breakfast on record. Christine felt horrible. She had been worried half sick herself, she had had no sleep, and the thought of Saturday in the shop, with guests coming to dine that evening and the theater after, appalled her. During the afternoon she crawled away from her floor and managed a session in the beauty salon. Lying relaxed under the operator's skillful fingers she longed for bed, tea and toast, a detective novel and lights out at nine. But Larry, with his extraordinary vitality which could take shrimp in its stride, would not agree with her. So dinner and theater it was, with Larry at his best and Christine at her worst. She did not look as tired as she felt but she looked tired, and Larry was infuriated beyond all measure when one of their women guests, surveying her hostess, said in sprightly accents, "Are you sure you don't work your charming wife too hard, Mr. Clarkson? She does look terribly worn out!"

Afterwards when they were home again and Christine was wearily dragging herself out of her garments, Larry, wide awake and fit, insisted upon discussing the theme of the play. Christine answered listlessly. He stopped and stared at her. "I don't believe you saw or heard anything!"

"Very little," she admitted. "I was interested in the clothes, though . . . didn't Fleurette do them?"

"Clothes!" repeated Larry. "An important play and the best acting of the season, and all you think about is *clothes*. Can't you forget your job, even for an evening?"

9

Christine stared at him for a moment. Then she said slowly:

"Larry, I don't know. I want to say, Yes, I can; and that's true, as far as it goes. Yet I suppose it's always in the background."

"That's the trouble with women. Single track. I can lock up the works in my desk and come home, and have a swell time, with no strings to it, but you — "

He was perfectly amiable, the slight testiness of his question had vanished. Christine, sitting on the edge of her bed, smiled at him. She said, caressingly:

"You're a goof. Perfect, of course. What you are trying to say is that you can forget business — when it suits you. But what about the evenings we're alone and you keep me up till midnight talking policies and figures and economies?"

"That's different. Partners, aren't we?" He sat down beside her, pushed her with the flat of his hand, catching her off balance. Christine collapsed, and lay still, her arms crossed behind her head. Larry, leaning over her, said urgently, "Well, aren't we?"

"Of course we are, darling. Do get up. Hurry. I'm so tired I could scream."

"Do," he said tolerantly.

She opened her mouth and instantly his big hand came down over it. "For heaven's sake!" he warned. "What would Mrs. Finley think?"

They laughed, idiotically. They were young, they were in love, they were, fundamentally, happy. But Christine, despite her fatigue, did not sleep. After the lights were out she lay there thinking, wondering why she and Larry were so dissimilar in their reactions to business, after hours.

She decided finally that it lay in the viewpoints. Larry's was a bird's-eye, an airplane, view of the store; hers was a series of small, clear close-ups; his in a sense was impersonal; hers, personal. It was harder for her to wrench her mind away from the day's problems. His mind was divided into a series of compartments: business; home; outside activities. Hers was like an attic, she thought ruefully, all jumbled up.

There were times when Larry opened the door between one compartment and another, when he wanted to talk about the store, when he insisted upon it. There were others when the least mention of it irritated him. Christine sighed. Talk about understanding women. Why couldn't someone write a book on understanding men? They were so complex, so ornery, and unexpected, and temperamental! And so far as understanding women was concerned, the woman who wanted to be understood was crazy.

She said suddenly, across the space between them:

"Look here, Larry, if I'd married someone else and kept on with the job, I'd have been careful to divorce it from domesticity. I would have done my best to — to insulate it from the home fires. But I married *you*. And you're part of the job . . . it's all mixed up with you, I can't untangle it and that's why, Larry."

"Mpmph . . . grumph . . . khroo . . . !" remarked Larry, out of his dreams into which her voice penetrated faintly, a small, persistent buzz like that of a mosquito.

Now he sat bolt upright, coming wide awake.

"What's that?" he demanded. "Did you call me, Christine?"

He employed the aggrieved but responsive tone of the fond husband who has been awakened from his first, sweet sleep by a willful wife.

"I did not," she said firmly, "you're dreaming. Lie down and go back to sleep."

As the days wore on and Christmas came and went and they entered into a new year, Christine became more keenly aware of the difficulty of maintaining proper balance between the store job and her job as Larry's wife. It was so hard to know what to do, when to speak, when to hold one's tongue. . . . Take the business of Larry's secretary, Miss Hanson.

Miss Hanson had not been well since the autumn. She had worked hard, saved, invested wisely, and now it seemed to her that she could afford to retire. She gave Lawrence her notice and while she regretted his dismay — for he depended on her, she had been Howard's secretary as well — she was firm in her refusal to stay on.

"I can't go on, Mr. Clarkson," she said, and smiled, remembering the days when he was "Lawrence" to her, when, if his mother was ill, she had taken him to the matinee, bought his clothes, seen him off on a train for school. "I wouldn't be worth my salary to you after a while. I simply must stop. I've a little place in the country and a young cousin to keep house for me. But I won't leave until I find someone to take my place."

Lawrence grumbled. It was inconsiderate

of Maria Hanson to grow old and ill in service and to leave him in the lurch. While he grumbled he was thinking of something he could do for her. He would consult his father. Surely she deserved a bonus, and Clarkson's mustn't lose touch with her. She had been far too valuable.

"Have you anyone in mind?" he asked.

It appeared that she had; a young man in the accounting department. Clever, industrious, honest, with fine secretarial training. Fred Parker. She was sure Lawrence would like him.

Lawrence wasn't sure. He'd never had a man secretary. He didn't think much of them. They usually took such jobs as steppingstones to something else. No, he couldn't make up his mind about Mr. Parker. Let it ride for a little, perhaps he'd find someone himself.

Rita, to whom he went with his grievance, had a suggestion. What about her own secretary, Miss Ryder? She was a brilliant girl and knew more about Clarkson's than half the people in it. Rita would gladly surrender her and find someone else. Miss Ryder was wasted where she was, she was far too good for the work she did, she would do splendidly in Lawrence's office. Lawrence knew her, liked her, didn't he?

He did. Miss Ryder was a tall, attractive young woman, silent, deft, and deeply indebted to Rita Allen who had once befriended her at a time when she badly needed a friend. Rita had done it out of pure altruism. The impulse didn't take her often, but now and then she remembered her own difficult times and did something decent and generous. If later she turned her impulse to her own ends, that was something else again.

With Nancy on Christine's floor and Gertrude Ryder in Lawrence's office, Rita would be reasonably sure that little would escape her own attention.

Larry, speaking to Christine, was inclined, he said, to take Rita's recommendation rather than Miss Hanson's.

"Well," he asked, as she said nothing, "what do you think?"

"You really don't want to know," she told him, remembering something Mr. Austin had said to her, "you want me to tell you you're right. And I'm not sure."

"Why?"

She couldn't put it into words. She couldn't tell him that because Rita urged the cause of Gertrude Ryder she, Christine, opposed it. She knew nothing about Parker, and so far as the superiority of male over female secretaries went she had nothing to go by. Male secretaries didn't annoy you by getting married and quitting; if they married, they stayed. On the other hand, they often considered secretarial duties a stopgap, as Larry had pointed out earlier in the conversation. And women were supposedly more loyal, more concerned with one's interests.

So she said nothing except, "Of course, it's up to you, Larry."

He looked at her keenly. "You and Rita don't hit it off as well as you used to," he remarked, "because of Nancy." He shrugged. "If women would learn to keep personal antagonism and disagreements out of business . . ."

She said hotly, "Rita has been hostile to me ever since I came. I've tried very hard to be friendly. At first I thought she was cooperative. I know better now. Only last week when it was a question of that imported tweed . . . just because she knew I wanted it . . . she as much as told me she had precedence — first choice . . . that her department was established long before mine — and — "

"Must we go into that?" Larry said wearily. "I thought you'd got it all off your chest before this."

Christine, at boiling point, subsided. But Miss Hanson came to her a little later in the week.

"I know your influence with Mr. Clarkson,

and I'm not being disloyal to him, Miss Carstairs . . . I'm acting in his interest. Miss Ryder has been closely allied for too long a time with one department. This makes for bias in favor of that department. You may think that in a secretarial position that wouldn't matter. But, believe me, it does. There are ways of bringing requisitions to Mr. Clarkson's attention . . . oh, a hundred things. About Fred Parker . . . I think he'd be very nearly perfect. Miss Carstairs, if you could persuade Mr. Clarkson . . ."

"I'm afraid I can't, Miss Hanson," Christine told her. "You see, I'm in a difficult position. I have no right to interfere, or use my influence. I'm sure you see that. If I were not in the shop, it would make a difference. You understand?"

"I'm afraid I do," admitted Miss Hanson, sighing.

So, after the first of the year Miss Hanson retired, Gertrude Ryder moved up to the office off Lawrence's, and he reported that she was shaping up nicely. Miss Hanson had instructed her in her duties, but the girl was intelligent and quick to learn by herself. He added, gratuitously, it seemed to Christine, that he was grateful to Rita.

During the winter Christine was confronted by several new problems. One was the problem of entertaining the executive heads of departments. This appeared to be an old Clarkson custom which she was expected to carry on. In Howard's day it had not been difficult. Howard usually gave three or four dinners a year, at some smart hotel. Mrs. Clarkson had long been an invalid prior to her death and the entertaining had been done outside save on rare occasions such as the opening of Christine's department. Now, with Christine as hostess, it appeared that Lawrence expected her to entertain their associates at home.

She planned her first dinner, for twenty, with the utmost care. Caterers to help in the kitchen, an extra man to assist Oleson . . . flowers, place cards, bridge and game tables set up. She could not leave it to Mrs. Finley; in the midst of preparations housekeeper and cook had an argument which she had to settle . . . discovering it was not the first time, and each had a complaint, at the zero hour.

She wore a new frock, and looked charming. She *was* charming. She knew it and wondered anxiously if she were not too charming. It occurred to her during the evening that as Larry's wife and Clarkson's employee she was in something of a spot. If she appeared overcordial, they would say she gushed or patronized; if she was not cordial enough, it would be said that she was high-hat.

Her fellow designers were included, and with them she felt perfectly at ease. If sometimes she disagreed with them, if often it was a case of dog-eat-dog, that was business and to be expected. She liked them all, personally. Rita was there of course, very much in her element, a little too friendly . . . a little apt to put her arm about her hostess, call her by her given name with what seemed to Christine some ostentation.

There were others whom she did not know so well . . . the wives of the men, of course, and the husbands, if any, of the women. She did her level best, kept the groups moving, and when at last it was over was able to say to Larry, a trifle anxiously:

"It went off very well, I think."

He was unconcerned. "Why shouldn't it?" he asked. He'd had a good time, he liked playing the host, and watching him, Christine had wondered if he had assumed, unconsciously, a touch of the lord-of-the-manor attitude. The thought amused her and she laughed silently, fighting a wild desire to call him "squire."

"I wonder if they really like coming?" she mused aloud.

"Why wouldn't they?" he demanded in astonishment. "Of course they do, they look forward to it."

Did they? Or was it politics, duty, curiosity? Wouldn't they rather be let alone? There'd be some among them who would gravitate naturally toward Larry and herself, in friendship, apart from business association. But the majority wouldn't. And despite the fact that their guests were competent, clever people holding down excellent jobs, without whom Clarkson's could not function, was there not a trace of condescension in the Clarkson social get-togethers — the company summer outing on an exclusive scale?

A day or so later Rita encountered Christine as she walked through her department and linked her arm in hers.

"Grand party," commented Rita, "the other night."

"I thought so," said Christine.

"Of course," Rita went on carelessly, "everyone had a wonderful time . . . but, oh, my dear, people are maddening. You can't please everyone."

"Meaning — what?"

"Nothing. One or two . . . oh, a little clique perhaps . . . feel that a party of that nature is terribly shop. Literally. You know how people are. They hate to be pigeonholed . . . they feel that if they aren't good enough to be entertained more formally . . . or do I mean less formally? . . . with others, outsiders — All very silly, I think."

Christine thought that over. What was Rita's motive? Surely it couldn't be just to make her feel that the party had been a flop, that she had been guilty of a real breach of hospitality? She asked Larry casually, "Have you ever entertained the store people with outsiders . . . mixed grill, as it were?" and Larry answered, without much interest, "Oh, occasionally . . . a big shindig now and then. Why?"

"I thought perhaps . . . it would be more fun for them," she replied, feeling her way.

The next time, toward spring, the Clarksons gave a buffet supper, asking the world and his wife: the store executives, department heads, lesser fry, and an equal number of their outside friends. It was the most difficult evening Christine had ever spent. She had worn herself out thinking up amusements, distractions, oiling the machinery which would run things smoothly. And on the surface people had a good time. Janis, looking exceptionally pretty, had come with Francis Austin and was making herself more than agreeable to everyone. But Christine sensed a certain feeling of hostility among some of the store contingent. The trouble was, she thought afterwards, dismayed, that some of the others were customers and customers talk too much! The idea of the Vanorman woman getting Ellen O'Day in a corner and telling her what was wrong with her spring collection! And as for Harriet North informing Mr. Bergman that his mink were mice! Or was it cats?

Bergman was the head of the fur department.

No, it wouldn't do, and there were repercussions. Some of them reached Lawrence, routed via Rita, through the indefatigable Miss Ryder, and he became disturbed. "I told you it was an error of judgment," he informed Christine.

"Larry, you didn't, you agreed with me."

He said, with infuriating kindness, "Well, you have to learn by experience. I'm pretty dumb about these things, I admit. But another woman might have known. Rita, for instance. If you'd consulted her."

"Rita suggested it," she said coolly.

"She did?" But it was obvious that he didn't believe it. Christine, raging, knew that she couldn't convince him. Rita had managed that nicely.

A little later Lawrence came down with a bad case of flu. Christine, her hands full of spring orders and spring activity, told herself bitterly that he might have picked another time. But she was terribly worried. Lawrence was a sick man, and a bad patient. He was the despair of his doctor and a trial to his wife. "I won't have nurses!" he roared. "They terrify me."

"Yes, you will," said Christine, "someone has to look after you when I'm not home."

So nurses were installed and Lawrence alternated between lion and lamb. The first few days he was decidedly lamb, too ill to be belligerent. Later the leonine qualities asserted themselves but his day nurse, Miss Lang, middle-aged, commonsensical, knew how to manage him.

Christine had a night nurse for him, but he wouldn't hear of it after the first few days. When he was a little better he sent her packing. Surely Christine, sleeping in the guest room, could look after him . . . he'd sleep all night.

In a sense he did, but she didn't, stealing in half a dozen times to be sure he was covered, to put her hand on his forehead and convince herself that his temperature hadn't risen. And of course he woke frequently, to demand water, to take his medicine, to announce that he hadn't slept a wink and would she come sit with him, he ached in every limb, his head was killing him, and altogether he needed attention.

When she came home, very tired, after being up the night before and a day in the shop, Lawrence, weak, irritable, convinced that the shop was going to the dogs without him, demanded her instant attention and a report on everything that had happened. When she left, mornings, heavy-lidded, half dead for sleep, he gave her a list of instructions as long as her arm. She was to see this department head, send Miss Ryder over, telephone his father, deputize in his place and see a wholesaler, an insurance man, a heaven-knew-what . . . in addition to her own work.

Convalescent, he was lonely. Miss Lang bored him, and was not too easy on the eyes. Couldn't someone come in and amuse him? Janis volunteered and more than once Christine came upstairs to find them laughing together like a couple of conspirators, falling silent on her arrival. Rita took her lunch hour and came to eat with him from a tray, as Christine found herself too busy to take more than fifteen minutes for a glass of milk, a sandwich and a look at her patient. Miss Ryder came and took dictation. And finally the doctor came and said that Lawrence might go back to work.

"But I'd prefer that you went somewhere for a week or so. . . . I suggest Virginia."

"I can't do it. I've been away from the office almost two weeks. I feel swell. What's the idea? I'd go nuts, if I took a vacation now."

"I wasn't thinking of you, my boy, that is, not much. I was thinking of your wife. She's been under considerable strain. It's a marvel she hasn't picked up the bug herself. I don't want to have her on my hands."

"Christine?" said Lawrence, sincerely astonished. "Why, she's fine. She hasn't had a thing to do — what with the nurses and all."

"You fired your night nurse."

"Oh, sure, I didn't need her. Slept like a baby. Christine wasn't even disturbed," said Lawrence cheerfully.

Mrs. Carstairs, coming to dinner, remarked that her son-in-law looked marvelous and her daughter wretched. "I'm sure you've been overdoing, Christine."

"Nonsense," said Christine quickly, "I'm in the pink."

Her mother shook her head solemnly. "I don't believe it," she said; "of course, any woman who tries to work and run a house and take care of a sick man — "

Christine said something, anything. Later Lawrence remarked, irritably:

"Sorry you had such a tough time while I was sick."

"Larry, I haven't complained."

"No? I thought you had. I inferred from

what your mother said — "

"Oh, Mother!" She tried to laugh. "That doesn't mean anything. You know how she is about jobs and marriage. Terribly reactionary."

"I know, but I had an idea that perhaps you'd said something. I wish you'd say it to me. I don't like being talked over by your family. It's all right for some crazy kid to run home to Mother with this and that kick. But when it comes to a grown woman . . . "

She said angrily:

"That's not so. I don't. Or if I do, it's natural enough. Just because I married you doesn't mean that I'm deaf, dumb and blind where you're concerned. I'm not disloyal. How about you and your father? You talk about me plenty. Don't bother to contradict. He's said things which could have come only through you. About the department. Problems I've discussed with you because they're your business. I see no reason why you should pass it on. I know your father still has a good deal of authority. But he's no longer the executive. And I do resent it, Larry."

"Well," said Lawrence, too amazed to be angry, "that's pretty funny. I can't discuss your department with my father, the head of the board, simply because you're my wife. That's a new angle!"

They did not pursue the subject. People were coming in after dinner, among them a member of the South European nobility, a dashing, dark-eyed creature who knew the Clarksons socially, and who was now trying to wheedle Lawrence into giving her a job as stylist.

Christine was aware of the Contessa's ambitions. The Contessa was an opportunist. She had Lawrence where she wanted him; he was considering her informal application seriously. He believed that she would lend atmosphere to the shop. Christine did too. Atmosphere — air . . . hot air . . . empty space. The Contessa would come high. She would work assiduously at her job for a couple of weeks and then would take to coming in after luncheon. She would bring her friends to the shop and a few would buy, but most would not. She would expect discounts. She might even expect to wear Clarkson clothes gratis and run an expense account at the smartest restaurants. She would want to manage Rita's fashion shows. For once Rita and Christine were in accord. The Contessa mustn't come into Clarkson's.

But the Contessa did.

This occurred shortly after Lawrence's return to the office and the announcement was received by Christine with mingled amusement and annoyance. Larry was too good a businessman, she thought, calming, to let the woman lead him around very long. He'd probably get rid of her before autumn. And besides, on the day she learned of the Contessa's manufactured staff position, something much more important occurred.

Her mother called her at the shop, a most unusual procedure. She was so emotionally upset that Christine, her heart cold with fear — what had happened? was Janis ill? — had to speak sharply to her before she could tell a coherent story. No, Janis wasn't ill; Janis had gone downtown that morning, ostensibly to shop. And had just phoned that she wouldn't be home. She had a job. At Williamson's. Modeling.

Williamson's was three blocks down the Avenue. It was a specialty shop, a Clarkson competitor, a little less expensive, and a little larger.

"But how did she get the job?" demanded Christine. "There are hundreds of professional models out of work."

"Larry got it for her," said Mrs. Carstairs.

"Larry!"

She remembered Janis's coming to see Larry, when he was ill — with books, flowers, puzzles. She remembered their silence, when she came upon them suddenly, their suppressed amusement.

She said finally, "Well, don't worry. She'll tire of it. I'll come up and see you tonight." Then she hung up, cutting short her mother's protestations, and went straight to Larry's office.

Miss Ryder was with him. Well-trained, she sidled out, almost closing the door. Christine didn't notice. She said, standing at the desk:

"Did you get Janis a modeling position at Williamson's?"

Lawrence grinned. He was quite aware that Christine was angry, he had known she would be. Temper sharpened the edge of her beauty. He answered casually:

"I gave her a letter. After that it was up to her. I explained that we hadn't a place for her . . . but . . . as my sister-in-law — "

"You knew I didn't want her to model!"

"I knew you didn't want her in Clarkson's," he said mildly, "and believed you were right. But I saw no reason why she shouldn't be somewhere else. You are making a mistake, Christine, trying to keep her a parasite, idle, too much time on her hands. She'll only get into mischief. It's a lot better that she be started off right, isn't it? She'd get a job on her own eventually. And I'm afraid I can't share your opinion that a store position is beneath the young lady's dignity. I think it will be damned good for her."

"How could you!" cried Christine. "You have no right . . . how *dare* you go over my head!"

10

Larry looked at her in stupefaction. She was white with anger and against her sudden pallor her eyes were very dark and her mouth very red.

"Go over your head!" he repeated incredulously, feeling like a subordinate confronted by an infuriated superior.

She said, and her voice shook:

"You *know* how I feel about Janis."

For a split second he had wanted to laugh. She looked so absurdly pretty, in anger, and the situation was, for him, supremely ridiculous. But now the amusement passed and his temper rose to challenge her own. He said, with infuriating control:

"Yes, I know how you feel. And I think you're wrong. You've done the worst possible thing for her, wrapping her in cotton wool, keeping her idle and dissatisfied. And as for my not having any right . . . that's a very curious thing to say to me, Christine!"

"When I married you," she reminded him, "I didn't give you permission to run the affairs of my family."

A desk telephone rang. He picked it up, spoke briefly into the transmitter. "Send him in," he said. Then, replacing the instrument, he looked up at his wife.

"I'm sorry," he told her, "but I have an appointment. We'll have to continue this interesting discussion — after hours."

Christine left the office, almost colliding with an unknown man outside and not even seeing Miss Ryder, who looked after her with bright and speculative eyes. A little later in the day Miss Ryder reported to her former boss.

"They had a row," she said with satisfaction. "I could hear them in the outer office."

Rita raised her eyebrows and smiled slightly. "What about?" she inquired.

"Her sister . . . Clarkson got a job for her . . . at Williamson's. Carstairs was furious."

"Silly of her," reflected Rita lightly. "Personally I think it was no favor to Williamson's. The girl hasn't the brains of a grasshopper — I wouldn't hire her in my department."

Christine went through the rest of the day mechanically. She made more than one mistake, rectifying it just in time. Everything went wrong. Materials she had ordered were delayed. Fitting appointments were confused. An order was canceled. Ada Reagan was ill and could not report for work. Nancy was smoothly insolent.

Shortly before closing time her head ached dreadfully. Nervous tension tied the nape of her neck into agonizing knots and her skull felt as though it were being hammered. Walking toward the private lift to her own apartment she was not encouraged by the sight of Larry talking with the Contessa. The Contessa was dressed for the street, and very well too. She looked relentlessly chic. It was apparent that her head did not ache. And evidently she was urging Larry to join her in some social occasion, for Christine heard her say, as she passed them:

"All work and no play. .. you know what happens. Come, you look tired . . . there will be amusing people . . ."

"Well" said Lawrence, "I shouldn't — but — "

He did not notice Christine; or if he did, he gave no sign.

She went on upstairs, took off her clothes, ran a boiling hot bath and got into it, a cold compress on her eyes, the aroma of pine bath salts all about her. If Larry came in, she did not hear him. Later, more refreshed, her headache lessening, she dressed and went into the living room. Larry was not home.

She wished that he would come soon. The

pain in her head was much better, she felt rested and refreshed. Lying there in the bath she had determined to talk over Janis's problem with him seriously and without rancor . . . trying to show him the dangers and pitfalls Williamson's would probably provide for a girl of her sister's temperament. Surely she would be able to make him understand? It had been stupid of her to lose her temper. Larry had meant no harm. He simply did not comprehend the situation; manlike, he took a broader, more tolerant view. He didn't know Janis as she did, but she might make him know her.

So, emerging from her bath, running a comb through her lovely hair, pressing the soft waves into place, reddening her lips and powdering her oval face, she smiled at herself in the mirror. How silly of them to quarrel when they loved each other so much! She put on her prettiest hostess gown, the one Larry liked so much. And went out to wait for him.

Sitting on the deep divan, her head thrown back, her arms relaxed and her eyes closed, she thought, What on earth is wrong with us . . . all the petty squabbling and bickering? Surely not everyone goes through this? She reviewed the materials of which their marriage was built: love, passion, tenderness, a mutual goal, a shared interest, a partnership. . . .

But was it, she wondered suddenly, the shared interest which was proving a stumbling-block to harmony instead of, as she had believed, providing the basis for that harmony?

She was afraid of the thought and put it from her. How appalling to think that a business relation which had been a perfectly happy one before marriage should, because of marriage, alter in aspect. It couldn't be true. If it was true, then her mother had been right, all the old-fashioned people were right and there was nothing in the modern belief that, in marriage, the enduring element is partnership.

Dinner was announced but Larry had not returned. Christine sent word to the kitchen to hold things back a little. When she was alone again she gave herself over to her solitary meditation. . . . She had forgotten Janis, she had forgotten everything but herself and Larry. She thought back, reviewing their first months together, in the shop, and the first months of their marriage. She thought of their little quarrels, about Rita, about Nancy, about a hundred and one small things which amounted to very little but totaled to an alarming sum. Constant petty bickering undermined foundations, set the icy waters of distrust seeping through the gaps, widening them, making a breach in the walls. Big differences of opinion were different . . . you could compromise perhaps; or they came like storms which cleared the air . . . but . . .

Suddenly aware of a most enormous fatigue, she found herself wishing that Clarkson's was a closed book to her, that she need know nothing about it except what Larry chose to tell her, that she was waiting like any average wife for her husband to come home from work with nothing more to report of their brief separation than an unsatisfactory servant, a new hat, a bridge party or a matinee.

If we were to have children? she thought . . .

But they weren't to have children, not for a long time. Well, perhaps not very long, but long enough for Christine to make a success of the custom clothes department. That had all been settled before their marriage. It was no longer alarming to consider childbearing after thirty. And she had wanted to work in Clarkson's without the interruptions a child would cause, for some years to come. "We've plenty of time," she'd said, and Larry had agreed with her. Later, when the department was established, an old story, she could take "time off." Apparently it had never occurred to either of them that she might take time off — indefinitely. When she had considered the alterations in their lives which a child would make, she had thought of them as temporary only. She would take a leave of absence, have her baby and after a proper interval return to work. Trained care would be more efficient than any she was competent to give.

She looked at the clock . . . a small enameled affair with jewels set around the face, a rather rococo gadget which had been a wedding present. Larry was terribly late. She began to worry. He had been angry with her, he had probably gone to the club . . . perhaps he'd met with an accident . . . perhaps . . .

She remembered the Contessa and her fear left her and anger returned, burning up like a rise in temperature. If he'd gone somewhere with that — that meretricious, mercenary, utterly futile woman . . . and left her to wait for him! . . .

He came in, cheerful and gay, hungry, he announced, as a movie star on a reducing diet. He had completely forgotten their quarrel. He slung his things about the foyer and made his entrance — *prancing,* she thought, looking at him coldly, and bent to kiss her. He smelled of the gardenia in his buttonhole, of good bourbon and better tobacco.

"I suppose I'm very late," he said contritely.

"Almost an hour," she told him; "dinner will be ruined."

"I could eat the wreck of the *Hesperus,*" he answered her, "let alone the ruin of a good dinner. You know cocktail parties. One thing leads to another. . . ."

Christine rose and led the way to the dining room. She said, as she was seated, "I had no idea you had an appointment. . . . I would have arranged things differently."

"I hadn't," he said, "but just before closing the Contessa asked me if I'd like to go with her to a cocktail shindig. Half the current visiting royalty would be there. It sounded interesting and might be good business."

"Don't delude yourself," said Christine coolly, "visiting royalty finds it difficult to buy a pair of stockings at Clarkson's — for cash, that is. We've carried several such accounts before, you know."

He looked at her, astonished.

"Not peeved, are you?" he asked, and meant it. "I'm sorry, darling. I didn't mean to stay so late. It was really most entertaining. I wish you'd been with me."

"Obviously the Contessa didn't," said Christine, "or she would have taken steps."

"Oh, come," said Larry mildly, "she probably didn't think about it. Nowadays people aren't sticklers for formalities. Besides, I intended to stay only a few minutes."

"I saw her talking to you," said Christine.

"Oh, you did? Why didn't you join us then?" he demanded.

Christine didn't answer and Larry went on, "By the way, I met a very unusual girl at the party . . . Sara Thorpe. She writes that clever advertising for Morris Brothers. . . ."

Christine looked up, her anger and hurt momentarily forgotten.

"Sara Thorpe," she repeated. "I've seen her, although I never met her. Dark, good-looking girl?"

"Yes," said Larry enthusiastically, "that's the one. Lord, she's amusing. I tried to talk to her about her work but she'd have none of it. Not after office hours. She's been in Hollywood, on a vacation, and she does imitations. They're pretty cruel but immensely funny. She's a swell person, I liked her. You'd be crazy about her," he went on, with bland masculine exaggeration, "and she's a great friend of Yorke's, I understand. It seemed to me from something that was said that she knew him pretty well at one time."

"I never heard him mention her," Christine said.

"Well, he wouldn't tell you about all his girls, would he?" inquired Lawrence. "She said she was anxious to meet you — "

"How nice of her," Christine murmured, but Larry was too content with life, with several old-fashioneds, the party he had left, and his rescued dinner to take offense at her tone.

After dinner was over he wanted to go out. He felt, he announced, like a million dollars. Couldn't they go to a movie or something?

"I'm tired," Christine told him, "and I'm not dressed. Larry, do sit down — you make me nervous, the way you prowl around. I want to talk to you about Janis."

"Janis!" He had forgotten all about Janis. Now he looked crestfallen and reluctant as a little boy.

"I'd forgotten," he admitted. "Look here, Christine, must we go into all that again? I didn't want to butt into your affairs, nothing was further from my mind. I believed sincerely — I still do — that Janis would be better off working. Let her give it a try . . . why not? She's a good kid, a little flighty perhaps but she'll settle down. You've had so much responsibility for so long that you take a pretty gloomy, narrow view. Give her a chance. If it doesn't work out — well, we'll know what to do. If I could get her hired, I can get her fired," he concluded serenely.

It was true, and for a moment she almost disliked him for his easy way of settling things, his capacity for moving pieces around on the board. Then recalling some of her long and lonely thoughts, she smiled at him. She'd dismiss the Contessa and the cocktail party. She couldn't blame Larry, really. She had been unkind to him, they'd quarreled, it was the most natural thing in the world for him to go out with gay impersonal people rather than come upstairs and face her, wondering if she'd pick up their hostility where they'd left it.

"All right," she told him, "have it your own way. And if you'll wait for ten minutes, I'll dress and we'll go out to a movie."

But when they went out of the house and started downtown in the clear spring night, Larry himself decided against the motion pictures. "Let's just buzz around," he proposed, "and perhaps stop in at your mother's . . . not too late . . . and see how the kid made out."

She had thought of this but had not suggested it and now that he had, she smiled at him gratefully. "I'd like that," she said, "better than Garbo."

They turned and drove through the Park and then on uptown to the apartment. Mrs. Carstairs had gone to a friend's for bridge, but Janis was at home, bemoaning her feet, excited, nervously keyed up. She seized Larry and kissed him. She kissed Christine. "Don't be cross with me, darling," she begged, "I'm having such a grand time."

Williamson's was the last word in everything, she told them; everyone was so helpful . . . the girls were swell . . . the department head was an angel.

Christine laughed and shrugged, although she felt a good deal more like crying. Janis in one day at the shop had picked up, it appeared, most of the jargon. She paraded for them, delicately balanced, her hips a trifle obvious. She was, she announced, catching on.

When they were leaving Christine held her close for a moment. "Do watch your step," she murmured, "in more ways than one. I — I can't approve. But . . . oh, I do hope you'll be happy."

"Larry," cried Janis, "don't let her go emotional on me. I have to be hard-boiled. She'll have me all to pieces in a moment. You'd think I'd eloped instead of gone to work!"

"Have you told Francis?" asked Christine, at the door.

"Frank? Of course. I called him up and said, 'Who do you think this is?' And he said, 'Janis, of course.' And I said, 'Miss Janis to you, you mug. I'm a woiking-goil now.' And was he mad! He was furious. He called me all sorts of names. I hope the operator wasn't listening. If she was, she got an earful. And he called you names too."

"Me!"

"You. And when I absolved you . . . 'she didn't do it,' I said, 'she disapproved. Larry helped me' . . . what he said about Larry!"

"He'd better say it to my face," Larry informed her, yawning, "as I'm bigger than he is."

They drove home almost in silence, Christine sitting very close to him, her head against his shoulder. Once or twice she sighed.

"Janis?" he asked her; the second time, "Still worried?"

"No, not Janis. I suppose now that the blow has fallen I'll have to accept it. It wasn't a sad sigh or an anxious one — just happy. And a little tired. I've had a pretty bad headache most of the evening."

He was instantly all contrition.

"You poor kid, why didn't you tell me? We wouldn't have gone out. I would have put you to bed."

"No, it did me good to go out; Larry, I've been thinking about our vacation this summer. Have you made any plans?"

"No, not exactly. I thought — late in the season . . . if you could stick it out till then. I don't mean too late. . . . I realize you have your autumn models to consider. . . . Of course Father expects us to be with him."

"I know," said Christine, "but, Larry, if you could see your way to taking an early holiday . . . and a longer one? Say six weeks, if you could manage it — and go to Europe?"

"Europe! Six weeks! It's out of the question this year," he said firmly. "I'm sorry if you've set your heart on it, but I can't be away so long, and besides, I don't want to go to Europe . . . I'd get no rest . . . dragging around sightseeing or staying in some infernally fashionable place and making the rounds. No . . . two weeks, three even, if I can arrange things, down on the island . . . that's my idea of a holiday. Riding, swimming, plenty of polo and tennis. . . ."

"But," urged Christine, sitting up, "I wasn't thinking of a holiday exactly. I was thinking of work. I've got to go abroad, Larry. It's essential. . . . I must see what the French designers are planning. I want to be in England at the beginning of the season and in Paris . . . perhaps the Lido. I think I owe it to Clarkson's."

"You're crazy," said Larry flatly. "You're an American designer. What's the big idea? Besides, Rita goes over every so often — "

"That's for her department," said Christine, "and not for mine. I know I'm an American designer. What has that to do with it?"

"Well, I'm not going to let you go," he said. "I've never heard of anything so insane. You know I can't get away with you . . . and your plan is worse than it sounded at first. I'd have a swell time, wouldn't I, looking at collections — !"

"I wouldn't be allowed within a mile of 'em," said Christine, laughing. "I wasn't thinking of openings. I was thinking of people. Real people. The best-dressed women in Europe. I was thinking of going where they'd be and seeing with my own eyes what they are wearing . . . and then coming home and being two jumps ahead of them. That means I'll have to go early . . . some time in June."

"You'll *have* to go. You don't mean to say you are thinking about this seriously, even though I can't — and wouldn't — go with you?"

"But, Larry," she said despairingly, "it's my job!"

Nothing was settled that night, or for many nights thereafter. But when he found that he could not move her, Larry spoke to his father. To his amazement, Howard, in town for a brief appearance at the theaters, agreed with Christine.

"She's right," he said, "and she's the logical one to go. Let her, Larry, make it six weeks, give her an expense account."

"But — "

"Well," said his father, "you married her and expected her to go on working. You can't have your cake and eat it too. If she stayed at home and didn't know a gusset from a drape, or whatever you call 'em — professionally speaking — she'd take your holiday with you, at any time you arranged it, and at any place, and be glad to get it. But this is different."

"I can't see it," said Larry stubbornly. "After all, she's only one of several of our designers, if you want to put it on a business basis."

"Officially, yes," said his father, "unofficially, she's the head, and you know it."

The argument went on, but with Howard on her side, and Rita — for Larry had consulted Rita and found to his amazement that she, too, was against him — Christine had her way. She consoled him as best she could.

"If you think for a moment I won't be dying of loneliness . . . hating every minute I'm away from you. And when I come back . . . we can go down to the Island week-ends . . . "

"What about my vacation?" he demanded. "Do you expect me to take it alone?"

"But, darling, I couldn't go with you, especially if it were late. I'd be up to my ears in work. Besides, you'd fire me," she said, laughing, "if I took two holidays."

"I've half a mind to fire you anyway!" he told her.

She thought, It's all very well, but he's behaving like a spoilt child. There's no reason why he can't come with me. Clarkson's won't go to pieces just because he takes six weeks off. If he wanted to, he could.

He said, gloomily, "Oh, all right. I'll go down to the Island while you're away and take my fortnight then. I can't afford more time."

Victory wasn't particularly cheerful. Larry went around like a man caught in the crash. They quarreled over nothing and were reconciled, the more passionately because of their impending separation. Once during a disagreement which lasted the better part of two days, Christine rang up Nelson Yorke. She had seen in the paper that he was back in town after a West Indian cruise.

"Could you take a workingwoman to tea?" she inquired. "I'm quitting early."

"What," he demanded when he faced her over a small and secluded table, "is on your mind?"

"Nothing," she replied, smiling, "only I'm a little tired of being scolded. You never scold. You flatter. It's fun."

"I've never seen you look so lovely," he told her gravely. "But what's wrong?"

She told him. When she had finished she said, wearily:

"I don't want to go, Duke. For a couple of pins I wouldn't, yet I think I should. In a way

I can't blame Larry. He doesn't want a wife who rushes across the ocean at the drop of a new hat. Yet, he could come with me if he wanted to. I suppose," she ended, "we're both plain selfish."

"Forget it," counseled Yorke, suppressing his conviction that Lawrence Clarkson was considerable of a fool, "and drink that champagne cocktail. It's good for you. Six weeks will pass . . . and you'll be home again. And next time he will go with you. You're perfectly right, of course. That reminds me, something very funny happened to me in Puerto Rico."

He told her the story, which was amusing and slightly ribald, and watched the sparkle come back to her long brown eyes and her lips curve in laughter. "Now," he said contentedly, "that's better, isn't it? Tell me more about yourself."

"There isn't much to tell." She put her elbows on the table and her chin in her cupped palms. "You *are* a nice person," she said, "you—you take everything so easily . . . as a matter of course. You don't get jittery. I like that in you. I suppose I shouldn't have come complaining to you with all this, it sounds disloyal to Larry. It isn't. We're awfully happy, Duke. Just at the moment it's . . . the job or Larry's personal wishes. Makes a decision hard, doesn't it? Yet the job *is* Larry. I can't make him see that. And it's true."

"Of course," agreed Yorke, "it's true. And you're a very pretty creature. But you won't be if you go on frowning like that. Uncrease. Relax. Thank you. When are you sailing?"

"June." She named the boat and the date. "Duke, I'm scared. I'm afraid that at the last minute I'll run down the gangplank howling like a baby and refuse to go. I can't refuse. I said I'd go and I must. It's the right thing to do. It's part of my work . . . or it should be."

"You'll go," he prophesied confidently, "and I shouldn't be at all astonished if Larry followed you on the next boat."

She flushed a little. "Duke, you don't really think . . . " Then she shook her head. "No, he won't," she said sorrowfully, "I know him better than you do."

"Obviously. But why won't he?" Yorke said. "I should."

"Oh, you." She laughed at him a little.

"Yes . . . perhaps, after all, I shall."

"Don't be absurd," she said sharply. Then she laughed again. "I can't have unattached gentlemen following me to Europe."

"I wouldn't put it just that way," he said easily, "and perhaps I didn't mean the next boat. But as it happens I had planned to go abroad this summer, Christine, and it might be in the cards that we'd meet."

11

The days that remained to Christine before sailing went by quickly. Too quickly, she thought, grasping at them desperately. She had placed herself in a situation familiar to almost every woman who loves her husband and who goes counter to his wishes, believing herself right, convinced that more than a surface principle is involved. She had hours of doubt, and hours of sheer exasperation, with Larry, with herself. She told herself, over and over, It's only six weeks, but that didn't seem to be much consolation. Rita, who had seemed extraordinarily and disarmingly friendly since Christine's decision, said lightly one day just before Christine sailed, "Of course, I envy you your trip and I think it very wise . . . except . . . " She laughed and shook a red-tipped finger at the younger woman in a manner which Christine described to herself as arch. "But don't worry. We'll keep an eye on Larry for you."

Well, I like that, thought Christine indignantly, not liking it at all.

Larry, as the time approached, appeared more resigned. He still grumbled, still, as she expressed it to her mother, "withheld his consent," but he busied himself with the details of her departure, saw to her letter of credit and her passport and visas, changed the cabin she had selected to a larger and more luxurious accommodation, supplied her with letters of introduction and gave her several commissions to execute for the shop.

Their last days together were sweet and disturbing. Christine spent a good deal of her time fighting an inclination to burst into tears, fling herself into his arms, announce that she was wrong, she didn't care what happened to the custom salon, she wanted to stay home, with him, and Europe could vanish beneath the sea, like Atlantis, for all she cared. Larry, too, waged a victorious battle with himself, sternly suppressing the urgings, the demands and the pleas that cried out for utterance.

Christine both hoped for and dreaded the hour before sailing, which would find them alone, so it was with disappointment that she learned that a farewell party had been planned for the midnight departure. Practically everyone she knew came to the boat and some had come uninvited. There were people from the store, Rita dominant among them, smart and self-contained, acting as if she were hostess, as if she were to be the voyager. Howard was there, his blue eyes bright, and Nelson Yorke, who wandered in casually, and as casually wandered out. But he didn't leave until shortly after Sara Thorpe's arrival. She came with the Contessa and one or two others from the shop. Christine had met her, briefly, during the previous week when she and Larry, dining alone in a quiet restaurant, had seen the dark, handsome girl at a neighboring table. Restaurant introductions are of necessity hurried but the impression remained with Christine of a good-looking young person tremendously sure of herself.

This was not dispelled when Sara came to the boat, wished Christine a pleasant passage, and then devoted herself to Larry. She was, Christine realized, regarding her more closely, utterly removed from the adjective pretty, or beautiful. Dark, tall, tremendously vital, with a slow, caressing voice and eyes which were an astonishing steel-gray, she had a clear-cut and interesting personality. Christine could not imagine her ill at ease or at a loss for words, yet a few moments after she thought this she saw her in both situations, her hard, shining, chromium-plated equipment failing her completely.

This was when Yorke strolled into Sara's line of vision . . . and turning saw her, and stopped to speak. Christine, standing with Janis and their mother, happened to be near.

"Well, Sara, it's been a long time," he said, smiling.

Sara said something, stammering, it seemed to Christine, although she could not catch the phrase, but she watched the girl flush slowly until the olive skin was suffused.

"You're looking very well," commented Yorke lightly, "but then you're always well. How's the work coming?"

Now she spoke more clearly, almost defiantly.

"As usual," she said, "and it's beginning to bore me."

"Of course," agreed Yorke, "it would. Your temperament demands pursuit and not capture. Sitting on top of the world would fatigue you."

He smiled at her and went back to Christine and her family. She told him, "Your orchids are the acme of extravagance . . . a pound of them, at least. And do you really think I can read all those books and eat all that fruit in the short space of four and a half days?"

"Well, you can try," he suggested, "and don't spare the horses. If my orders were properly carried out, there are more orchids in the steward's icebox."

Janis said admiringly:

"He does everything in the royal manner."

"And so, also in the royal manner, I'll take my departure," Yorke said, laughing. He held Christine's hand closely. "I may see you," he reminded her, "in a couple of weeks, or less."

Looking up, she was aware of Sara Thorpe's eyes on them, filled with an extraordinary hostility. The regard made her self-conscious. She withdrew her hand, said something casual, and watched Yorke leave the cabin. Larry, standing with his father, came over to her. He said, "You look tired, darling."

"I am. It's only a little while before we sail. Can't you get rid of these people?" she implored him.

"Well," said her mother, "that's not very kind of you, Christine."

Mrs. Carstairs had been crying, not too obviously. But her little nose was pink, and her eyes were swollen. She hated farewells and she disapproved of this trip. It was outside of nature, a young woman leaving her husband, to flit around Europe by herself. Larry should have put his foot down, she thought, and had told him so more than once.

"But I tried," he said ruefully; "give me credit for that, at least."

Janis put her arm through her mother's.

"Don't be ridic," she said kindly, "can't

you see that Chris wants to be alone with Larry? Let's get going. Besides, it's past your bedtime and I'm plenty tired myself."

Christine drew Howard aside for a moment. She asked, anxiously:

"You'll look after him, won't you? Now that the time's almost here and I can't back out, I've the most corroding doubts. Not that I haven't had them all along."

"We'll look after him," he agreed amiably, "you're to have a good time, get all you need and come back to us brimming with new and marvelous ideas." He patted her shoulder gently.

She said, because she was emotionally worn out, and forgot that she was speaking to a man who had, she believed, never really liked her and who had not tried to win her confidence, "But I'll miss him *so much* — "

She saw something cloud the bright blue eyes . . . it was fleet, it vanished before she could interpret it — pity? regret? self-reproach? And it came to her suddenly and with a terrific impact, that Howard had been glad she was going — against Larry's wishes, and for that reason had taken her part and thus furthered her plan. Glad she was going, glad to have Larry to himself for a while, afraid of her influence, hoping that perhaps her very self-will would lessen it. She stared at him, almost frightened. She thought, But I haven't taken him from you, there's no reason for you to feel toward me as you do!

The pearls around her neck, which Howard had given her, felt cold and hard and heavy.

Howard said, smiling:

"I claim the usual privilege." He kissed her cheek charmingly. He was a delightful old man, really, and quite aware of his audience, watching the gesture, thinking that very thing. But in his heart there was a stirring of compunction. He was not aware that it had reached, briefly, his eyes. After all, his son's wife was a thoroughly nice person, a decent, attractive, hard-working girl. He had disliked her because Larry had chosen her and he, Howard, had had no hand in the choice. He had disliked her because he disapproved of women working with their husbands in business, he thought it wrong, dangerous. He had been delighted at her decision to go abroad. Minor in itself, it showed that her ambition was greater than her sense of the fitting, and greater perhaps than her love for Larry. It would cause a little rift, and would serve its purpose. So, earlier, he had felt no compunction in counseling Larry to let her go. He could base his argument smoothly on the good of the store. He was too fond of his son and too biased to have thought for a moment that

Christine had married Larry without love. But he had told himself, sardonically, that she had loved at the right time and in the right place. If the boy hadn't been president of Clarkson's — ?

Now he wasn't so sure that Christine's falling in love had been — fortuitous.

For a moment Christine forgot that look she had seen, the troubled thought it had brought to her, and remembered only that this was Larry's father, who also loved him. So she clung to him, briefly and without words, and there were tears on his cheek, not his tears.

Howard released her, and cleared his throat. He said, "You'll want to be shut of all this," regarding with sudden distaste the guests, the champagne bottles in their buckets, the massed flowers and packages and baskets. He straightened his shoulder and proceeded to manage things in his own manner. In less time than she would have believed possible Christine found her hand clasped and her cheek kissed and the final words spoken and then quiet and a door closing and Larry.

He took her in his arms and she began to cry.

"Larry, Larry, I wish I weren't going."

"It's a fine time to discover that," he told her with indignation. He kissed her, shook her gently. "Buck up, old girl . . . you can't quit now."

"You'll write — and cable?"

"I'll write and I'll cable and I'll phone you," he told her.

They were silent for a little while, holding each other fast. The warning cry sounded for the first time. "All ashore that's going ashore . . . all ashore that's going ashore — "

"You'll have to go," she told him brokenly.

"Not yet. There's plenty of time."

"No. Please go. It would make it more difficult . . . go, now."

She kissed him again, said, "I'm not coming to the gangplank with you . . . take care of yourself, darling, please take care of yourself."

She watched him to the door and then shut her eyes against its closing. When she opened them again, he had gone.

Joining his father at the gangplank, Larry said, trying to cover his own emotion, "Poor kid, she was pretty cut up about going." He grinned suddenly. "If she isn't the stubbornest, damnedest . . . sets her heart on it, gets her way, and now she's sorry."

"She's a woman," said his father philosophically. "I wonder if we were right after all, letting her have her way?"

"Of course we weren't," said Larry, "and

what do you mean — '*we*'? It was your doing. You kept hammering at it in that board-of-directors manner of yours and talked me into it. *Talked* me into it! You pushed me into it!"

Walking down the pier he stopped suddenly and swore aloud, to his father's amazement.

"What's that for?" asked Howard.

"Nothing. Something I forgot to ask Christine."

"Send her a wireless."

Larry grunted and continued to march through the press of people. He couldn't tell his father that he could hardly wire his wife and demand what the hell did Nelson Yorke mean by saying he'd see her in a couple of weeks? He'd overheard that, had meant to ask her about it when they were alone, but had forgotten, as who would not forget under the circumstances?

"The crowd's outside," he said, "they're all going on to a night club or something. Think I'll duck. . . . I'm hardly in the mood. Coming home with me? The spare room's ready and we'll send around for your bags. Lord, but I'll be lonely," he concluded.

"I'll come," answered his father, "for a little while. And you'll be down week-ends."

"Sure," said Larry. Walking to the car he discussed his vacation plans. He thought, I wish he'd stay in town with me till then, but the heat gets him; he isn't as young as he used to be.

He was glad they were going home together tonight. It was like old times, the two of them keeping bachelor house. Yet not like old times. Entering the apartment he was keenly and achingly aware of Christine . . . everything reminded him of her. He need not go into their bedroom, need not open closet doors to look at the clothes hanging there on their scented hangers in their transparent bags, or the rows of shoes bearing the impress of her small and slender feet.

He began to wish that he had gone on with the party. Making his excuses to the others he had been aware of Sara Thorpe standing quietly beside him. He heard her say, "You'd better come . . . it's no fun going home to — emptiness."

Now how did she know that? he inquired of himself briefly, and then dismissed it from his mind.

Well, tomorrow was another day and Clarkson's was still Clarkson's and there was plenty of work ahead, even with summer setting in. Six weeks would pass quickly, if not quickly enough.

Howard stayed on for a few days and then went back to the Island and his stables and his kennels. Larry missed him greatly at first and then reconciled himself to loneliness. He wrote Christine by every boat, cabled and phoned her, for the first time, in London. Her voice came clearly to him, eerie and strange over the leagues of space. There was so little they could say. A good voyage. London was lovely. The weather was fine. She was all right. Everything was going well. She loved him.

Unsatisfactory things, transatlantic calls.

London *was* lovely, and the weather was fine. Paris was pleasant, and Christine looked up her old friends there, recalling the six months she had been there, an eager apprentice, frightened, lonely, ambitious. Now it was different. She was back again, a designer with a reputation, the loyalty of a great shop behind her. She went, of course, to the establishment in which she had learned the rudiments of her trade. The owner, that remarkable woman, greeted her enthusiastically.

"I should really bar the door."

Christine smiled. "You don't mean that, madame," she said gently.

"No, I do not mean it. You are very original. But America begins to threaten France for supremacy in design. I am not resigned. I hear, my little Christine, that you have married Clarkson's. I congratulate you."

That, as Madame would have had it, gave her to think. She had married Clarkson's . . . a dual personality, the shop and the husband. She felt like a woman who has committed bigamy, who owes allegiance to two masters and cannot serve either well.

She went everywhere that smart women congregated, a noticeable figure with her distinguished beauty and her charming clothes. She knew many people, others sought her out, Larry's letters provided her with company, flattery, entertainment. She executed his commissions, talked to him on the telephone about them, reporting her success. She did some judicious buying for the accessory department and saw one or two people Rita had asked her to see. She spoke excellent French, women found her disarming and men found her enchanting. It was all very gay, on the surface.

Nights were the worst. Days went by quickly, there was so much to see and to do. But nights . . . Coming home to the hotel rooms, the suite which Clarkson's had provided for her, wandering disconsolately under the high ceilings, from drawing room to bedroom, trailing her evening wrap, too fatigued to stand on her feet, too tired to sleep. And terribly alone. If she didn't have to come back to the hotel, if she could keep going twenty-four hours a day, it wouldn't be so bad.

She was therefore delighted when Nelson Yorke telephoned her that he was in town. She dined with him that night, and for the first time did not watch the other women, did not make her mental notes of this and that original, color contrast, a new neckline, a newer sleeve. She sat in a corner, her hands clasped on the table, listening to Yorke. He was a friend, someone who knew her and Larry, someone from home.

She was going, she told him, to the Lido for a little while and then she would return to Paris, sailing from there when her time was up.

"It's been successful?" he inquired.

"Yes, very. I've a lot of ideas . . . oh, not anyone else's, really my own. I see something, it suggests something else to me. . . ."

"Hearing from Larry?"

"By every boat . . . and he cables, of course."

"Strictly business?"

"Oh, strictly," she replied solemnly, "and he has telephoned me, three times. He's down on the Island now . . . with his father."

"I saw him, before I sailed."

"You did? He didn't mention it — how did he look?"

"Yes. He didn't see me. He looked very

well. He was with Sara Thorpe and another couple on one of the roofs."

"Yes, he told me about that party." She asked, after a moment, "You used to know Miss Thorpe, didn't you?

"I still do," he answered. "What a way to put it! And who's been gossiping?"

"Oh, not really gossip . . . but — "

"I was very fond of her, at one time," said Yorke quietly. "We had a rather stormy friendship. I think I told you once that I was not matrimonially inclined . . . if I changed my mind later, it had nothing to do with Sara and anyway I was forced to change it again. All very feminine." He laughed and said, after a moment, "Sara's a very interesting and a very brilliant girl. I have a great deal of admiration for her." He looked down at the wineglass he was holding, set it gently on the table. "Paris," he said, "is the pleasantest place in the world, with the right company."

"If you dare to say . . . 'Paris in the spring . . . ' "

"I won't. It's getting on for summer. Look, there at the door. That's the Duchess of—— " He mentioned a great name. "Pretty, isn't she? Not the usual run-of-the-mill duchess."

So, he didn't want to talk about Sara Thorpe any more. Christine noted that, was idly curious. Not that Miss Thorpe was anything to her.

She went to the Lido, white sands, blue water, gay, sun-tanned people in the minimum of clothing. And before she left Yorke joined her for a day or so, flying back to Paris the day before her own departure, in order to keep an appointment. Dutifully she wrote to Larry. "Duke has been here . . . it was very nice seeing him again."

When she was back in Paris with a short time left her before she sailed, Larry called her. He asked without preliminary:

"Is Yorke in Paris?"

"Why, yes, Larry . . ."

"Then you'd better leave."

"But, Larry . . ."

"Oh, I know," — his voice came to her with that strangeness associated with distance — "but there's been plenty in the New York papers . . . and I suppose the Paris *Herald*. Dining here, lunching there. I don't like it, Christine. It makes me look like a fool."

"Larry, you're crazy!"

She was outraged, her voice caught in her throat, she had to repeat herself. "Don't let's quarrel, Larry." She tried to laugh. "It's silly and, besides, it's so expensive."

"I'm not quarreling," he told her. "But I want you to stop seeing him."

"But we're old friends . . . Larry, I've written you every time I saw him."

"What has that to do with it? People are talking, I tell you. It has been borne in on me recently that half New York knows he's in love with you."

She replaced the telephone. The French operator rang her. "Madame was disconnected?" she inquired.

"No," said Christine, "I'd finished talking."

12

She had an appointment with Yorke for the following day. They were having cocktails with friends of his and planned to go on to dinner and the theater. She had looked forward to the cocktail party, there would be people there she had not as yet met, expatriate Americans who would, of course, bewail the fall of the dollar but who would be tremendously chic and maliciously amusing; there would be the editor of a great Parisian newspaper and members of the literary and diplomatic sets.

She telephoned Yorke the following morning after a sleepless night which left her worn and miserable.

"Duke . . . did I get you up? I'm sorry. Something's happened, I can't go to the party with you this afternoon and I'm going to beg off tonight too. I'm quite all right. It's just . . . "

How utterly absurd. She couldn't say, "My husband called me up last night and told me to forbid you the door." She couldn't, however, lie her way out of today's appointments, or if she could, she couldn't keep on lying till she sailed. She went on, with determination:

"I'd like to see you. No, not lunch, I have an engagement. I was going to the Louvre before. Yes, the Louvre. No, it's just that I made some sketches there before I went to Italy. I want to make some more. Oh, ideas. Very adaptable to modern costume . . . "

"What on earth are you talking about?" he asked, astonished.

She was, she knew, talking to gain time. She said, "Look here, come to the hotel before lunch, will you? Well find a quiet place and talk for half an hour. Twelve-thirty, then?"

When he arrived, impeccable, and curious, she took her courage in both hands.

"Larry telephoned me last night."

"Oh, I see." He caressed the smooth wood of his stick thoughtfully and smiled at her. "Indignant husband?"

She was grateful to him for guessing, and she was enraged that he had guessed. She tried to smile. He noted the careful application of her rouge, unusual in itself, as she rarely employed it, and the lines, the dark shadows about her eyes; he noted, too, the especial bravery of her lipstick.

"Something like that. Duke, I'm so utterly ashamed. It's so foolish of him . . . so . . . insulting to us both."

"No," he contradicted thoughtfully, "it isn't. It's perfectly natural. Come, smile. Chin up. Don't let a little thing like this defeat you. It would have been insulting — to me, at least, if he hadn't telephoned. I would have, in his shoes. I would have burned up the wires."

She said, hotly, "If he doesn't trust me out of his sight!"

"Don't talk in clichés, it isn't like you. What has trust to do with it? It's just a word, or perhaps a mood, or a frame of mind. Words, moods, frames of mind — and you, thousands of miles away!" He laughed and then was very sober. "I'm sorry, my dear," he said, "I wouldn't hurt you for the world."

"*You* haven't."

"But he has? It's the same thing. I have hurt you through him. I didn't mean to. No, of course, that isn't entirely sincere. I didn't will it. I could have spared you. I did not. I didn't want to."

"When I get home I'll have it out with him."

"By all means. Assure him I was summering abroad anyway. I'm leaving for Switzerland tonight, by the way."

"For Switzerland!"

"Yes, a sudden change of plans. Very sudden. Just came to me this moment."

He smiled again and added gently, "Me, I remove myself."

"Duke, it's all so silly," she began helplessly.

"Not very. He'd be a complaisant sort of idiot if he didn't exhibit some resentment. Christine, you're still in love with him?"

"I'm furious at him," she said, "and yes, Duke, I'm still in love with him."

"I thought so. Well, make him believe that. He's never been overfond of me, you know."

"He said," she began, "that people had talked — "

"Why not? They'll always talk. Let them." He began to laugh. "You haven't seen the recent American papers, have you?" he asked her.

"Not lately. Why?"

"Nothing. I was wondering about . . . Men are very peculiar — they have consciences. In the batch of newsprint which arrived on the last boat, the columnists are frying the usual fish. Poor fish!" He rose and looked down at her. They were conscious of constraint, of the people passing in the lobby. "I'll be off," he said, "see you in New York, I hope, in the autumn."

She rose and faced him.

"If you knew how idiotic I feel," she said;

"so unutterably self-conscious. I hate that."

He ignored that. "Christine, do you remember my offer?"

"Offer?"

"Either. Both. I was thinking of the first. Your own shop. At any time. It still holds good. I don't expect you'll consider it, ever. But if you should at some later date . . ."

She watched him leave, walking lightly, his head held high, his special aura of cool amusement with life following him. She liked him so much. He was a good, an exciting friend. No, not exciting. Of course not. Her thoughts returned to Larry. She'd not cable or telephone. She would wait till she heard from him again.

It was not until later that she remembered Yorke's remark about the American papers and then not until mail reached her at her bank. There were letters from Larry, impatient, ardent, and she read and reread them, conscious of the ache in her heart and her throat. They had been written so long ago. But one did mention Yorke. . . . "Aren't you seeing too much of the boy friend?" it inquired, with an attempt at facetiousness.

Her mother and Janis had written. One or two other people. And there was a typewritten envelope which contained nothing but clippings. No letter, no signature. There were three clippings, from columns, and all of them mentioned Larry . . . and Sara Thorpe.

"What youthful merchandise magnate has been seen lately in the hot spots with what brilliant young copy writer, during the absence in Europe of the former's beautiful wife?"

She crumpled up the clippings, threw them in a wastebasket, fished them out again, smoothed them, reread them and tore them into tiny strips.

Larry. So that was what Yorke had meant. Larry, mentioned in the gossip columns in connection with Sara Thorpe! Yet he had the effrontery to telephone her across some three thousand miles of air and land and sea and demand that she stop seeing Nelson Yorke. It was intolerable.

A letter she had overlooked dropped out of a bundle of old and uninteresting newspapers. It was from Howard, a chatty note, reporting on the latest litter of puppies and on Larry's vacation. "He had a quiet enough time with me, and very dull he found it without you, my dear," Howard wrote. "We all miss you and are glad you are coming home."

It was the first letter she had had from him. She folded it and replaced it in its envelope. It had been sweet of Larry's father to write to her, almost as if he liked her.

She did not hear from Larry again before

she sailed. Nor did she communicate with him except to cable him the brief, official notice of her sailing. On the way over, she waited for word by wireless. None came until the last day out when the flimsy message was brought to her on deck. She tore it open.

"Meeting you tomorrow love Larry."

Terse, and disappointing. Yet what had she expected? "Forgive me for not trusting you, do let Yorke know we expect him soon for a week-end, I adore you."

She laughed at herself shortly, to the alarm of the seasick bride in the next steamer chair. She put the message aside, looked out at blue water and a cloudless sky, closed her eyes and lay back. She had rested physically on this passage home, sparing herself, taking her meals on deck, avoiding the other passengers and all the usual feverish shipboard activity. As a result she looked and felt well enough. But mentally and emotionally she was worn out, fretted, and completely unable to achieve stability.

She told herself that this new and publicized association of Larry and Sara Thorpe concerned her not at all. He had met and liked her before Christine's departure. No one could expect him to stay at home and mope for six weeks. Why shouldn't he go out with her — with anyone, for that matter?

But she was not resigned. She hadn't especially liked Miss Thorpe, the little she'd seen of her. And now after thinking about her for, it seemed, days on end, she was possessed of an utterly illogical dislike far stronger and more disturbing than a mere casual not-liking.

She tried to argue herself out of it. She stated the facts of the case coolly and dispassionately and said, in effect, "See here, my girl, this won't do at all. You insist upon leaving Larry for six weeks because you believe that your job demands it. You are hurt and upset because he won't come with you. And when you hear he is amusing himself at home with, not a group of people, but one especial person, you go off the deep end . . . you're as silly and jealous and as afraid as a schoolgirl. But you aren't a schoolgirl. You're a grown woman, with experience and common sense, a *modern* woman. You are in love with your husband and he is in love with you. A dozen Sara Thorpes wouldn't matter, they'd signify exactly nothing. So snap out of it, I tell you, and be quick about it!"

It didn't do any good. When it came to a battle between the reasoning brain and the unreasoning emotions the emotions won every time, hands down. Christine hated herself. Was it because she was a woman, because in a woman, no matter how intelligent, intelligence is subordinate to emotion?

If she could only talk about it to Larry, if only she could say, after their meeting, "See here, darling, I've been an idiot. I deserve a scolding. Ever since someone sent me those clippings about you and Sara Thorpe I haven't been able to eat or sleep or do anything but worry myself sick and rush around stirring up tempests in every available teapot. Tell me I'm a fool. And then kiss me and hold me close and I'll try to forget it. Larry, you aren't really interested in her, are you?"

Yet she couldn't . . . because of Nelson Yorke. They had quarreled over Yorke and were she now to assume the attitude of a jealous wife — not that it would call for much assuming — Larry would think, and very logically, that it was a defense gesture, a coverup, a carrying of the war into the enemy's camp. Talk about the pot calling the kettle black! That's what he'd think and there was no getting around it. If it hadn't been for Yorke . . .

She tried to think about herself and Yorke. She was forced to be honest and she disliked it. She couldn't dismiss it with; Well, what of it, we are old friends, I was homesick, I like him, it was nice to see him. . . . She could say it and mean it, but that was surface excuse.

She couldn't look herself — or Larry — in the eyes and announce that Yorke wasn't in love with her, or if he were, that she had no knowledge of it. Because he was, in his way, and she knew it and had always known it.

That she did not love Nelson Yorke, and never had, provided no excuse. She could tell herself, in all sincerity, that she had not encouraged him to believe that she was, or ever could be interested in him. But that didn't mend matters. It provided no excuse for going out of her way to see him, for she had gone out of her way, had telephoned him before her departure for Europe, had had tea with him, had refreshed and renewed herself with his admiration.

The woman doesn't live, Christine told herself, staring at the sea, whose soul doesn't preen itself and purr like a cat in the sun of an admiration she doesn't return and doesn't perhaps even want, consciously.

Because of her intemperate passion for Lawrence Clarkson and the strong magnetic pull between them, all their differences became exaggerated, assumed an undue importance. If they had not loved each other so much, they would not feel the terrific antagonism which rose between them at times. Yorke provided a sort of brief respite. She could go — had gone — from Larry to him to be comforted, because he asked nothing of her, because she had no emotional urge toward him, because he flattered her vanity and salved her pride.

You couldn't explain this to a man, least of all to the man whom you loved. You couldn't go to Larry and say, "Larry, because I'm so terribly in love with you, because our every encounter strikes sparks, because we antagonize and wound each other, I can turn, deliberately, to Nelson Yorke. You see, I don't have to give him anything, neither love nor hate, tenderness nor passion. I simply accept what he brings me . . . I delude myself into thinking he understands me. He doesn't, of course, any more than you do, or any more than I understand myself."

On the surface, of course, it was absurd of Larry to object to her association with Yorke during her trip. Her slate was perfectly clean, technically. She gave nothing, she offered nothing. But when she looked below the surface she was ashamed.

On the surface, then, it was just as idiotic for her to object to Larry's interest in Sara Thorpe — if it was an interest. But what lay beneath it she did not know. That was what alarmed her.

Her ship docked the next day. Larry was there, waiting; she stood at the rail and saw him and felt physically sick with excitement. They greeted each other, conscious of the crowds about them, the stir and confusion of the piers, she felt his arms about her, his mouth on her own, and heard his "Lord, it's good to have you back." She could respond to these and forget everything else for a brief moment, kissing him, stammering how much she had missed him.

But later, waiting by her luggage for the customs official, constraint fell upon them and they spoke of trivial things . . . the weather and the shop and had he heard from Janis and her mother and why weren't they here to meet her?

"I asked them not to come. Your mother hasn't been well."

"Larry! I didn't know, she wrote but didn't say a word. Is it serious?"

"Don't be frightened. A little cold . . . I told her not to dream of coming up from the cottage . . . We'll go down this week-end. Janis is coming along to the house tonight. She's working, of course."

"Yes, I'd forgotten. How are things at the store? Is your father well?"

"He's fine. Everything's all right. It's been a good season, considering everything. Rita's laid up, broken wrist."

"Oh, I'm sorry. How did it happen?"

"Slipped on a rug one evening, at home. She'll be back to work in a week or so."

"I must go see her. Larry, you look marvelous, so tanned and husky. I believe you've put on weight."

"You look all right yourself," he said inadequately, and regarded her as if he could not get enough of looking. "That's a pretty outrageous hat."

"You don't like it?" She looked at him anxiously. "I thought it had something. It's the original model . . . I thought, with certain modifications, I could suggest it to — "

But he had forgotten the hat. He interrupted, "Where in hell is that man? Oh . . . coming this way. Sit tight. It will soon be over. You had a good crossing?"

"Scarcely a ripple. I was a little tired, I think, with all the activity of the last few days in Paris, but the voyage set me up. I could lick my weight in wildcats. And I've brought home some marvelous ideas. I wrote you about the Louvre? I have some sketches . . . You wouldn't believe that the robes of the Doges inspired me to think of hostess gowns, would you?"

He wasn't listening and she didn't care. She was talking just to be talking. Saying anything, because so much was unsaid between them.

When they reached the apartment she found it filled with flowers in welcome: from Larry, from friends, from Janis. The servants were glad to see her. Even the housekeeper unbent sufficiently to murmur that they had missed her.

The boat had docked at noon. Luncheon was waiting for her, all the things she especially liked, cool salads, cold cuts, iced coffee. New York, reported Larry, splashing cream into his glass, had been intolerably hot for the past week. One of the usual heat spells which astonished people so much and yet were so common to a Manhattan summer.

After luncheon he lit a cigarette and regarded her. "I've got to get downstairs. A conference. I'll get away early."

"I'm coming with you," she said cheerfully.

"No, not today. Stay here, rest, unpack. Time enough to go back to work next week. Tomorrow's Friday. We'll pull out and go down to the farm tomorrow evening. You can run over and see your mother Saturday. I've seen her several times. She likes the new cottage and Janis gets down week-ends and she has that Mrs. Fraser staying with her."

"Wait, Larry . . . don't go yet . . . I want to tell you something."

"It can wait." He took her in his arms and

kissed her. "You must never leave me again."

"I shan't." She clung to him, half crying. "Larry, it's been so terribly lonely."

"You're telling me!"

"Wait. Let's say it now, and then never again. About Duke Yorke. Oh, don't draw away like that. I was — terribly angry. When you phoned, I mean. . . . "

"I gathered that. You hung up on me," he said.

"I know. I hoped you'd call . . . later . . . or next day . . . but you didn't. I . . . It was foolish of you, Larry. He's nothing to me, nothing. Only I was so homesick, so really lonely. I'm sorry if there was gossip. There wasn't any basis, Larry. We lunched together, had dinner several times, he introduced me to some people who were helpful and some who were merely amusing. I didn't see him again, after you phoned, except to tell him that I couldn't see him . . . I mean, you can't break appointments without some excuse. It didn't matter. He was leaving for Switzerland anyway."

Larry flushed angrily. He felt like a fool. "You told him that I phoned and — !"

"Larry, of course not!" She thought, It's the first time I've lied to him, but I must to save his face. He'd loathe thinking I'd said he was — jealous. And what else did it amount to? "Of course not. I had a perfectly legitimate excuse. It was just a cocktail party we were going to and I told him someone connected with Clarkson's was unexpectedly in town and I had to do the honors. And as he was going off to the mountains . . . "

Unnecessary for Larry to know that the Switzerland trip was an afterthought. Yet, she thought, watching his face, seeing that he believed her, how could he be so fatuous? How could he believe that she made no excuse other than . . . "Sorry, I can't have cocktails." It was stupid of him, or was it merely a universal stupidity, a desire to believe what one wished to believe?

He said, "Forget it. Perhaps I was crazy to call you. And I never liked Yorke," he admitted unnecessarily, "and when I thought of you together . . . I — I guess I was a fool. I'm sorry. We won't talk about it again. I'd had a couple of drinks and something I overheard got under my skin."

He hadn't overheard anything. Rita had spoken to him, directly. She'd said, "I wonder if dear Christine is being wise? After all, everyone knows that Yorke offered to back her before she took the position with us. I'm sure she just doesn't think. But . . . alone as she is . . . over there . . . it does make a difference. . . ."

"It's all right," said Christine, smiling, "even if he hadn't gone away I would have managed not to see him again. Only . . . when he comes back to town? We can't afford to be made ridiculous, Larry. I mean . . . the best way to stop that kind of talk is to be seen with him, casually, together."

"I suppose so," he said gloomily, "but it's a long way off; don't worry about it now. Meantime," he added hopefully, "he may slip off an Alp and break his neck." He looked at his watch. "I've got to run," he said.

Christine put her arms about him. "I'm so sorry," she said, low, and wondered why she was sorry — whether it was because she had lied to him, or because she had caused him a moment's anxiety, or because she knew that, after all, things could never be wholly clear between them, being man and woman.

"I'm the one," he said, "forgive me."

She went with him to the door.

"What's the conference?"

"Oh, advertising," he replied vaguely. "We've made some changes. I'll tell you about it tonight. Get some rest and do your unpacking. I've put your mother's phone number in your address book in case you want to call her."

"I do — 'bye, darling."

She went back into their bedroom, smiling.

Everything was all right. She had forgotten the heart-searching and the involved emotions which had attended her across the Atlantic. They were as the white wake of the ship, dissipated, gone forever. All that mattered was that things were right between them. She thought, Silly, how trifles loom when you're separated.

In absence you had no reassurance of touch and clasp and kiss. In absence it was difficult to conjure up even the features of the beloved. You were accompanied by ghosts and memories, you exaggerated everything. But once home, where you belonged, everything was sane again. Being away was like waking in a dark room in which the familiar furniture becomes strange and menacing. Return was like drawing up the shades and letting in the sunlight. How safe everything looks then, how known to the heart, the shadows dispersed and the fear dispelled.

She had forgotten Sara Thorpe.

She telephoned her mother, supervised her unpacking, bathed and dressed. Then she thought of Rita. She felt kind toward everyone in the world, even Rita, toward whom she had no great reason to feel kind. She thought, I'll call her.

She did so and presently was talking to her, commiserating with her on her accident, promising to run in and see her, telling her about her trip . . . and then . . .

"What do you think of the changes in the store?" asked Rita.

"Are there any? I didn't know . . . I've not had time . . . "

"Well, in the advertising department . . . didn't Lawrence tell you . . . Fellowes was leaving?"

"No," said Christine, "he didn't." And still no premonition took her.

"It all happened very suddenly. He hasn't been well for some time," Rita told her, "and his resignation took effect at once, about a week ago."

"Did Steele take his place?" asked Christine. "I hope so." She liked Roger Steele, assistant to Mr. Fellowes, and had thought for some time that he would make a better thing of the department. Fellowes was old and crotchety and rather too conservative for the times.

"Well, no, he didn't," Rita told her. "I am surprised you haven't heard. Sara Thorpe has the job."

13

There was silence. Then, "Did you hear me . . . are you still there, Christine?" Rita asked urgently.

Christine thought, Yes, I'm still here. She thought further, I've got to keep her from knowing. But she couldn't. She couldn't say lightly, Why, of course, he did tell me, in fact he asked my advice . . . it had slipped my mind. No. There was no way of deceiving Rita. She took a long deep breath and as Rita said again, "Christine?" she answered, very steadily:

"Yes, I'm here. I was just thinking. It's splendid. She's enormously clever."

"Oh," said Rita, "I thought for a moment we'd been cut off." Her voice was perceptibly tinged with malice. "It's odd Lawrence didn't tell you," she suggested.

Christine laughed, She managed it very well. It was the secretly amused laughter of the beloved woman and it made Rita, on the other end of the wire, wince . . . it was patronizing, even pitying.

"My *dear,*" said Christine, "we've had other things to discuss — we haven't seen each other for weeks . . . and we hadn't very long together."

She thought, I'm an astonishingly good actress. Her throat hurt, her eyes were suffused. If only Rita would say good-bye and hang up.

"Of course," agreed Rita, a little blankly. And Christine laughed again.

Someone knocked at the door, and she welcomed the interruption. She called clearly, "Come in," and then said into the transmitter, "I'm sorry, Rita, I have to run . . . I'll try to get over to see you. Hope you'll be a lot better soon."

Presently she replaced the receiver, got rid of the housekeeper who had come to consult her on a minor matter, and when she was alone again, rose and walked restlessly about the room.

She stopped to stare at a great growing mass of phlox in a squat vase, without seeing it. She thought, I'm making a fool of myself. Why didn't he tell me . . . *why didn't he tell me?*

Perhaps he believed it none of her business? Yet it touched her vitally in her relation to the store, no matter what else might be involved. Or didn't he consider her part of the store, in her twofold capacity: as a working unit and as his wife?

She remembered the clippings. She hadn't kept them. Thinking of them she was now convinced who had sent them. Rita, of course! Rita with her protestations of friendship and her pleasant way of stabbing one in the back! To think that she had been taken in by her — ever.

The pieces of the puzzle fell into place and she saw Rita as she had always been, resentful, jealous, spying on her through Nancy, making things as difficult as possible for her. But she couldn't go to Larry and say that. Larry thought Rita was pure gold. So did Howard.

She went to the private telephone which connected directly with the store, but her hand dropped from the instrument. She couldn't call him, demand that he come upstairs immediately and render an accounting. She couldn't do — anything.

She sat down in a low chair and began to cry helplessly and forlornly, as a child cries.

After a time she rose and went into the bathroom to hold cold compresses to her reddened eyes. She searched in the medicine cabinet, found triple bromides, and took one, drinking the fizzing mixture with distaste and reluctance. But after a time she felt steadier, more sure of herself. She went out into the living room and glanced at the clock there.

Larry had promised to come home early.

She picked up a morning newspaper and lit a cigarette. Turning the pages of the paper she came upon the Clarkson advertisement and stared at it for a moment. Yes, that was pure Sara Thorpe. The sketch of a perky hat, an amusing jingle beneath it; a generally sophisticated yet confidential tone to the copy, like amusing gossip heard at a hotel bar; a little mild fun-poking at Clarkson's itself, at the Clarkson tradition. Yes, the entire tone of the advertising had changed. It was smart, knowing, disarmingly frank. It would sell merchandise, she thought dully. The more conservative among their customers, those who might easily be irritated at this new orchestration of an old song, probably didn't bother to read advertisements. They'd just keep on coming to Clarkson's to buy the things they'd always bought.

She put the paper aside and was conscious of the fact that her hands were wringing wet. It is usually very warm in Manhattan in late August, of course . . . that was the reason. Yet her feet felt cold and her head hot. She rang and asked for iced tea. While she was drinking it, ignoring the small thin cucumber sandwiches which appeared with it, the doorbell rang and Howard came in without ceremony.

Christine rose to greet him. Her first startled thought was that he was the last person she wanted to see. Her second thought that she was gladder to see him than anyone else in the world. He came in, chipper as a lark, his blue eyes bright, his white beard aggressively tended.

"I should have waited till tomorrow," he said. He took her hands. "You look a little thin." He kissed her cheek. "I wanted to come to the boat but thought perhaps . . . well, a welcoming committee of one is better. Told the boy I wouldn't be in town until tomorrow and then came anyway. May I have some of that tea?"

"Of course. I'm so glad you came. You were sweet to write me . . . I missed you," she told him, smiling, and realized as she said it that it was the truth.

"Did you? I missed you too," he said, and added as if astonished, "more than I expected to. You and Larry coming down for the weekend tomorrow night? We'll all drive down together."

They talked of her trip and of the weather and, "How do you think Larry is looking?" he inquired. They spoke of the farm and Howard announced proudly that the last litter of Llewellins had 'em all beat. Then he asked abruptly:

"What do you think of the new advertising?"

Christine twisted her hands together in her lap. She said carefully, "I just saw it a minute ago. It's very clever."

"It's too clever," remarked Howard, frowning. "You know, Christine, it's not wise to be cleverer than your customer. And not all of our customers are wits. I don't like it. Smart aleck. Sort of take it or leave it. I was very much opposed to the change but I hadn't a chance. Larry had sold everyone else on it. Well, we'll see how it works out. Larry accused me of not liking the girl — this Thorpe woman, I mean — of being prejudiced personally. Well, maybe he's right. I *don't* like her. But I pride myself on believing that, like or dislike, I wouldn't be influenced by that. What do you think of the setup?"

She had had time to get herself in hand.

"Well, I hadn't heard . . . until just a little while ago. But Sara Thorpe's very brilliant, and we have to move with the times."

She had made a mistake and a bad one. She knew it as soon as the blue eyes flashed at her and the sagacious old face fell into lines of amazement.

"You mean to tell me Larry hadn't told you!"

"There wasn't much time," she explained

hastily, feeling her way. "It all happened quickly and recently. And we didn't" — she tried to smile — "talk shop the little time we had together today."

"Oh," said Howard, "I see." She had an uncomfortable feeling that he saw more than she wanted him to see. She said eagerly:

"But I'm sure it was wise. Of course, I don't know Miss Thorpe very well, I've met her only twice. But she impressed me as a person who knew her business. Larry doesn't often make mistakes."

"No," said Howard, "he doesn't. I'm beginning to realize that. Good girl," he added suddenly, to Christine's astonishment.

He drank his tea, jiggled the ice in the glass, and made as if to rise. "I must be going," he said, "see you tomorrow."

"No," said Christine, in a panic, "no, don't go. Please stay for dinner, Father Clarkson." She had never called him that before, she had always avoided any direct form of address if possible. She was not aware that she had said it now.

"You could drop the Clarkson," he suggested, smiling. "Thanks, but I'll go along, you and Larry have a lot to say to each other."

"No, really." She was imploring him now, her eyes more desperate than she knew, her hand on his sleeve, detaining him. "I — I brought you something . . . and there's so much to tell you about . . . I saw Bianchi in Paris. . . . "

Bianchi was their Italian exporter. Christine went on, "And I have some sketches I'd like you to see. I want your advice . . . I — "

Howard thought, Something's wrong, I knew it as soon as I set eyes on her. The Thorpe woman? Nonsense, the girl's crazy. There couldn't be anything in that. But his heart gave an uncertain leap. Larry had been — pretty insistent, and there'd been all that stuff in the papers. And once Larry had brought Sara Thorpe with several other people to the Island for a week-end. Howard began remembering. His bushy brows were drawn together. He thought, She's got the stuff — and he wasn't thinking of Sara now — she wouldn't let me know if she could help it. She's loyal.

That was the ultimate trait; the trait he prized so highly, loyalty. He had preached it in his business over all the years, he demanded it from his employees, his friends, and his son. He looked for it in his kennels and was never disappointed, which was one reason why he liked dogs.

"I'll stay, if you like. Matter of fact, I hoped you'd ask me. I don't like mooching around the club alone or with a couple of useless oldsters like myself. Larry won't be pleased though. He'll want you to himself. I should have stayed where I belonged and waited till you came down tomorrow. But I couldn't. Wanted to see with my own eyes as soon as possible how you were."

"I'm fine. And so glad you came." Christine went into her room to get the tortoise-shell cigarette case she'd brought him, and the amusing, gay ties. She found them, and the portfolio of sketches. She was thinking, He is glad to see me, he likes me, he's my *friend*.

When Larry came in he found them together, their heads over the portfolio. Howard was groaning and smiting a sketch of a Medici bonnet.

"Do you mean to tell me that women will wear that?"

"When I get through with them, they will. Look . . . a hostess gown, velvet, along these lines, girdled with a woven rope of lamé . . . and I talked about special costume jewelry to one of the French designers. Heavy, almost massive . . . see, like this . . . I thought we could put some in, in my department, made especially for these gowns. . . ."

"Well," cried Larry, at the doorway, "and everyone ignores a starving man!"

He came in, clapped his father on the shoulder, asked, "What are you doing here with my wife?" and kissed Christine. Howard said, stretching his long legs, "If you will leave her alone you must expect competition. I'm staying for dinner and I don't think you'll like it. Not that I care."

"Of course, I'll like it," said Larry heartily. Too heartily. Christine and his father watched him, and he was conscious of their regard.

"Hey, what's up?" he demanded. "You look like a couple of conspirators. Where'd you get the case? Pretty swank, sez I."

"A lovely lady brought it to me from Europe," replied his father.

"I brought you one too," said Christine consolingly, "and something else." She went to get his presents, the case and the crystal links. While she was gone the two men looked at one another. Howard said carelessly:

"Christine insisted on my staying. Took pity on me. She looks a little fine-drawn, but I expect that's the trip and the excitement. We were discussing the new advertising."

"Oh," said Larry, "you were . . . I haven't had a chance to tell her . . . I mean — "

Christine came back with her little packages. After suitable comments had been made, Larry said:

"Father says you've been discussing the advertising. Like it?"

"Very much," answered Christine smoothly,

and Howard grunted, "Well I don't and that's that."

"Oh, you'll come around," prophesied Larry, amused. He looked, they both saw, a trifle relieved. "There wasn't time to write about the changes," he went on, ignoring the fact that cable companies could be persuaded to operate for a fee, "but I knew you'd approve. Then I found out that Sara was anxious to make a change."

Sara. . . .

"Yes," said Christine and smiled brilliantly, "it was lucky for her, wasn't it? And for us." Howard, watching her, was uneasy. He thought, She's overdoing it. He thought, Wish I hadn't stayed, hate these rumbly sort of thunderstorms which never get anywhere, don't break out and have it over with; if I hadn't stayed they might have had a bang-up row and cleared the atmosphere; as it is, it will be all the worse when it happens.

The household had been informed that the senior Clarkson would be dining with them. The cocktails came in, just as he liked them. Presently they went in to dinner.

Larry asked, eating his shrimp:

"What have you been doing with yourself all afternoon, Christine?"

"Oh, entertaining a very charming gentleman," she said, smiling. "Before he came I unpacked and fiddled around, and I talked to Rita."

That, thought Larry and his father simultaneously, is where she heard about the changes in the advertising department.

Janis came in before dinner was over. She looked, Christine saw at once, keyed to the highest pitch — and very pretty. She had left someone waiting in a taxi, she informed them, she was going on to late dinner on a roof. No, she wouldn't have coffee.

She talked for fifteen minutes. She adored her work. She adored having Christine home again. She adored the cottage they had taken this summer. No, she wouldn't be able to get down this week-end. She had promised to drive out to Rye to a house party.

When she had gone, as she had come, a whirlwind, Christine looked at Larry.

"So she doesn't go down every week-end."

He said uneasily, "No, I suppose not. She's met a lot of people, she's asked out a good bit."

Howard said, "I think you should take a hand, Christine. The kid's having a pretty sensational sort of time. Not that I know about it firsthand. But I do hear things."

"What about Frank Austin?" asked Christine. "Surely . . . in six weeks!"

Had she been gone only six weeks? It

seemed a century. Larry shrugged.

"In the discard, if temporarily. The current boy friend appears to be Sam Pierson."

Christine set down her coffee cup with a clatter. She knew Sam Pierson, the merchandising head of Williamson's. She said, appalled:

"But he's married!"

"Not very much, he isn't," Larry told her; "he's been separated from Mrs. Sam for a long time."

"He's still married," said Christine steadily, "and it wouldn't make it much better if he were divorced . . . or a bachelor."

"Come," said Larry tolerantly, "don't get wrought up. You do get pretty excited over nothing. Christine, Janis is old enough to take care of herself. You can't wet-nurse her forever."

Howard said quietly, "I agree with Christine, not that my opinion's been asked. Sam Pierson isn't the type I'd want a daughter of mine to run with — and Janis is young and inexperienced."

"Well, if she is," said Larry impatiently, "it's Christine's fault. She's kept her in an incubator."

Christine leaned back against the divan and closed her eyes. Howard looked at her and said, "You're tired . . . I'll be going along. See you tomorrow." He came over and kissed her, put his hand on her shoulder and kept it there. Then he looked at Larry. "You're a lucky so-and-so," he told him, smiling, "and you don't half know it."

Larry took his father out to the elevator in the foyer and presently returned. He sat down beside Christine, put his arm about her, drew her close. She did not resist him. Nothing in her resisted him, not even her mind. She leaned against him, her eyes closed, and rested. He spoke first, a little awkwardly:

"About Sara Thorpe . . ."

Now was the time. To push him away, to cry out, Why didn't you tell me, if only you'd told me! But she was too tired. This last bit of information about Janis had, she told herself, taken all the tucker out of her. Tomorrow she would know how to deal with it and with other things. Not tonight. She felt like one of her own models in its initial stages, flimsy and basted. If someone pulled out the basting threads —

She said with her head against his shoulder and her two small hands in his big clasp:

"Never mind about her now. About anything. I'm so tired, and so glad to be home. I think I'll take your offer."

"What offer?" he demanded.

"Vacation till Monday. I'll potter around

tomorrow, we'll go down to the Island after closing. Monday's time enough. Larry, are you glad I'm back?"

Her lethargy was dissipated suddenly, terror sharpened her tone. His arm tightened about her. "Need I tell you?"

"I suppose not. But do. Tell me a lot of times." She turned, clung to him. "I'm frightened," she said, in a half whisper.

"Of what?" he demanded.

"Oh, everything. Life — it's so short, so hideously short. Death . . . I don't know. I wish I hadn't gone away. There's that gap, that blank, those six weeks, I can never find them again, can never share them with you. I wish I'd stayed home," she said unconsolably.

He said anxiously, "Look here, you're worn out. You'd better get some sleep."

"No, I'm all right. And I'm perfectly wide awake. I don't want to go to sleep . . . I just want to sit here with you and keep reassuring myself that I'm home, that we're together."

Half an hour later she slept quietly against his shoulder; moving with great caution in order not to disturb her, he rose and picked her up in his arms. As he reached the bedroom door she opened her eyes and smiled at him. She said, "You forgot to do just this, over a year ago, but now — the bride comes home."

14

On Monday morning Christine returned to Clarkson's. The week-end had been like an isolated dream, hardly related to life. She had willed it to be so. She had deliberately kept herself from questioning Larry about Sara Thorpe, from even approaching a discussion. She had gone to see her mother and had closed her mind to Mrs. Carstairs' querulous complaints about Janis. That, too, could wait. She would not have her homecoming utterly spoiled. She could not return and find herself in the midst of recriminations, quarrels, misunderstandings. It would have been very easy, but she wouldn't let it happen. She had to get back in touch with Larry again, had to pick up the threads of their life before she could afford to go beneath the surface of laughter, tenderness, love. She had the strangest feeling which was that if she and Larry misunderstood each other now, on the heels of her return, they might never straighten things out again.

She rode with him, swam, watched a game

of polo, a tennis match, motored to the club Saturday night to dance. She went to the kennels with Larry and fell in love with a clumsy-footed puppy. She played hostess to the people who dropped in for lunch and for tea or cocktails and for supper on Sunday.

They drove back, very late Sunday night, and on the following morning hurried through breakfast, having overslept. Going down in the elevator, she smiled at him.

"Back on the job," she said. "Glad I'm here?"

"You know — "

"I didn't mean at home, exactly," she told him.

"Then," asked Larry, astonished, "what did you mean?"

"Never mind, darling. You're just a little denser than usual today," she said, laughing.

Her department, exclusive of Nancy, who was, Christine was pleased to discover, on her vacation . . . although why she needs a vacation, thought Christine — welcomed her with open arms. She had a very full and busy day, getting reorganized, swinging herself back into the tempo of the store. She would have her work cut out for her to get ready for the fall opening. But she had her sketches, the materials were ordered. Things would get under way and she would be ready, she told herself.

During that first week she had time for scarcely anything outside the store. Larry complained that she might as well still be in Europe. Rita came back to the shop, her arm still in a sling, and before the week was up Christine made her appearance at a department conference. It was, she soon saw, an advertising conference and Sara Thorpe presided at it. At least Larry presided nominally but he listened to Miss Thorpe's crisp suggestions with a paternal pride which Christine found maddening. It was as though he had brought the girl up by hand.

She had seen Miss Thorpe on her second day at the shop. Larry had brought her upstairs to lunch. "I want you two girls to get acquainted," he said fatuously. Sara seemed willing. She was affable in her clear-cut manner, and she looked, Christine saw with despair, as pretty as it was possible for her to look. She said, smiling, "I hope you don't think we put one over on you, Miss Carstairs."

Christine smiled in return. She said gently, "But you did. And I wish I'd thought of it first."

Sara looked at her hostess with some admiration. She was a little amused. It was, she felt, a direct challenge.

"I'm so glad you feel that way. Larry and I

have cooked up quite a mess of pottage. Hope you'll approve."

"So long," said Christine, "as my department gets a full bowl, I'll approve all right."

"Of course . . . " Sara began. Christine went on smoothly:

"But, of course, the advertising department is out of my jurisdiction."

"Don't you dare sit there and tell me that you aren't the Guiding Hand," exclaimed Sara, and was pleased to see Larry frown.

"No," said Christine, "I'm not. I haven't the slightest influence with Larry. But then he wouldn't try to tell me what to do in the cutting room, either."

Larry's drawn brows relaxed and Sara said something swiftly. It wasn't much. Just a reminder of something he and she had seen together . . . an entertaining incident . . . a man in a high hat, sitting in an ash can in front of a Park Avenue apartment at an early hour in the morning.

That night Christine asked carelessly.:

"What on earth were you and Sara Thorpe doing around an ash can at two in the morning, anyway?"

Larry laughed. "Oh, coming home," he answered. "When I learned she wasn't exactly satisfied with her job I began to see how well she'd fit in with us. It took a little persuading though. I saw her a lot, one place and another, and kept hammering at her. She's a stubborn youngster. She does a lot of outside work, you know, wanted to give up advertising entirely and write, with maybe a public relations special job on the side now and then to help her over the lean times. But I persuaded her finally. Then before we had everything all set, we worked out a sort of skeleton organization for her. After she came into the shop we worked together late, some nights, and had dinner after or went somewhere for a drink and a bite. She's marvelously co-operative."

"Yes," said Christine, "she must be," and although he looked at her sharply, he could for the life of him find no fault with her tone or her expression.

Well, if no offense meant, none taken.

She thought she knew where she stood. Thank heaven, she hadn't gone off the deep end and accused Larry of all sorts of things on her return. He admired Sara Thorpe. He was genuinely proud of her. He felt that she was an asset to the store. He liked her, she flattered him. So far, so good. If it went no further, even better. He didn't, Christine believed, or tried to believe, think of Sara as a woman, an attractive woman, in relation to himself, as a man. And he never would, if Christine could help it.

What Sara thought was another matter and how she felt was something else again. Christine didn't know. Couldn't. But she'd find out.

Meanwhile, in addition to her increasing and exacting work she had other things to think about, notably Janis. She saw Janis once or twice briefly during that first week, but over the second week-end Janis was down on the Island. It was then that Christine determined to speak to her.

She drove over in the small roadster alone, that Saturday afternoon, and picked Janis up at the nearby tennis club.

"Am I going home with you?" inquired Janis, very slender in her linen shorts and silk blouse.

"No, were having a mob down. Larry's doing. He loves a party. But I wanted to talk to you. Let's drive."

They drove out into the country and turned off on a dirt, tree-bordered road. Summer was all about them, drowsy summer, slipping steadily toward sleep. Hay in mounds and stacks, and blackbirds flying, and goldenrod drowsy and heavy at the roadside. A sky that was blue and faintly misty and the green leaves of the trees dusty and drooping.

"What's on your mind?" demanded Janis.

"Darling, you know. Sam Pierson."

"Oh, so my little brother-in-law's been talking. Well, it's none of his business!"

"Perhaps not. But it's mine. Janis, don't be a fool."

"I'm not. And I wish you'd leave me alone," said Janis angrily. "I like Sam. He's all right."

"He's married," Christine reminded her.

"Oh, don't be childish, Christine. You are perfectly absurd. What if he is? He's been separated from the woman for years."

"Has he any intention of getting a divorce?"

"She won't give him one," said Janis, "and what difference does it make? I don't want to marry him any more than he wants to marry me, but I like to go around with him. He knows all the answers. I'm free, white and over twenty-one and I'm hurting no one."

"What about Francis?"

"Oh, Frank." Janis shrugged. "Well, what about him?"

"Aren't you hurting him? He's too fine a person to merit such treatment, Janis."

"If you think so much of him why didn't you marry him yourself?" asked Janis. "Lord knows you could have had him for the asking any time you wanted."

"But I didn't want."

"Then why assume I do? Frank's all right, he's a swell person, but he treats me as if I were two years old and made of Dresden china into the bargain. Besides, I'm not interested in catching a man on the rebound. He spent a whole evening once telling me how much in love he'd been with you and how I took your place. Nice going, wasn't it? I don't want anybody's leavings."

So that was it, thought Christine, light dawning. Janis had fallen in love with Frank — and Frank had made the usual masculine mistake of a full confession of past emotions. Of course, Janis had known that Frank and her sister had been close friends, had known that Frank at one time had wished to marry Christine. But knowing it was different from hearing it, from him. She could have saved her funny, foolish little face by all sorts of excuses; Frank and Christine's youth, their long knowledge of each other, propinquity, family relationships. But to have him tell her solemnly, "I was in love with your sister, now I'm in love with you . . ." Christine could have shaken him. Men were intolerably stupid. They were honest at the wrong time; and dishonest at the wrong time. Poor Frank!

She said mildly, "Well, really, Janis, I wouldn't look at it like that. Frank and I were kids together."

"He's older than you are."

"Oh, the years don't matter. It was a sort of

expected thing . . . you know . . . his father wished it, and so did mother. He was — well, railroaded into thinking himself in love with me. But it was over long ago, before I even met Larry. And I was never in love with Frank, you know that."

"Yes," admitted Janis grudgingly, "I suppose I do. Which makes me wonder what was the matter with him?"

Christine dissolved into helpless laughter. "You idiot! Must there be something wrong with any man with whom I don't fall in love? If that's the case then there's only one man in the world who's entirely all right."

"Oh, you and your Larry! Still," said Janis thoughtfully, "you did like Nelson Yorke."

"Not enough. And that's what I'm trying to get at. You like Sam Pierson. But you don't like him enough."

"How do you know, I'd like to inquire? Look here, Christine, I know the facts of life. Don't sit there like a schoolteacher, and an old maid one at that. I know what I'm about. I — well, Sam amuses me and I see no harm in it. I go out with him, shows, dinner, that sort of thing. House parties, gobs of other people, friends of his. There's nothing funny about it. Of course, Mother went off the handle because I went to his apartment — "

"Janis!"

"Good Lord, Christine, that sort of attitude went out with the flapper. A girl can go to a man's apartment nowadays without expecting her family to appear with shotguns. We went for cocktails, after closing at the store and then on to dinner. And he hasn't any etchings! And he didn't tell me there would be other people there! You've been reading a book or something. Snap out of it — "

Christine said, after a minute:

"I'm a perfectly tolerant person, Janis. I realize that times change and conventions alter or go by the board. Basically there's nothing wrong in your going to Pierson's apartment for a cocktail . . . not if it doesn't seem wrong to you or — Pierson. If it does, that's something else again. That's just being silly and defiant and taking a dare with yourself, so to speak. But despite all the new standards and new freedom and — well, license — appearances remain. And you might regret it, that's all. I can't forbid you. You're on your own now. But — oh, Janis, please, please don't make yourself a laughingstock and an undeserved reputation just because — "

"Skip it," suggested Janis briefly, "I'm not going to disgrace the family honor."

There was no use. It was like talking to the girl through a glass wall. Christine drove her back to the cottage, stopped for a moment with their mother and then went on to join Larry feeling helpless and very much alone. There was no use talking about the whole dreary business with Larry. She was afraid he might even agree with her, and too vehemently. She would be forced to defend Janis in, practically, the girl's own shallow words. Larry, very amiable about Janis and her job, would not be so amiable about Janis and the Pierson situation, once he knew more about it. He would probably feel that as a member of Janis's family he should seek out Sam Pierson and punch him in the nose. Which would be just lovely for all concerned.

She found herself wishing for Nelson Yorke. She could talk to him. She had confidence in his worldly judgment; he'd probably be tolerant enough of Janis but he'd see all the implications and the dangers. And he would advise her, Christine.

The autumn showing took place and was unusually successful. The town went Venetian and Van Dyck and Medici mad. Everyone who was anyone wanted the modified bonnets and the hostess gowns and the evening gowns, lavish, superb, with great dignity and richness . . . everyone wanted the costume jewelry. The custom department was rushed with orders and Christine ate and slept in snatches.

Larry was busy too. There were nights when he went back to work after dinner, and nights when he didn't come home to dinner, when he and Sara Thorpe had conferences after hours. He was perfectly frank about these. The fact that the previous department had acted more or less independently of Larry didn't seem to matter. The present organization worked hand in glove with him, a novelty which appeared to please him greatly.

Christine was not pleased. Nor was she pleased when it was borne in upon her that the majority of the advertising ignored her department entirely. During a departmental conference at which Sara was, of course, present, she went to the mat about it. She told herself, before entering the conference room, that her grievance was legitimate and had to do with the store and her department only. The fact that she had an emotional grudge had nothing to do with it. It was then that she discovered how difficult it was to detach herself. She hated herself for it. Larry could detach himself, why couldn't she?

The quarrel, discreetly conducted, boiled itself down to a three-cornered affair, with Rita, Sara and herself. Rita, of course, was on Sara's side of the fence and why shouldn't she be? She had no complaint to offer at the advertising. She was getting plenty.

Sara was markedly patient. She said, in effect, that the very nature of Miss Carstairs' department tied her hands. Miss Carstairs and her coworkers were not represented in the outside fashion shows which Sara's department, in co-operation with Rita, were planning to put over during the season. They couldn't be, any more than they could have their models displayed in the windows, for fear of copyists. The most that the advertising end could do was to run an occasional fashion note, almost a society item, which would feature the fact that the Clarkson custom-made frocks were seen in the best places on the best-dressed women in town. And this Sara had done.

Larry agreed with her. Rita agreed with her. Almost everyone followed their lead, including the other designers. It was perfectly true. No sketches of the custom-made clothes could be made available to the public through the medium of advertising. Sara couldn't do more than oversee the occasional copy which went out about the department, copy which was in the nature of an announcement.

That night Larry made the first overture toward hostilities. It was Christine's fault that he did so. She was tired, she was bruised with defeat, angry at herself, and it was impossible for her to dismiss that humiliating conference from her mind. All through dinner she kept going over and over it, trying to find some flaw in Sara's argument, trying to find a way in which she could convince her that the department was not receiving its full share of attention. Larry, who had forgotten all about the morning's fracas, because he chose to forget it, over a good meal, pushed his plate aside in exasperation.

"For heaven's sake, Christine, will you stop nagging and talk about something else? I'm tired, and I'd like to enjoy a meal in peace."

"I'm tired too," she said angrily, "but I can't just dismiss it. Of course, there's no use talking to you. You're on her side too."

"What do you mean, too?" he demanded. "And why on her side? Christine, don't be silly. You never kicked about the advertising before and you have as much now as you've always had."

This was perfectly true and she knew it. Knowing it maddened her all the more; she set her little jaw and looked at him with marked hostility.

"Mr. Fellowes always showed me some consideration," she cried. "It isn't so much the lack of space — and I think you'll find if you look up the records that my department is receiving less space — but it is total lack of consideration. I might just as well not sit in at a conference so far as Thorpe is concerned. She's been with Clarkson's a few weeks . . . and she acts as if she ran it. She leads you around by the nose. You didn't work overtime with Fellowes or look into Park Avenue ash cans with him. You didn't need to do research work then."

He said, "Oh, that's it, is it? Sore because I went out with her while you were away. Why didn't you say so when you came back instead of waiting till now?"

The pantry door opened, and dessert appeared. Hostilities ceased. Christine refused the sweet, and announced that she would have her coffee in the living room now. She left Larry at the table and when he joined her he was not in the pleasantest frame of mind.

"We might just as well go on with it," he suggested, "the evening's ruined anyway."

Christine shrugged, and the gesture irritated him. He said hotly:

"You don't like Sara and never have. This whole business is based on an unfair feminine prejudice. I don't deny that you have a right to your likes and dislikes, but like most women you can't keep them out of business."

"Like most women," she demanded, "what about you? I suppose you keep yours out of business! I suppose you hired Sara Thorpe without stopping to consider whether you liked her personally or not!"

"Of course I like her personally," he said angrily, "what has that to do with it?"

"I thought it had everything to do with it."

"Well, it hasn't. If I had despised the sight of her but believed she was the person for the job, she would have got it. A man doesn't run a successful business any other way."

"That's not true," said Christine, "you would never have taken her in Fellowes's place if she hadn't flattered you into it, if you hadn't had an interest in her which had nothing to do with business."

Larry began to laugh. His face, which had been set in lines of anger and annoyance, broke up into an expression of genuine amusement. He said, "Women are the damndest . . ."

"Well," demanded Christine, "what's so funny?"

"I was just remembering that you once told me that the gossips accused me of having a personal interest in you and employing you for that reason. You were pretty hot and bothered about it . . . or have you forgotten that?" he asked.

15

Christine rose and walked away to the windows. She pushed the draperies aside and looked down over the street. It had been raining and on the sleek wet blackness of asphalt the lamps made little pools of light, the cars moved with more caution, and from the distance the hoot of horns, the occasional squeal of brakes reached her.

She let the curtains fall in place and turned. She said, after a moment:

"I do remember, Larry. I was furious . . . at the people who said such things . . . and at myself, because I hoped it was true."

Now there was nothing he could say, she thought, looking at him. But he answered violently:

"Well, even if it was true in your case it doesn't follow that it must be in this."

"I suppose not," she admitted. She walked over and sat on the arm of his chair, and touched his cheek with her hand.

"If I could only talk this out with you," she said wistfully, "but I can't. I try to and all I do is confuse, cloud the issues."

"What is the issue, exactly?" he asked her. At her nearness, his face softened, his anger was appeased. He caught her hand in his own and put it to his lips. He added, as if in astonishment, "Why do we quarrel so much, Christine?"

"I don't know, darling," she said sorrowfully. "I — I was hurt. I thought you might have told me . . . about Sara Thorpe, I mean."

"But it happened so quickly — "

"I know. Yet if you'd cabled . . . "

His mood changed. He said irritably, "But it had nothing to do with us — with you, Christine!"

"Why not?" she cried at him. "I'm your wife, I head a department in your business. I had a right to be consulted."

"Oh, come now," he told her, trying to keep his temper, "that's going a little too far. Surely you don't expect me to consult you every time I fill a position?"

"No . . . but I am part of the business, Larry. And your wife. I thought — when I married you . . . that we would talk things over . . . everything — no matter how trivial. I thought it was a partnership."

He said, smoothly, "But surely I'm permitted to use my own judgment in matters not materially affecting your department?"

"Oh, Larry," she said in despair, "don't take that attitude. That employer-to-employee tone! Haven't I some rights as your wife?"

"The trouble with you, Christine," he told her, "is that you can't separate the two."

"But — *must* I?" she asked him, astonished. "And can you?"

"I can," he said firmly. And wondered, fleetly, whether he could. This rumpus about the advertising, for instance. In all fairness he had been forced to agree with Sara. Christine's department was getting its quota of advertising, and that advertising was limited in its scope by the very nature of her work. He had tried to view it as though Christine, as a person, as the woman he loved, as his wife, did not enter into it. It hadn't been easy.

She said, "Larry, we aren't getting anywhere. I mean, we work together, after a fashion, we share an interest in a business. Why? So that the shop will be a success, in order that we shall have a good income. Is that all that such a partnership amounts to? I mean, isn't there anything more, something beyond success and money? I thought there might be. I didn't know what, but it had to be more than that. I mean, is it enough, just working together for more money to put back into the business, more money to spend, to keep up our end socially? I thought because we worked together we'd be so much closer than most husbands and wives. But we haven't been, we've quarreled more, it seems to me, pulled apart; I don't understand it, and it frightens me."

He said stubbornly, "I don't know what you're driving at. And if it's the job that worries you . . . well, any time you want to quit . . ."

"But I don't want to," she cried, "and you know it. And a few months ago you wouldn't have dreamed of saying that! Are you tired of having me around, taking too much interest in what you do and decide? Is that it?"

"Oh, don't twist my words," he told her wearily. "I didn't mean anything of the sort. I'm just trying to find out what's wrong and looking for a remedy. I'm perfectly happy as we are. If only you wouldn't get ideas."

Ideas? Sara Thorpe? She said hotly, "If you mean Miss Thorpe . . . Can't you see what she's doing to you, Larry, making excuses for seeing you out of hours, working overtime? You never took so personal an interest in the advertising department before. She's clever and ambitious. She wants more than the authority over her department, she wants a finger in every pie. She'll flatter you till she gets it. No, don't interrupt me. You haven't listened to my advice on anything, anything at all. You've laughed at me. The Contessa. That was a stupid thing to do and you know it. I tried to tell you, you wouldn't listen. People are no longer intrigued by a title . . . there are too many of them, a dime a dozen. She worked you for all you were worth. What trade did she bring with her? None that mattered. A few women with a good deal of façade, and nothing more, who didn't pay their bills. And she's borrowed money from anyone who had ten dollars. She's not worth her salary, let alone anything else. Since I've been back I've heard she's made the most amazing demands. And I've heard about the bills she's been running up, expense accounts . . . bills at theater ticket agencies, at restaurants."

He said shortly, "She's leaving . . . the first of the month. I found out things too."

But you wouldn't, she thought, come and tell me, admit your mistake. Aloud, she said:

"You took Rita's part when we had trouble over Nancy Redding. It wouldn't occur to you that Rita dislikes me, planted her niece in my department to spy on me — and Miss Ryder in your office to keep tabs on you. I could talk my head off about Nancy, advising you against Miss Ryder, but you wouldn't listen to me. Every move you make in your office goes back to Rita. I don't know why she wants the information. But no matter *why* she wants it, she gets it."

"That's absurd," he said easily, "what on earth — " He laughed shortly. "You are letting your imagination run away with you, Christine."

She got up from the arm of the chair and went over to a little sofa by the fireplace. She said, after a moment:

"That's what you think."

"You don't like Rita," he reminded her, "or Nancy. So you invent — situations. The same holds true of your attitude toward Sara."

"You would think that. Your Sara and Rita are very good friends. They lunch together, see each other evenings. Oh, I have ways of knowing things too. It's dog-eat-dog in this business, more's the pity. Rita will get her share of advertising. Sara will work for Rita, see that her sales go up. In her turn Rita will do Sara favors. You'll see. But there's no use telling you — you think I'm blind and prejudiced."

"Aren't you?" he asked. "You've practically admitted that you don't like either of them."

He rose. As she did not answer, he said, standing over her, looking down:

"If you'd try to detach yourself . . . if you'd let me manage my end of things . . . I interfere very little with yours . . . I give you every assistance, I do not permit the fact that you are my wife to influence me one way or another. If you feel that your department is not getting the co-operation it should, we will take it up, in conference, where it belongs. On the other hand, if I should feel that your department is not turning in as good an account of itself as I expect, I would not hesitate to say so, and to try to find out the reason — with your help. But this nonsense about spies and malice . . . this idle gossip. I do expect to come home and have the normal life any man desires, away from business. I don't expect to have every little grievance on your part carried to the dinner table. It's intolerable."

She spoke very quietly:

"I'm sorry you feel that way about me, Larry. I don't suppose it's any use asking you to believe that my personal feeling toward Rita and toward Sara Thorpe hasn't warped my judgment. And we won't talk about it any more . . . out of business hours."

Lawrence smiled at her.

"That's my girl. Are you terribly tired? No? Get on your bonnet and we'll go for a ride. It's a grand night. Let's drive up Westchester way for a breath of air."

So far as he was concerned it was over, although from time to time he would remember things she had said, and it would make him uneasy. Driving out of the city, taking, beyond New Rochelle, the less traveled roads, he was conscious of a deep feeling of resentment toward the girl who sat quietly and close beside him, her little hat in her lap, the wind blowing through the silken mass of her dark gold hair. He could no longer be perfectly unself-conscious when he worked and talked with Sara Thorpe. He'd watch Rita, and, yes, the Ryder woman, with new, if reluctant eyes. He hadn't believed a word Christine had said; had put it down to her absurd, feminine, unreasoning dislike of the other women, almost indulgently, for a man expects lack of reason and of logic from women. Now he was quite aware that there would be times when he would feel suddenly uncomfortable in Sara Thorpe's presence, wondering if, after all, she was using him for her own ends, wondering if the things she said, or left unsaid, were not dictated by diplomacy and politics rather than by a genuine liking for himself, which she had given him to understand.

On such occasions he would probably find himself thinking that women know more about women, after all. It was all confusing and distasteful.

For a little while nothing more was said. The store was busy with its seasonal activities.

Christine and Sara maintained an armed truce. Once, alone with Larry in his office, Sara said, sighing, "Miss Carstairs — that is, Mrs. Clarkson, doesn't like me. I wonder why?" and Larry laughed awkwardly, angrily conscious of his embarrassment, and said, "What nonsense, she likes you very much."

"That's sweet of you," said Sara, smiling, "and so very transparent!"

He had to show her that it wasn't true. Sara must be asked to the apartment. How? There was one way, the usual departmental dinner was given; Sara came, and made herself extremely agreeable. Rita, watching from the other end of the table, smiled.

Rita and Sara were good friends but Rita had more than met her match. Her carefully careless questions as to the exact state of affairs between Sara and Larry met with little response. Sara always knew the answer. "Oh," said Sara lightly, "I adore him, he's a grand person . . . but he's very much in love with his wife . . . isn't he?"

In Sara's argot "adoring" meant little, and Rita knew it.

During the autumn Nelson Yorke returned to town. Christine showed the clipping to Larry. "I'm going to ask him to dinner," she said. No beating around the bush, as he had with Sara's invitation. Larry looked glum.

"Look here, must you?"

"You said there was gossip," she reminded him, "I haven't forgotten. And this is the way to scotch it. We'll have other people . . . Janis and Frank perhaps, and — suppose we say Sara Thorpe," she added and was fully conscious of malice.

They dined and went to the theater. On the surface it was as pleasant and well-mannered a party as you could find in all Manhattan, three extremely attractive men, and three more than average pretty women. But there were undercurrents.

Janis was sulky, she had quarreled with Frank all the way to the apartment. Therefore, she flirted outrageously with Nelson Yorke, who was tremendously amused . . . although now and then a raised eyebrow questioned Christine, secretly.

"I don't know what's got into Janis," Francis said plaintively to Christine; "ever since she began going around with that Pierson person she's been utterly unlike herself."

"Please," advised Christine, "please be patient with her. She's just issuing a general challenge. It's part being on her own, and part youth. And we're trying to sober her, and she hates it. She'll snap out of it — "

"I hear you had a marvelous time abroad," said Sara to Nelson Yorke. She smiled at him, her dark, vivacious face alight. "I read about you." Her tone changed, she said carelessly, "What a very lovely woman our hostess is . . . she's at her best in evening dress, don't you think?"

"She's always at her best," replied Yorke calmly.

He had a moment with Christine standing by the fireplace, a liqueur glass in his hand.

"You're worried. What is it?"

"Lots of things, Duke. I wish I could talk to you."

"Any time. Just let me know when and where. If I can help —"

Sara wasn't far away. She couldn't hear, but she could see. She felt as if she were bleeding internally. There was no use, she would never get over it, she couldn't. One nail does not drive out another. It seemed to her that the memory of her stormy association with Yorke had clouded all her skies. There was nothing he had ever said to her that she did not remember . . . "No, Sara, it wasn't love . . . let's be honest about it, my dear. It was sweet and exciting, but it wasn't love. It's not in me to love anyone. . . . I wish I could . . . even without hope. Perhaps I'd be a complete person if I could." She remembered that now as she watched him standing with Christine. He was looking at Christine. . . . Sara would have given half her life to believe, Once he looked at me like that. But he had never looked at her like that. He had regarded her with amusement, with friendliness, with passion. But never like that.

She walked over to where Larry stood with Janis and Frank, and with a gesture detached him. They stood together by the windows and smoked. She said, "Mrs. Clarkson — " she made a little movement with her hands — "she's very beautiful," she went on. Then she laughed. "You look as proud as — the father of twins." Larry laughed at her. "Do they look proud?" he demanded. And Sara said, "I'm sure I don't know, I never had the pleasure." She gestured again toward Christine and Yorke. "But we aren't the only people who think her beautiful," she said. "Duke does obviously, and he's an expert."

She spoke a moment later of a poem she had had in one of the smart weeklies and upon which Larry congratulated her; and of a short-story recently purchased by one of the more literary monthlies. She said, sighing, "I don't suppose I'd like doing them so well if I had to earn my living that way."

But she wouldn't talk about how she earned her living. That was a rule. If she and Larry worked together and went out to dinner, the store was not mentioned during the meal.

"Let's eat a lot — and drink a little — and relax completely," she'd tell him, "and to the devil with Clarkson's for the time being."

He liked that in her, very much. It was restful, a relief. It wasn't restful in the way it is when a man comes home to some woman who knows little and cares not at all about his business. That's a sort of sofa cushion interlude. No, Sara stimulated, amused and entertained, you were perfectly aware of her intelligence and alertness, and you knew that once the recess period had passed she could snap right back into her other role, that of businesswoman, wholly and completely. It was a masculine trait, he had never encountered it in any other woman. Most women got their two personalities mixed; most women, he thought, and told himself that, of course, he was not thinking of Christine, were too apt to bring drawing room, or even more intimate tactics, into the office and office tactics into the drawing room.

Sara sat next to Yorke at the theater, with Francis on the other side. During a moment when the stage was darkened for a change of scene she murmured, "You haven't congratulated me on my new job."

"Indeed," he said, "I do, if my congratulations mean anything."

"I'm having," she stated, "a marvelous time."

"I judged so. Sara, be sure it isn't too marvelous."

"Just what do you mean by that?"

He said, as the lights flared up and the stage became illuminated, "You know. You were always quick on the uptake. If you do anything to make her unhappy — "

Her heart shuddered and there was a bitter taste on her lips.

"What an admission! So it's as bad as that."

"As you like," he said, "but I'd prefer to say — as good as that."

Sara saw little of the rest of the play. She believed that she sat there hating Nelson Yorke with every fiber of her being. But it wasn't Nelson Yorke she hated. It was Christine Clarkson, with her dark gold hair and long brown eyes, her air of distinction and friendly dignity, her rare laughter and quick, lovely smile. Didn't she have enough? Hadn't she Larry, a grand person, an assured position, both in and out of business? Must she have Nelson Yorke as well?

Having isn't keeping, thought Sara. Larry could further her ambitions and, lacking love, ambition would have to do. Women had risen to vice-presidencies before this. If she worked with Larry closely, made herself necessary to him? Perhaps after a time. . . . She liked him, he was physically attractive to her. It would have to do. It had served, since Yorke, very adequately.

Sara knew with the intuition of a woman who loves one man, without hope, that Christine loved not Yorke, but Larry. This was somehow an added straw to the heavy burden of resentment. That Christine would dare, that Christine would not find Yorke worth loving! It was obliquely an insult to her, Sara.

She could not hurt Christine through Nelson Yorke; but she could hurt her through Lawrence Clarkson.

Christine did not see Yorke for some weeks. Then one day after Christmas Janis telephoned her.

"I'm going South," she announced, without preliminary.

"When? With whom? Janis, for heaven's sake!"

"Oh, after the middle of the month. Sam's taking his vacation . . . he has a place at Palm Beach . . . half a dozen of us are going . . . we'll fly. They won't give me a vacation so I'm quitting. I'll find something when I return."

"Janis, you're out of your mind. You can't."

"Oh, but I can," denied Janis. "Mother is throwing fits. The fact that there'll be two respectable married couples to chaperone me doesn't seem to matter. You'll have to smooth her down. I've got to go, Christine. I'm crazy to go."

There was nothing more to be said over the phone, at the office. Christine's day went badly. She couldn't keep her mind on anything. She went to the weekly departmental meeting and her answers were so abstracted that Larry looked at her sharply and twice addressed her with veiled impatience.

She couldn't tell him. This must be handled carefully and by herself. It was her responsibility.

Yet she telephoned Yorke, the following day, and met him for luncheon. Larry found no explanation of her absence when he went upstairs — Mrs. Clarkson wouldn't be in, was all the information he elicited. He thought very little of it at the time, as for some time the routine of lunching together had been broken for one reason or another.

At luncheon Christine told Yorke of the difficulty in which she found herself. He listened, shook his head.

"If I go to see Pierson . . ."

"Christine, don't put yourself in such a position. This isn't a play, it's life. You'll only make a fool of yourself. He'll tell her, she'll hate you. Let her go. I have faith in her common sense. I have just one word of advice. See young Austin. He has common sense enough for two; too much for his own cause perhaps. He might find that he could take a vacation too. Florida's a nice place. If he chanced to be there . . . when she was . . . it might be just the right time, she might find it convenient to have someone to turn to. . . . I know Sam Pierson rather well."

"Duke, you're a genius."

"No. And it may not work. But somehow I think it will. Are things all right with you, Christine?"

"Yes," she said, "they're fine."

He didn't believe her, but there was nothing he could do about it. He let her go. "I'll walk back, Duke — it's such a grand day — " He watched her a moment before he got into his car. He thought, Rather than let Sara hurt her . . . He laughed. Was that the ultimate sacrifice, to consider marrying one woman in order not to hurt another? Cockeyed. But . . . after all, he liked Sara, he had been very fond of her. And he was lonely. Absurd! He was no Sidney Carton to choose the guillotine of another woman's exacting passion. . . .

At dinner Larry said idly:

"Where'd you lunch?"

She told him and added, "with Duke Yorke."

He put down his fork. "Yorke! May I ask why?"

"There was no special reason," she answered, "just something I wanted to ask him."

"Well!" Words literally failed him. Presently he said, "I stretched a point when I permitted you to have him here for dinner. You know how I feel about him, Christine. I was very tolerant about that Paris business."

"Were you? I thought we were agreed that you were not."

He said, stiffly, "I accepted your explanation. But, really, Christine . . . going out with him, behind my back."

"Hardly. I told you."

"You might have told me at breakfast."

"I wasn't sure I'd reach him."

"You mean . . . you phoned him?"

"I did. Does it make it so much worse?"

They were going out, for cards. They took up the discussion in the car, on the way to the Lintons'.

"You might at least respect my wishes in this one thing," he said, leaning away from her.

"Oh, Larry, don't be stupid. I wanted to ask Duke's advice. It doesn't matter what it was about. Nothing to do with us. Something I thought he might help me with — nothing of importance to you. You lunch with Sara occasionally . . . dine with her even. I don't like her any better than you do Duke Yorke."

"But that's different!"

"Why?"

"It's business."

"No, it isn't. You told me once that she never discussed business after hours."

"Yorke's in love with you," he said sullenly.

"Well," said Christine angrily, "maybe Sara's in love with you. How do I know? I'm not in love with Duke and I assume you aren't in love with Sara. So I can't see the difference. Here we are at the Lintons'. And if you expect me to know an ace from a trey . . . "

That wasn't, of course, the end of it. They had said all they had to say yet they said it over and over on their return home that evening with the result that Christine, worn out, went into a dreadful fit of weeping and Larry, frightened and contrite, comforted her, made the usual protestations, took the usual steps toward reconciliation. He did not learn Janis's plans for several days; in fact, not until the day before she left for the South. He was furious. He would turn her over his knee and spank her. He would see Sam Pierson and beat him up within an inch of his life. "Why didn't you tell me?" he demanded.

"Because I didn't want Janis spanked or

Pierson beaten. It's all right, Larry. I felt as you do about it and then I — I thought things over. I've had a little talk with Frank. He's going down to Palm Beach, by plane. He'll be with his aunt there. He's very sensible and he understands Janis. That is when he thinks about her with his mind and not with his emotions. He'll stand by. Don't worry, Janis isn't in love with Pierson, just getting a kick out of playing with fire. When she burns her fingers she'll run howling to the nearest person who'll supply ointment and a bandage. That's Frank's job."

Larry whistled. He said, staring, "You're pretty clever, I'll admit, it takes a woman . . . a man would wade in, regardless."

She felt a little uncomfortable. She hadn't earned that praise. Someone else had earned it. A man, at that.

So Janis went off to Florida and Frank went off to Florida and Mrs. Carstairs, to whom matters were not explained fully because of her inability to keep a confidence, was convinced that Janis and the world would come to a bad end. But it took Larry to argue her out of that, to Christine's secret amusement. And meantime letters came from Frank, he had seen Janis, she had appeared glad to see him, he was sticking around, Christine was not to worry.

At the store things went smoothly, until the day when advertising copy relative to a mid-season sale in the custom salon was omitted from the morning papers. Christine had had no time to look at the papers before going downstairs but when she arrived she found the department buzzing. She snatched the papers, ruffled through their pages, stared at the Clarkson advertisements and then marched herself into Sara Thorpe's office.

"Just how did this happen?" she demanded.

"I was coming down to see you . . . it was an oversight . . . someone," said Sara darkly, "will get hell for this."

It was her fault, but not deliberate. It had been an oversight. She had, she thought, checked the copy. She should have looked at the layout again before it was sent out. There had been some last-minute changes . . . but she had believed her assistant competent to handle them. There had been a misunderstanding. The changes were made, copy which she had intended should come out had remained and the custom department's announcement had been pulled out for space. "I thought," said the assistant, summoned and agitated, "that that was what you meant, Miss Thorpe. I thought you said the sales date had been changed."

"I said the sale on handbags had been changed. . . . This is a fine mess," said Sara;

"we'll be mobbed . . . and the sale wasn't to be until the day after tomorrow."

Christine said coldly:

"If you left less work to your subordinates . . ."

"I'm sorry," said Sara, "there isn't anything more to say. I was at fault. Your copy will be in tonight and tomorrow. You'll lose nothing. I'm thinking about the accessory department. I've had Miss Hawkins on my neck ever since I came in."

Christine went out, slamming the door. She went directly to Larry, with the newspaper. She told him what she had come to say and he said, "Lord, that's too bad. I'll have to see Miss Hawkins . . ."

"Oh, of course," cried Christine, "you don't stop to think that she did this deliberately — to annoy me."

"Are you crazy?" he asked sharply. "Why should she? Your department isn't the one that will suffer." He spoke to Miss Ryder through his desk phone. "Get Miss Hawkins up here from the accessories," he ordered, "and ask Miss Thorpe to come to my office."

He had forgotten Christine. She went on downstairs, listened to the comments of her coworkers, thought it all over. How silly; of course, Larry was right. It couldn't have been deliberate. The brunt would fall on the accessory department, not on hers. She thought wearily, Why can't I see things straight, just because I dislike the woman? It's so unfair of me.

She went back to Larry's office without ceremony. Miss Ryder tried to stop her, a confidential hand on her arm. "He's busy, Miss Carstairs, Miss Thorpe is — "

"I know," said Christine, brushing past her, ready to apologize, ready to do what she could to straighten things out.

She opened the office door, and shut it again quickly. She heard Miss Ryder smother an exclamation. She went past her without a word, and back downstairs and locked herself in her office. She sat at her desk and put her head in her hands. Later it would matter to her that Miss Ryder had seen what she had seen: Sara Thorpe in Larry's arms, clinging to him, Larry's tall head bent over hers.

16

For a long time Christine was conscious of nothing but pain, as sharply definite as anything physical. She told herself dully, *It's over!*

After a time she rose, gathered her things together and went out on the floor. Nancy passed her, turned and looked at her curiously. One of the other designers came out of a fitting room and Christine said, levelly, although her lips felt stiff and it was an effort to move them . . . "I — I'm going upstairs. I don't feel very well . . . a raging headache. Could you take over my fittings, Ellen?"

Ellen O'Day could, and would. She murmured something about aspirin and an ice bag. Christine nodded. The tension in the back of her neck increased and she felt wooden, as if she were no longer flesh and blood.

Rita came into the department shortly after Christine had left. She had a fashion magazine in her hand. Had Christine seen the sketches of her Borgia gowns? But Christine wasn't available; she had gone upstairs, Miss O'Day reported, suffering from a severe headache.

Rita crooned her commiseration and returned to her own occupations and preoccupations. It was not until noon, when she met her former secretary for lunch, that she discovered what she was certain was the cause of Christine's sudden indisposition.

Lawrence, coming home to luncheon, found his wife in a darkened bedroom with a compress over her eyes. His cheerful and noisy entrance was halted at his first glimpse of her.

"What's the matter?" he demanded. "Are you ill?"

She said faintly, "I have a wretched headache, Larry . . . no, there's nothing you can do. I'll be all right presently."

He came to the bed and took her hand anxiously, "Sure you haven't a temperature? Perhaps you're coming down with something. . . . I'll send for Dr. Rudd. . . ."

She looked up at his face bent over her there in the dim coolness of the room. Slow tears crawled down her cheeks. She hadn't lied to Miss O'Day. She had a terrible headache, caused by nervous tension and emotion. The back of her neck felt like a board, the top of her head was splitting. Nothing had done any good.

"Please go away," she said, with a tremendous effort.

In common with the majority of men, Lawrence Clarkson feared illness. He had never before seen Christine supine in defeat, at the mercy of her unhappy body. As his anxiety rose a species of vague anger seized him. He looked down at his wife, her hair a dark gold fan against the pillows, angry because he was frightened and frightened because he loved her so much.

"If you'd be sensible and let me send for Rudd . . ."

"No. Larry, please leave me alone."

He laid his cheek against her own for a moment. Straightening up he said, loudly:

"You've been crying!"

"My head — " she explained dimly.

"Shall I send Mrs. Finley in?"

"No — thanks. Larry, please go — your lunch is waiting."

He went unsatisfied, alarmed, closing the door with exaggerated care. Christine turned her face to the pillow and wept without sound. It hurt to cry, but it would hurt more not to cry. Why was she such a coward? The darkened room and the headache which explained it were means of escape, of evading the facing of the issue. Lawrence didn't know what she had seen. She was aware of that, from the instant he entered the room.

She was no sheltered woman of another

generation, believing that because her husband took another woman into his arms it meant that she had irrevocably lost him. She could forgive, possibly even forget, a sudden yielding to temptation . . . a drink too many, a pretty girl, a dance floor, a spring evening . . . oh, any one of a thousand settings and circumstances. But this wasn't a sudden temptation. He had been interested in Sara Thorpe for a long time. He had made over his advertising department solely in order to have her near him. What else was the explanation?

She put out her hand, changed the compress, tinkled the ice in the bowl. Someone who hated her was beating at her skull with hammers muffled in cotton wool. Someone else who hated her even more was driving red-hot splinters through her eyes.

Lawrence, eating his solitary meal with poor appetite, was divided between worry about Christine and with thinking about Sara. He had come up to luncheon feeling extremely masculine. It hadn't been like Sara Thorpe, as he knew her, to go to pieces over what was plainly a mere mistake. But in the midst of discussing the affair with him she had suddenly burst into tears . . . and had said hysterically that she was tired, that everyone had been hammering on her all morning, that she had so wanted not to fall down on this job.

He, of course, had no recourse other than to console her, and assure her that one mistake did not mean a failure. He had felt paternal and powerful and superior, putting his arms about her, patting her shoulder, making all the consoling gestures and murmurs. He hadn't dreamed that Sara had it in her to go all feminine and clinging and afraid. The quality which he did not approve of in her was her complete poise and self-possession. It made her appear hard. But she wasn't, of course, she was as feminine as — as Christine. Poor kid, it was too bad this had had to happen.

When he left the apartment after issuing worried orders to Mrs. Finley, he found Rita waiting for him in his office. The efficient Miss Ryder was nowhere to be seen.

Rita said, without preliminary:

"I'm so sorry, Lawrence. If Christine would let me talk to her — men are pretty blundering at times — but perhaps I could make Christine see that it didn't mean anything. It was stupid of you. . . . Why select your office as a setting? But I do want to help you."

Lawrence looked at her in utter bewilderment.

"What in the world are you talking about, Rita?" he demanded. "Christine's ill, she has a bad headache . . . why do you want to talk to her?"

"Larry, don't play dumb. Christine has a bad headache because she saw you and Sara Thorpe in your office this morning. I thought you two would have had it out by now. But I see you haven't."

"Sara and I? How on earth did you — " He broke off suddenly and the angry blood rose to his temples. "I see, Miss Ryder."

"Does it matter?" asked Rita smoothly.

It mattered a lot. So Christine had been in his office, had seen him and Sara . . . Ryder had seen too, and had straightway run to Rita. Christine, he reflected, as calmly as he could in the circumstances, had warned him against Ryder. But he hadn't listened to her.

He said furiously, "Look here, Rita, why should you take this upon yourself? You have no right . . . none, I tell you! If it has served your interests to put your own secretary in here to spy on me — "

"Oh, come," she interrupted, "don't take that tone with me. I'm only trying to help you out. It was unfortunate that Christine happened to open the door. Miss Ryder tried to stop her."

"Nice of her," he commented hotly.

She said, evenly:

"Christine has never liked Sara Thorpe. She resented it when you employed her. It will take a lot of explaining . . . this morning's affair, I mean. If Christine liked me better . . . However, I thought that if I could persuade her to see me . . . " She added, reluctantly, "I'm a good deal older than she is. I've known you a long time, I am convinced this infatuation doesn't mean anything, Lawrence. You're far too sane. But if your father hears of it — "

"*Will* you keep quiet?" he demanded. His voice rose, and he rose and stood at the desk, his hands flat upon it. "I believe you've lost your mind. There is nothing between me and Sara Thorpe — I'm not infatuated with her, as you put it. Whatever anyone saw this morning was perfectly innocent. The girl was tired, overwrought. She began to cry. Hell," he said with disgust, "I'm wasting my time explaining. There isn't anything to explain. And I'd thank you very much, Rita, not to meddle in my private life. I can manage myself. If there is any talking to do, I'll do it."

Rita faced him. She was perfectly white under the delicate application of make-up. "We've been friends for a long time," she said. "If we weren't . . . I'll pretend you didn't say what I just heard. I was trying to make things a little easier for you. Your mistake was in marrying a girl who is jealous of you personally, and jealous of authority in the store. It's a bad combination."

He said shortly, ignoring this:

"Miss Ryder's no longer necessary to my office. I'll have some people sent up from the agency today. And I'd be glad of her resignation."

She cried, "That isn't fair! I suppose you want mine too!"

"Do as you please," said Lawrence indifferently.

Rita left the office, shaking with anger. She would see Howard, tell him everything that had happened. She had gone to Lawrence with, she told herself, his best interests at heart. That she had gone on the chance of making a little more trouble she refused to admit, even to herself. When Ryder, over the luncheon table, had told her of the morning's occurrence Rita had been incredulous. She had believed that if ever Lawrence Clarkson turned from his wife, it would be to her. But it was not to her, it was to Sara Thorpe, whom she had cultivated carefully for her own ends. Her anger and humiliation had been beyond bounds. But her own position had seemed perfectly clear to her. She would enter into a conspiracy with Lawrence; together they would convince Christine of his innocence and in so doing, no matter how far his interest in Sara had gone, Rita would tacitly be allying herself with his wife, always the safer, the more strategic position.

She thought, hurrying back to her office where Ryder was waiting, faced with the unpleasant task of telling Ryder she was through and of the more difficult one of finding other work for her — that she must see Howard if she had to make the trip to the Island.

Lawrence sat down at his desk. He said to himself helplessly, She *couldn't* believe . . . it isn't possible . . .

It was possible. It was even probable. She did believe and she had hidden herself away from him, in a darkened room, pleading a headache as her excuse. She had been crying, he had felt the tears wet on her cheeks.

He thought, Why didn't she come right out and say so? Tell me what troubled her . . . if she trusts me as little as that . . .

He pressed a button, ready to speak into the annunciator, then remembered that Miss Ryder was not in the outer office. He picked up a telephone and called the personnel department. The simplest thing was to say that he had found, after all, that Miss Ryder was not satisfactory. Had they someone else available, or would they call the agency? He thought he might like to try a man secretary for a change.

That business concluded, and conscious of the gossip it would cause, he called a meeting he had scheduled for the afternoon. It would be long and tedious but it was important. He could not cancel it, he could not leave things and go to Christine now.

Shortly before closing he let himself into the apartment. Christine was up, she had slept a little during the afternoon, her headache was no longer so acute. She was in negligee, and lying on the divan in the living room when he came in.

She said, mechanically, "You're early."

"Yes." He sat down beside her and asked directly, "Christine, you were in the outer office this morning?"

"Yes," she admitted dully, then she sat up and looked at him. "Rita told you," she exclaimed, "and Ryder told her!"

"It doesn't matter. Why didn't you tell me this noon? Oh, my dear," he said unhappily, "all this time, to have thought what you must have been thinking . . . to condemn me without a hearing. That's not like you, Christine, not just, not kind."

"She was in your arms," Christine said inexorably.

"If you'd walked in on us — why didn't you? — you would have seen that it meant nothing. The girl was tired, at the end of her rope. She had made a mistake, she began to cry. . . . Darling, can't you understand? I don't give a snap of my fingers for her."

"How can I believe you?" she asked him forlornly. "You must have employed her because she attracted you. Otherwise why all the secrecy? You pride yourself on not being moved by emotion in business. Is it like you then to turn soft because a girl makes an error and cries about it — arousing, I suppose, all your protective masculine instincts?"

He had felt just that; it was so true that he could have shaken her with a certain amount of pleasure. He felt like a fool, either way you looked at it.

"Christine, you're getting things twisted," he began, "I swear — "

"Oh, don't bother," she said wearily. "What difference does it make? If you're in love with her — "

"I'm not in love with her, damn it!"

"Don't shout at me!"

"I wasn't shouting."

"Yes, you were. Do you want everyone in the house to hear? Rita will inform the store, so I suppose you'd as soon the servants heard too."

He said, "Leave Rita out of this," and did so because the last thing he wanted at present was a discussion of Rita. Christine took the words at their face value.

"Why should I? Just because she's been a sort of Sacred Old Guard around here for the last half century. She's in love with you. She always has been. She's hoped you would respond, and as she's your father's protégé, she felt she could dismiss the difference in your ages and her position in the store. She hates me, naturally, she's always made things unpleasant. Everything I do and say on the floor goes back to her. I've tried to tell you this, but you wouldn't listen. The good old Clarkson tradition! Rita is loyal! Rita carries the Clarkson banner! Then she planted Ryder in your office. I advised against that, you may remember. Everything *you* do and say goes back too. Ryder saw what I saw this morning. And now Rita has something else to think about. She's made a great friend of Sara Thorpe. If I'm not mistaken, she won't be as keen about her now."

He said, "I can't believe all that, Christine." But he knew now that she might be right, to a certain extent. Rita did know things almost before he himself knew about them. Once or twice she had erred in admitting her knowledge. There had been that conference, a few weeks ago . . . Rita hadn't been present and when he spoke to her about it she had offered him his own opinion, almost verbatim. It had seemed very clever of her, at the time. They thought alike, of course, on many subjects, having worked together so long.

Now it occurred to him that it hadn't been so clever as he thought — or it had been cleverer. Ryder had told her, of course, had read her the notes, possibly. Yes, that must be it. She couldn't assemble all those arguments by herself, she hadn't had time to think about them, she didn't know the background and she had given her opinion before the background had been made clear to her.

He looked down at Christine and wished with all his heart that she had not said what she had. He would never feel at ease with Rita Allen again. Of course, that was nonsense about her being in love with him. Yet he couldn't wholly dismiss it. He remembered, against his will, things she had said, had done, little situations which hadn't seemed to mean anything at the time, yet now, in the light of Christine's statement . . .

He'd always be self-conscious with Rita. His happy unawareness of her as a woman was destroyed. He'd thought of her as a friend, a working partner, an integral part of the business. Never as a woman. But since early afternoon his trust had been shaken. And now Christine was going on:

"Whether you believe it or not makes no difference to me. I don't care how Rita knew, I don't even care if she does know. Yes, I do. I've enough pride not to want to be made a laughingstock throughout the store. What really concerns me is Sara Thorpe. You say you aren't in love with her, that you haven't any interest in her. Very well, prove it."

"How?" asked Lawrence. "Christine, you're utterly wrong, you're taking this far too seriously."

"It is serious, to me. There's just one way you can convince me it isn't serious to you."

"How?" he asked again, trying to keep his temper.

"Let her go," said Christine simply.

Lawrence stared at his wife in horror. He spoke slowly. "But I can't, Christine. You must be out of your senses!"

"I'm beginning to think so," was her quick reply. "Nothing adds up, nothing makes any sense. So you can't. Why not, may I ask?"

"But it's absurd," he argued, "it isn't fair to her. She hasn't done anything. . . . No, don't interrupt me. If I had a habit of firing an employee for a first mistake . . . well, how many would we have left? Christine, do be reasonable. I repeat, the girl means nothing to me. I like her, yes. I admire her. I think she's clever and an asset to Clarkson's."

"You don't find her personally attractive?"

"Of course I do," he replied savagely, "any man would. What do you think I am?"

"I'm wondering."

He went on, ignoring the interruption.

"Because I'm in love with you and married to you doesn't make me blind and deaf and dumb. Didn't you say something to me like that once? Of course, the girl is attractive to me. But I'm not in love with her. I don't want her. I never have. When will women get it through their heads that because other women are attractive to their men, it doesn't mean catastrophe, emotional scenes, divorce courts. It hasn't anything to do with my loving you. It doesn't make me unfaithful in word or deed or thought. Can't you see that?"

"No," came her answer.

"Then," he told her, "you aren't what I thought you . . . a little different from other women. Can you lie there and tell me that other men aren't attractive to you . . . Yorke, for instance?"

He was carrying the war into her camp. She cried:

"Yes, I can. He's not attractive to me. Not in that sense. Oh, he's attractive in the way of looks and manner. And he's a good friend. I like him. But in that other way — no, he isn't, Larry. I — I wouldn't want to be in his arms, not even for a minute. I couldn't. That's the difference in our loving. In any intimate sense other men, all men, are repellent to me. But you — you can take little interludes like this morning in your stride and think nothing of them."

"It wasn't an interlude. What did you expect me to do — throw her out of the office?"

"There's a long gap between throwing her out and taking her in your — Oh, what's the use," she went on, "we'll never get anywhere with this. It just boils down to one thing — will you dismiss her or won't you?"

"No," he said, "I won't. I won't because it isn't fair to her. It wouldn't be fair to any employee to whom you happened to take a dislike. I've had to lean backwards with you, Christine. Just because you are my wife, I can't afford to let that influence me. There have been times when it would have been easy, when we didn't see eye to eye on certain things. I've had to forget our relationship and look at everything from a purely business standpoint. I'm looking at this that way, now. Sara Thorpe has done good work. She's been here a short time. She has done nothing to merit dismissal, and nothing you can say or do will make me feel otherwise."

17

There was a long silence. The telephone rang and Lawrence was summoned. He returned to inform her briefly that his father wanted to see him, that he would run down, at once, and have something to eat there. She need not wait up. He'd take over the guest room on his return.

He was gone, she was alone, lying there on the couch, refusing, later, the tray Mrs. Finley sent to her, and shutting herself in her room, to go back to bed and stare into the darkness.

She couldn't repudiate her ultimatum. She dared not. If Sara and Lawrence were as guiltless as angels, Sara must still go if only to prove that Christine Clarkson's husband loved his wife more than the Clarkson tradition.

She slept finally and was still sleeping when Lawrence knocked at the door next morning. She roused herself with an effort and sat up. Her head was fuzzy and dull and was sore to the touch, but it no longer ached. She was emptily hungry and her eyes felt like something left out overnight, but she was more or less herself. And for a split second she forgot what had happened, wondered why she was alone in the room, called, or started to call, "Come in, darling . . ." But before the last word escaped her, she had remembered.

Lawrence came in, and she thought frantically, I must look like nothing on earth! He didn't look very well himself. He had a telegram in his hand.

"This came," he said, without further greeting. "I opened it. I thought it might be important. It's from Frank Austin."

The wire was brief. Frank and Janis were to be married in Palm Beach as soon as his father, her mother, Christine and Lawrence could reach there.

Christine exclaimed, pushing back her hair from her forehead, and Lawrence said presently, "It's fine . . . it's what you hoped, isn't it? I'm sorry I can't get away."

He thought, uncomfortably, of his interview with his father. Rita had reached Howard by telephone, apparently, crying into the receiver that Lawrence had demanded her resignation. Howard had elicited some of the facts from her and he had sent for his son.

He was not pleased with him, nor with Rita, nor with Sara Thorpe. He was quite patently on Christine's side. Lawrence had been a fool. Rita had been a fool. Sara was a minx. Christine must be pacified, placated. There had never been a Clarkson matrimonial scandal. There must not be one now. Rita was too valuable to the store to lose. Howard would see her, frighten the daylights out of her, put her in her place, and the Thorpe woman must go.

Lawrence was tired of hearing that Sara must go. He said so, hotly. Sara did not deserve a dismissal, she would stay on. As for Christine, if she didn't trust him —

"What has trust to do with it?" Howard had demanded.

Christine was saying:

"You could get away if you wanted — for a few days."

"I suppose so," he admitted, "but I don't see the object of it in the circumstances. I've had all night to consider, and perhaps a brief separation might do us both good. When you've talked to your mother and made your plans, let me know."

Christine, Mr. Austin and Mrs. Carstairs left by plane. Lawrence took them to the airport, brushed Christine's cheek briefly with his lips in farewell. The foolish tears thickened in her throat as she watched him go, her mother's voluble exclamations and speculations falling on deaf ears. Why couldn't Janis come home, demanded Mrs. Carstairs, and be married like a Christian?

In flight, watching the country unroll beneath her without recording the sight, Christine thought a great many childish things. If they crashed . . . serve him right, all the rest of his life he'd remember her as he left her . . . remember last night. But she couldn't, she mustn't. The cold fine sweat broke out on her forehead under her little hat, dampened her fine hair, prickled along her sides. She swallowed convulsively. Austin, leaning toward her, asked anxiously, "Not airsick, are you, Christine?" She shook her head. She was not airsick. Let him turn his attention to her mother, who was beginning to feel anxious about herself. She, Christine, was sick with fear, sick that she might never see Lawrence again, never feel his arms about her, his mouth upon her own, in love.

She thought, I'll compromise. If he'll get rid of Sara Thorpe I'll — I'll leave the store. . . . I'll find something to do . . . there must be something. I could take lessons, go to art school, try to find whatever I've lost along the way. If I'm willing to give up my work, can't he give her up, in return?

If he can't?

She couldn't go back to him and pretend that things were as they had been between them. Some radical change had to be made in their lives. She had given him what amounted to an ultimatum . . . a challenge: Choose between us, she had said, in effect. She could not crawl back and say, Never mind, it doesn't matter, perhaps you aren't in love with her, let's pretend that you're not.

The ocean was very blue along the Florida coast, the Lake was bluer still. There were patios and cool fountains and delightful people, music, and the palms swinging in the breeze and bright cabanas along the white beach. There were flowers and green hedges and wheel chairs and bicycles. Christine had never been to Palm Beach. She found herself thinking, Lawrence and I must come here one day. And then turned her thoughts away.

Francis was as usual, only his eyes and the nervous grasp of his hand betrayed him. Janis was subdued, thought Christine, too subdued for a bride. Christine worried over that — until she saw Janis look at Francis. Then she ceased to worry and began to envy.

They were married in the Austin house on the Lake, which Austin had opened on his arrival. It was small, the inevitable Spanish type, charming. Mr. Austin, deciding to remain for a few weeks, urged Christine and her mother to stay on, but Mrs. Carstairs refused. She would go home by train, she added firmly, she hadn't proper clothes for a visit, she had engagements she must keep in New York. Old memories of splendor died hard. She had recollections of Palm Beach which she did not intend to stir up any more than she could help. But to her astonishment Christine elected to stay, "If I won't bore you," she had added.

Austin assured her that she would be very welcome. "You'll keep me from dashing down to Long Key to see how our youngsters are getting on," he said. "Perhaps Lawrence will join you?"

But that, Christine regretted evenly, was impossible. Larry, she believed, was too busy. Unless, of course, he found that he could get away, which she doubted.

She had a word alone with Frank, just before the pretty, quiet wedding. She hadn't dared ask Janis anything. Janis had volunteered, "It was just one of those things, Chris. I got to seeing him down here and realized what an idiot I'd been."

Sam Pierson was not mentioned.

Frank was more communicative. They had a short time together but he made the most of it. He couldn't thank Christine enough for her advice. Suppose he hadn't come on down, opened the house, played the carefree bachelor? Janis had appeared glad to see him when they met, then a little resentful, on the defensive. He'd been asked to Pierson's. Too many people, noisy, too much to drink, lax behavior. He'd hated it, because of Janis.

Nothing had been said, he had been careful not to antagonize her and then the night before he wired Christine, Janis had suddenly appeared at his house. She had come in evening clothes, in a wheel chair, at two in the morning. He had been sound asleep and she'd rung and rung, and the servants the agency had engaged for him hadn't heard. Finally he had wakened and gone down, thinking the ringing was done by a telegraph boy. There she stood, shivering, half crying, the incurious chairman stolidly waiting for his money, accustomed, it seemed, to scenes at all hours of the night. She hadn't said anything but "Take me in, will you, Frank?"

He had questioned not at all at the moment; had paid the man, closed the door, and then she had laughed and cried, she had left all her clothes at Pierson's, could he lend her pajamas? "I hadn't enough money," she said, "to go to a hotel. I couldn't show up at this hour and ask them to trust me. I didn't bring much, enough for tips and oddments. Hadn't much, as a matter of fact. What I had I lost tonight. They got to playing poker."

It appeared that the variety of poker into

which the game developed became distasteful to her and after she had settled her small bets she had gone up to her room. Pierson had followed her.

Frank did not press her further, she was worn out, hysterical. He heated milk, finding no other sedative in the house, furnished pajamas and a guest room. But after she was in bed she called him and he went in to find her huddled up in one of his bathrobes, despite the warm night, her teeth chattering. She was, she said flatly, afraid. And then she had asked if he could forgive her, ever, for being such a fool. "I thought I could take care of myself," she said; "I found I couldn't."

This was the story which Christine heard, not in detail, but by implication. Janis had fallen asleep finally and Frank had sat beside her during what was left of the night, holding her hand, listening to her childish breathing. He had sent the wire as soon as the office was open.

And Pierson?

Oh, he admitted, he'd gone gunning for Pierson despite Janis's pleas. He believed that a sound thrashing could be effected without causing too much of a scandal. But Pierson wasn't at home.

The rest of his guests were, and it appeared that Sam, poor dear, had been called away unexpectedly. They were vague as to his destination. He had borrowed a car.

Christine said, "Frank, all my life I'll be grateful that you were here."

"Your doing," he reminded her blithely, "and now — Lord, look at the time. Let's get going. I'm pretty nervous, never having been married before." He took her hand and held it. "You always wanted to be a sister to me," he said, smiling, "even when I wasn't content with a fraternal relationship. Well, you have your wish. The best thing I can pledge you is that Janis and I will be as happy as you and Lawrence."

If only he hadn't said that. She forced a smile, said, "Futile dream," and wondered why she bothered to save her face. And wept at the wedding, in the traditional manner, and the others could not guess that her tears were for herself.

She wrote Lawrence that she was staying on for a time . . . to think things over. Meantime her mother was returning to town. . . . Mr. Austin was making her very comfortable . . . it had been a lovely wedding . . . she would let him know her plans. The department, she felt, could spare her for a week.

Thinking things over wasn't easy. She couldn't. Her mind made little pictures: some foolish, some secretly lovely, all important to her. Lawrence in a temper over a dress tie, Lawrence gulled by that impossible Contessa and sheepish about it, Lawrence walking on the beach bordering Peconic Bay, Lawrence riding through the Long Island woods, Lawrence standing beside her watching the tennis matches.

She couldn't go back. She couldn't return to the store and the apartment with all this between them, and pick up her life as though nothing had ever happened. She couldn't return to quarrel with him. There had to be another way.

She had brought only a few necessary things. Now she shopped for more, and at another time it would have been amusing to buy one of her own Southern models at the Clarkson branch in Palm Beach. Nothing was amusing at the moment. Mr. Austin left her alone a good deal. He was there when she wanted him, not at any other time. Once he inquired, "Something's bothering you, Christine?" and she nodded. "Yes," she told him, "please don't ask about it — yet. I'll have to work it out my own way."

She had one letter from Lawrence, demanding her return, pleading with her almost incoherently. She read it until she knew it by heart and then destroyed it. Howard wrote her also. He announced bluntly, "This is all a very silly business. Come back home. By the way, I've a pup all picked out for you."

Howard gave his dogs only to the people he loved. Now he was giving her one. He did care for her, then, he wanted her to return. Oh, why couldn't Larry see that it wasn't just Sara Thorpe? It was the whole impossible situation, their association in the store, unnatural and nerve-racking.

She had worked hard to attain a reputation. Her work was part of her. Could she, in justice to herself, give it up?

One evening about a week after the wedding Christine was alone in the house except for the servants. Mr. Austin had gone to Bradley's with some friends. She was sitting reading in the cool, two-storied living room when the doorbell chimed and a caller was announced: "Mr. Yorke to see you, Mrs. Clarkson."

Christine dropped her book and fled into the hall. "Duke!" she cried and gave him her hands. "I'm so glad to see you. When did you get in?"

"Very recently. I chartered a plane. Why wasn't I asked to the wedding?"

"How did you know?"

He said coolly, "Through your mother. I called you at the apartment and was told you were in Florida. I couldn't seem to connect with Lawrence. So I went uptown and saw Mrs. Carstairs."

"Come in," she said; "don't stand there. Let's go out into the patio, it's cooler."

The patio was roofed with stars, and the tiled floor was white with moonlight. There were trees whispering, and the scent of flowers and a wall fountain tinkling into a little pool. Christine's face was a pale blur, her eyes very dark. She wore white, a fragile gown, utterly appealing. She looked very tired and immeasurably lovely.

They sat down together on a long curving bench. Yorke lighted a cigarette and smoked a moment thoughtfully. Then he asked, "Can you tell me what's gone wrong, Christine?"

"What makes you think anything is wrong?" She tried to laugh. "I needed a little rest . . . heaven knows, Europe wasn't a vacation. Janis's wedding gave me the opportunity."

"Stop stalling, my dear," he replied gently, "I've seen Sara."

"Oh!"

"You needn't say it just that way. All I know is what she told me. That she burst into tears in Larry's presence the other day and that he did what any man would do under the circumstances. There seems to be some confusion about the whole affair. Rita Allen appears to be in it, and the old man. Rita went to Sara with a tale of how she had disrupted your household and Sara sent in her resignation and Larry refused to accept it. It's all pretty muddled. Tell me, won't you?"

She said hotly, "What's the use! You know a great deal already and take a lot of things for granted."

"All right. What are you going to do after you leave here?"

"I haven't decided."

"Life is short, you haven't much time," he warned her, "the longer you stay away the harder it will be to return, Christine. Sara is very ambitious. You can understand that. She is also very clever. I am convinced that she does not care for Larry, and never has. I am sure she finds him attractive — what woman would not? She can be perhaps a little unscrupulous when she finds someone both useful and attractive. But this has nothing to do with caring. You see, I know her pretty well. You will not think me the world's prize ass with a touch of peacock if I say that Sara, as you know her, is partly my fault? And whatever you think about her and Lawrence, I am reasonably certain that Lawrence doesn't give a hoot for her. But if you leave him too long, if you let him feel misunderstood and oh, very, very misjudged and innocent, all the childish things men do feel, you are running a strong chance of heading him her way. And Sara, being Sara, and human nature being, as I've heard somewhere, human nature, she'd be a star-spangled idiot not to make the most of it. This is merely a warning. Further deponent sayeth nothing."

She replied, quite forgetting that she had meant to never say it, "Oh, I do believe him. I must, or lose what little reason I have left. But I asked him to let her go — from the store, I mean — and he wouldn't!"

"Neither would I," murmured Yorke. "You don't know much about men, do you? Me, I've never liked spinach. My mother used to say, 'You must eat spinach, Nelson, it's so good for you.' So I wouldn't. If she'd said, 'Don't touch that spinach, it will make you ill,' I suppose I would have clamored for a bathtubful. Men are like that, even when they grow up. Remember the priceless 'I say it's spinach and the hell with it'? Perhaps Lawrence feels that way, aside from any ideas he has as an employer and not as the husband of a very charming woman. Women are like that too. Lots of 'em don't like spinach," he concluded mildly.

She said humbly, "Oh, I know it, Duke. But, you see, I made a point of it. I can't . . . I can't *crawl* back now. It's beyond endurance to think of it. Besides, it all goes deeper than just that."

"I suppose it's your pride," he said thoughtfully; "a funny word, an odd quality. If people would crawl a little more! Not that I like crawlers as a rule. It isn't your pride, darling. You're afraid. Afraid that Lawrence is right and you're wrong, afraid to admit it, afraid that once having admitted, he'll have the upper hand. You'd hate that. Or you *think* you'd hate it, consciously. Unconsciously, I wonder. I often ponder whether this partnership, equality business isn't pretty much overrated."

She answered resentfully, "You think I'm childish."

"No," he told her, "I think you're a woman." He rose and she rose also and faced him. He said, "Look — I've a plan — "

She never knew how it happened, whether it was, after all, herself who made the blind gesture but suddenly she was in his arms, crying her heart out. He touched her hair, murmured something, held her close. She felt relaxed, almost at peace. She didn't love him, but he was kind, he loved her, he was sorry for her.

Christine drew herself away. She tried to smile. She said, "I'm so ashamed, please forgive me."

Starlight poured down, and moonlight and the palms sang in the wind. Christine, finding her handkerchief, was aware of the warm, insidious glamour of the night. But Yorke said easily, "Don't be silly. You had it coming to you. I'm not assuming anything. It was just a good cry. You'll feel better and I feel very important, and protective, and all that. It's a pleasant, wholly masculine reaction."

He was talking to give her time to recover herself but now she exclaimed and then was silent, standing quite still, looking at him. She had said to Lawrence that she couldn't have borne the touch of another man's arms. And all the time Lawrence had tried to tell her, just this, in reverse. Tried to tell her that he could hold Sara as Yorke had held her, and feel nothing, except a little human pity and kindness.

Those moments in Yorke's arms had not been repulsive to her, they had not revolted her, she had liked being there, held, comforted, at peace. And Yorke loved her. But Lawrence didn't love Sara.

She began to laugh. Yorke looked at her a moment and then shook her. "Snap out of it," he demanded harshly.

But she couldn't stop laughing. It was so awfully funny, so terribly funny, so bitterly, devastatingly, marvelously amusing. She laughed . . . and went on laughing. And Yorke slapped her, sharply.

Christine stood with her hand to her cheek. The blow had hurt and sobered her. She said, "Thanks, Duke. I had that coming too."

"I'm sorry, my dear," he said. "You'll forgive me? I don't as a rule go around hitting women — openly. Have you a wrap? Well, go fetch it. We'll go out and walk along the Lake for a bit. . . . Great thing, exercise."

A little later they walked along together under the palms. She said, breaking a silence, "Duke, I've been very silly. I don't mean Sara . . . and Larry, I mean . . . myself . . . a lot of things. I can't explain. But even if Larry lets Sara go, it won't fundamentally make the difference I thought it would. It's the store that's come between us. I'm jealous of it, in a way I can't explain. It just doesn't work out, my being there. Yet I can't give up my work . . . or must I?"

"No," he said, "of course not, and that's where my plan comes in. I've made you this offer several times before . . . I'll make it again. Let me set you up in your own shop."

She said, brokenly:

"You're sweet." It came to her suddenly that she wished she could love him. It would have been so much simpler to have fallen in love with Nelson Yorke. But she hadn't; she couldn't. She loved Larry; she always would. She went on, after a moment, "But I can't, Duke. It would mean the end of everything between Larry and me."

"Need it?" he asked her. "It's a business proposition. If he's big enough to see that it means your steady happiness, you will achieve a real adjustment between you. If he isn't big enough, Christine, you haven't lost anything worth keeping no matter how much it wounds you at the time. I won't be in the picture at all, my dear, if that is what troubles you. I'll make all the arrangements, tie you up tighter than a drum. So much interest on my money, so much repayment over a period of years, all arranged through the bank and my lawyers. I'll be just something on a balance sheet. I'm going abroad, perhaps to live there indefinitely, perhaps for just a few years. It depends on Sara."

"On *Sara?*" she asked incredulously. "Sara Thorpe!"

"Yes," he answered gently, "That's one reason why I came down . . . to tell you. We're going to be married on my return."

She murmured helplessly, "Duke — I'm so happy for you."

"No," he said, "you're not. You don't understand at all. For a long time I've been telling you I'm in love with you. Well, that's true, still true. Being a woman you won't understand why it doesn't interfere with my loving Sara. You see, she needs me. You don't, not really. You need a black column in an account book, and a place of your own, and your work and — after hours, Larry. You don't need me to love you. Sara and I will be very — comfortable. It's time I settled down. Ever since I saw her again, on the night you sailed, I've been wondering — about her, about myself. I don't belong in your life, Christine, as a man, as your lover. Perhaps, if this breach with Larry were to widen, you might turn to me. But it would always be second best and you'd hate having second best. You'll work this out for yourself, and for Larry. If he doesn't understand, if he can't make himself see, well, you've your work, a place of your own, something to attain. Think it over. I've interfered considerably in your life. Sara has interfered too. This may make some sort of amends. I don't know."

She stopped, clung to his arm. She said faintly, "I'm — so tired."

He hailed a passing wheel chair, and put her in it and gave the boy Austin's address. Then he stood beside it, hatless, and smiled at her.

"I'm leaving tomorrow," he announced. "Telephone me before eight at the hotel" —

he gave her the name — "and tell me if you have reached a decision. Then, before I sail, we'll have everything under control."

She said, "Duke, whatever I decide, I'm so grateful . . . and I hope you'll be very happy."

He said, "When two lonely people find each other, after a long time, and know they need each other, something approximating happiness comes out of it. Good-bye, my dear."

He stood there watching the chair as it went toward the Austin house. He thought, She'll have to work it out. He thought of Sara. His heart warmed. She had said, frankly enough, "I've been playing the field. It wasn't your fault. I was a fool. I thought you could possess the person you love completely. You can't. No one can. This business with Lawrence Clarkson, it didn't mean anything. I might have gone further with it in order to hold my job or to get a better one. I didn't stop to think about his wife. I never have stopped . . . Duke, you're in love with her?"

He said, "It isn't what you call being in love, Sara. And she's in love with her husband. So let's forget all that. You and I, we're misfits in a way. But we know each other, we respect each other, after our own fashion, and so, if you'll have me, and no questions asked . . . ?"

He thought of Christine and her pride. Sara

hadn't any. He was glad of it. He felt under the deepest possible obligation to her because of her complete lack of reservation. She had learned one lesson, she would not irritate and frighten him by her possessiveness. She would give, she would no longer demand. In a deep sense they belonged together.

Christine lay wakeful until the dawn crept in at her wide windows and in the patio the birds sang and scolded, about the fountain pool and in the palms and vines. If she accepted Yorke's offer . . . ?

This was a big thing, bigger than the other thing she had asked of Larry. She would have to ask him for, in a sense, her freedom . . . freedom of action, decision. It had no such trivial basis as the dismissal of a woman she disliked and distrusted. It had far-reaching roots, and on his attitude toward it the rest of their lives would depend. She could not go back into the shop, that much she knew.

She telephoned Duke Yorke before eight. "All right," she said as evenly as she could, "I'll take your offer."

"Good." He gave her his lawyer's name and address. "Tell me when you plan to return and I'll make the appointment for you. Everything will be arranged between you and him and the bank. I won't be there, Christine. He has my power of attorney in this. You're to have everything you want — and don't spare the horses. And good luck — "

"I won't see you again?" she cried.

"No, not for a while. When will you reach town?"

"I'll leave by train tomorrow," she answered. "It will give me a little more time to rearrange a lot of thoughts."

Presently she replaced the telephone and went back to her room wondering how wisely she had chosen. Yes, she believed it was wise, no matter what came of it. Only an important decision could bring herself and Larry permanently together — or wrench them, permanently, apart.

She told Mr. Austin that she must return to New York and listened to his lack of enthusiasm. "I thought," he mourned, "that Larry might join you here, a little later, after all."

"No," she said, "he can't get away." She smiled at him. "You don't know how much good it's done me being here with you."

"You haven't told me what's troubling you . . . I assume something is. Don't shake your head at me, you admitted it once and you can't fool me now."

"I won't burden you with it," she told him, "I'll work it out myself, soon, Uncle Austin. Don't worry. I'll manage."

"You will," he assured her, "and, I hope, in

the best way for your enduring happiness."

Was then unhappiness written clearly on her face for anyone to read? she wondered.

She telephoned Lawrence, telling him when she would return. She would come straight home, she said, from the train, and see him there.

Opening the door with her key, she was greeted by a bundle of silk and affection, all awkward paws and a pink industrious tongue. She bent to take the setter pup in her arms, the chauffeur grinning behind her, with her bags. "When did this arrive?" she inquired of Mrs. Finley, who stood sedately welcoming in the hall.

"He's been here a few days," replied the housekeeper austerely, "and he's more care than comfort." Yet her eyes softened as she looked down at the dog. "Mr. Clarkson telephoned a little while ago," she went on, "he'll be home any moment now, he was tied up in a conference, he told me. There's a letter came with the dog," she concluded.

There were flowers in the living room and even in her bedroom. And Howard's letter was propped against the mirror of her vanity table.

"Here's your pup," it read, "his name is Pete. I'm glad you're home, and I'll see you very soon. Love."

That was all. But it was signed, "Father."

What, she wondered, panicky again — as if she had been anything but panicky all the long way home — would Howard say to her decision?

She changed from her traveling suit, brushed her lovely hair, superintended the unpacking of her bags. When she heard Lawrence's key in the door her heart misgave her, she felt almost faint with excitement, suspense.

She went out to meet him. What they would say, how encounter after their parting, she did not know. She had no time to wonder, for his arms went out and she was in them, holding to him as if her salvation depended on it. She spoke, half crying, "I've missed you so."

"I've missed you," he told her. It occurred to her that he looked thin and drawn. She said, frightened, "You've been ill."

"Just a cold. It didn't matter. What matters is that you've come home — to stay. You have, haven't you, Christine?"

She replied slowly, "Larry, I don't know."

The dog brushed against her feet and looked up at her with eyes of an instinctive devotion. She spoke to him absently. Then she said, "Larry, let's talk — now."

She led the way back to their bedroom, and closed the door. She motioned him to a deep wing chair and then sat down on the side of the bed. She began, "It would be easy — not to — for a while. I mean, we could be together — the rest of this day . . . and tonight . . . and never a word said. But someday we'd have to talk. Tomorrow, next day, it doesn't matter. Let's talk now. I've tried to plan what I'd tell you. That's why I came by rail instead of air . . . so I'd have time, to think, to arrange things in my mind. I didn't get anywhere."

He said dully, "Christine, if it's still Sara . . . she's left, I refused her first resignation. But she stayed out, recently, and wrote me that she was to be married and that in the circumstances I'd forgive her leaving without notice. Christine, does that make things right between us?"

She answered, leaning forward, her small face grave and pale and her long eyes almost black with concentration:

"Larry, it wasn't Sara, really. I — oh, in any other circumstances I would have been angry, frightened, said more than I meant, come to my senses and realized that you spoke the truth, in every word. She was just a symbol of the thing that's come between us — just as Rita is a symbol, and Nancy Redding, as all the gossip and bickering and inner politics have been symbols."

"What do you mean?" he asked her, his face very still.

"Clarkson's. Larry, can you understand when I tell you that it's been Clarkson's all along? Not Sara. I saw something, I put one interpretation on it. That was because I've grown narrow and blind and stupid. Because of Clarkson's. I don't belong there, Larry. Not as your wife. If I weren't your wife, yes. Look at it this way . . . I've a job, a dozen jobs. I'm your employee, I work for the success of my department, that's for your success too. I'm your wife, which means your companion, your lover, your partner, in a sense which has nothing to do with the store. I'm not your partner in your business. It's a twenty-four-hour-a-day job and it's too much. I can be one thing or another. I could sacrifice the job to the man, stay home, hear one side of things only, forget the store except as it affects you. No gossip, no chiseling, no toadying to me because I'm your wife, therefore must have influence. I could help people even more because I could put them first and you second. I could help you by being utterly unbiased when you present a problem to me. That might be a solution — one solution, Larry. The other is — "

"Wait a minute," he broke in, looking at her intently. "You mean you'd quit, give up your work, be idle, waste yourself? What would you do?"

"Your — our house runs itself," she answered, trying to smile, "so I'd do as other women do, I suppose. Take a hand in something, civic work, charity, social — it doesn't much matter. Learn to play a better game of contract, make women friends who think of a shop as a place in which to buy things . . . or else join classes, perhaps at the Art Students League, and pretend that it would be my chance to pick up broken threads and develop the artist I once believed I could become."

He asked, "You'd be willing to do this for — "

"No, don't say it. Not for you. You don't want it. You look at me as if I'd struck you. But you want me as you first knew me, with my job to do, with an interest in the things you care about. I'm simply telling you that I *could* do this thing, because our happiness is essential to me. Oh, you must be convinced that I'm not thinking only of myself," she said unhappily.

He answered, as if bewildered, "No, Christine, it isn't that. But *I've* been happy."

"Not entirely, Larry. Can't you understand, we love each other, we have been married so short a time. All the little quarrels and bickering we have had haven't meant much to you in the long run, you've forgotten them easily enough because there were the reconciliations.

But lately we ceased to quarrel, we came to grips with something which seemed more at the time, terribly important. Yet it was trivial, and you knew it, of course, and I pretended I didn't believe it. I made it important because it cloaked something more vital, much more vital." She looked at him, put out her hands, instantly covered by his own and said, with her voice breaking, "Darling, I can't have you and Clarkson's too. I must divorce one of them."

He said soberly, "I see," and his grasp tightened on her hands. He added, "But — without your work? No, Christine, you'd be miserable. I can't let you."

She said swiftly, her heart pounding, "There is another way. Nelson Yorke came to Palm Beach when he learned I was there. He offered to back me in my own shop. As he has offered before. My own work, my own place, standing or falling on my own ability. And I haven't been quite truthful with you. It isn't just an alternative. It's what I mean to do. The other — staying home, giving up my work . . . you'd hate it, Larry, and I'd hate it. I told Duke I'd accept his offer. I am to see his lawyers tomorrow."

He was white and his eyes blazed. He cried: "Yorke . . . you'd take this from *Yorke?*"

"Yes," she said steadily, "I'd take it from

him. He is my very good friend, but that has nothing to do with it. I'd take it as a business proposition. Friendship had nothing to do with it. It will be arranged through his bank and his lawyers. He will not even be there."

Larry said, after a moment:

"And if I offered it to you, Christine, if I said, 'Take my money, use it, set yourself up in business, consider me a silent partner — ' "

She asked, low:

"You'd do that?"

"Yes," he told her. He released her hands, searched in his inside pocket, took out a folded sheaf of notes. "I talked," he said slowly, "to my father and I thought things over. I came to much the same conclusion you have come to . . . so I set down figures . . . worked it out on paper for you."

She took the notes and turned them over, glancing at this column, at the other. Larry had gone to a good deal of pains, with his estimates. The tears ran unchecked down her face and stained his careful writing. She said:

"That you thought of it means so much."

"Then," he told her heavily, "you'd rather take Yorke's money?"

"Yes," she replied, quite steadily, "Yorke's. Or anyone's. Not yours. Can't you see? Oh, *try* to see, Larry. If I accepted this" — she riffled the pages with her fingers — "we'd be in business again — together. Differently, but still together. It wouldn't work. It couldn't."

He asked, "Why not?"

"You know why. I'd be answerable to you, for everything. I wish to be answerable only to myself."

"You'd be answerable to Yorke," he told her.

"Financially only. But if you back me, it is far more than a financial responsibility, Larry. It becomes an emotional problem immediately."

"Let me understand this clearly. If I am opposed to your taking Yorke's money, then what?"

"If you are opposed," she replied and twisted her hands together so that he would not see how frightened she was by their shaking, "I will take it — anyway."

"That is final?"

"Yes," said Christine. She was not aware how her eyes pleaded with him, nor how white her face, nor how the careful reddening of her lips seemed like an affront to that pallor.

He rose and walked to the windows, standing with his back to her.

"Yet a little while ago," he reminded her, "you said you were willing to give up everything, to stay home."

"I did not say I was willing," she told him, her lips trembling. "I said that I could. But that's not what you want. You want me, as a complete person, with a job to do, with an interest outside of yourself yet related to you because we love each other. You don't want half a woman. And I'd be just that."

He said slowly, still with his back to her:

"And Yorke has always been in love with you."

She sighed. "I think he has cared for me, for a long time. Larry, is it possible for you to believe me when I say that his caring has nothing to do with this offer . . . except that a wish to be kind and to help me has sprung from his affection for me? Will you believe me when I say that since I first knew you no other man has interested me, even remotely, and that before I knew you I never fancied myself in love either with Nelson Yorke or anyone else? Will you believe me when I tell you that I feel free to take this offer without any qualms or reservations . . . and that aside from a perfectly natural and comprehensive gratitude my acceptance of it in no way concerns me emotionally?"

She thought she did not breathe, she fancied her heart did not beat in the interval before he moved or spoke. Not long ago he had asked her to believe him, in a matter which involved her trust in him and which, as she saw it now, was in no measure as important as this matter, which also involved trust.

While she waited, conscious of unbearable suspense, of an almost physical faintness, he turned from the window and came over to her. He lifted her from the edge of the bed and set her on her feet. He held her very close.

"You love me, Christine?"

"Yes," she said, "I love you. Whatever happens, it's you I love."

"Nothing else matters," he told her, "except your happiness." She looked up at him and saw the sweat standing on his forehead. He breathed as a man breathes who has run a race and is exhausted, not knowing whether he has lost or won. "Whatever you do," he told her, "and however you do it, will be all right with me. If this is your way . . . then take it, just so long as you don't take the way which leads you away from me."

She spoke his name, and raised her mouth for his kiss. And stood there for what might have been a second and what might have been an eternity. When she drew away a little she was laughing, a little brokenly, and Larry said, "You're trying very hard not to cry."

She thought, It's cost him so much, and it's been harder for him than I'll ever know. He's a big person. I haven't known how big. He measures up — small things upset him, he can face large issues. If he hadn't, would I have gone through with it? I don't know . . . I'll never know.

She released herself from his arms and smiled at him, her eyes luminous. She had no sense of victory, none of the emptiness which invades the conqueror when, having defeated the enemy, he is himself exhausted and knows neither peace nor triumph. No, it was not victory she experienced but a sense of unison and completion.

The pup whimpered at the door, scratching. Christine, freeing herself, went to turn the knob and let him in. He cast himself at her in an ecstasy, and Larry said, smiling:

"Pete loves you already."

She said, "Your father's giving him to me — it's like being knighted." She knelt to take Pete in her arms and looked up at Lawrence, her face alight with a charming and delicate malice. "He never gave you a dog!"

"Yes, he did. Two. I kept them at the farm . . . they died . . . the last one shortly before we married."

"Oh, I'm sorry." She rose, with the setter in her arms. "You can share Pete," she offered.

"Half?"

"Let's not put it that way . . . just — yours," she said, "and mine."

He took the dog from her, set him gently down. "Christine — there's another thing. Rita . . ."

She said firmly, "You'll have my resignation tomorrow. Poor Larry, losing all his help!" She laughed. "Rita!" she said scornfully, "to a woman emancipated from Clarkson's but pledged to its president, Rita somehow no longer seems very important."

She heard exasperated exclamations and a faint calling of her name. The pup ran off eagerly. It was Howard coming through the hall, and announcing loudly, "Came up in a damned taxi and we ran into a truck."

Christine ran to meet him, to take him into the living room, to ring for cocktails and make a great fuss over his well-being. The dog leapt at their feet, clumsy, adoring, upsetting a little table, and looking at them with frightened and beseeching eyes.

"Glad you're home," Howard grunted. "Hope you'll stay there. Kiting off to Florida . . . How's Janis? I want to send her a present."

"She's fine," Christine told him, "and she sent her love to you."

"Won't have much to spare now." He cleared his throat, hesitating, "Larry tell you he's lost his high-power advertising female?"

Christine laughed. She said mildly:

"Yes. I already knew. She's going to be

married . . . to Nelson Yorke."

Her eyes met Larry's and danced at his expression of outrage. Why didn't you tell me? his regard demanded clearly. She shook her head at him, and smiled secretly. She was glad she hadn't told him. This way she was certain she was secure.

Howard grunted. "They're a match. Bet it turns out all right."

He leaned back, waiting for the cocktails. Christine thought, We won't tell him, just yet. Funny, she was beginning to think in the plural.

Howard put out a hand to scratch Pete's ears. He said, "Dogs are the only living beings which love you for yourself and in spite of yourself, and if they make any bones about it they bury them under the parlor rug!"

"Oh, I don't know," said Christine. She was standing by Larry now, and she put her hand in his.

Howard regarded them and smiled. Under the heavy brows his bright blue eyes twinkled. He thought, Had me scared for a little but they've weathered it, somehow, it doesn't matter how, I suppose, looks like everything's going to be all right.

The cocktails came, and Howard lifted his glass. "I don't suppose Lawrence bothered to tell you I've come for dinner and then I'll be getting back to the farm." He snapped his fingers at the pup. "This rascal's mother, she hasn't been up to snuff. I'm kind of anxious about her."

He raised his glass.

"Well," he announced cheerfully, "here's to you — both of you."

They drank, and Howard was outraged.

"Don't you know any better than that?"

But they smiled at each other. There would be discussions and explanations and long talks, before everything was completely clear; there would perhaps be disturbance ahead, and dangers. But they'd meet them. For the first time in their marriage they had met on a basis of absolute equality and understanding and for the first time in their marriage each had realized how much the other was loved.

"What on earth are you grinning about?" Howard asked his son explosively.

"I was drinking," Lawrence replied cheerfully, "a little toast of my own. To a new partnership."

He smiled at his wife. A partnership, she thought, while Howard said aloofly, "Well, you needn't be so mysterious about it. How about some dinner?" A partnership . . . theirs? Or Sara and Duke's? Or could it be, in a sense, her business venture with Yorke? She would never discover, she knew instinctively that he would not tell her and for a moment she looked at him as if she saw him for the first time, a stranger, with thoughts concealed from her, with mysteries she might not probe . . . and in that moment she fell in love with him all over again, all the more helplessly and completely because she knew it would no more be the last time than the first.

Oleson appeared at the door.

"Dinner is served," he announced gloomily, as if fearing the worst.

"Thank God!" said Howard and rose stiffly to his feet. "What *are* you two mooning about? I'm not going to stand here all day waiting for you to make up your minds. I could eat the hind leg of a mule!"

He followed Oleson without ceremony, and if he knew that Christine and Larry kissed briefly but satisfactorily behind his straight old back he gave no sign.

Christine, from the head of the table, surveyed her two men. She said happily, as if making a discovery:

"I'm home."

And so she was. This was where she belonged, this was sanctuary, and excitement, and peace. What happened below these floors would not matter to her except as it affected Lawrence. From this place she would go out in the morning and to this place she would return at night, a free woman with her work to do and a woman happy in the compulsion of her return.

The employees of THORNDIKE PRESS hope you have enjoyed this Large Print book. All our Large Print titles are designed for easy reading, and all our books are made to last. Other Thorndike Large Print books are available at your library, through selected bookstores, or directly from us. For more information about current and upcoming titles, please call or mail your name and address to: